ISOLATION

LOVE, LOSS, LEVERAGE, MURDER

A Novel by

C.L. BLUESTEIN

SEDUCTION series • Book 3

ISOLATION:
Love, Loss, Leverage, Murder

ISBN Print: 978-0-9966210-6-9
ISBN audio: **978-0-9966210-7-6**

2021 Edition V.6.0

Editor: Anne Frasier Walmart

SEDUCTION SERIES REVIEWS

"Good read!!! …I didn't want it to end. Nor did I want to put it down." L.V.

"A good thriller. Story progresses well; plot line clear. Author weaves modern technology into the lives of the characters along with slowly revealing the past. Well done." B.T.

"…great read that incorporates positive ideas on some modern issues." F.A.

"Wild story. Great ending!

"Very enjoyable. Imaginative story line and characters. The ending was great. Couldn't put it down." Gracieon

"A great, fun read. Excellent story line with enough twists to hold your interest, but not so many as to feel contrived." Mozartnyon

"Excellent read! I am an avid fan of Coben, Crais, Parker, Silva, Child, Eisler and now I can add Bluestein to the mix." A.B.

"Loved the series. Can't wait to see it as a TV series or a movie." L.S.

"An intriguing mix of fact and fiction with story lines woven into a surprising conclusion. Couldn't put it down." C.M.

"This book's a page-turner. Couldn't put it down." M.B.

"Politically savvy thriller threads its way through covert politics, those leveraging wealth and power by manipulating the most vulnerable within the dark, chaotic reality of betrayal and greed. DECEPTION, 4th in the Seduction Series, holds your attention. Big screen ready." B.T.

"The series would make the coolest TV mini-series... wonder if any TV writers are looking for brilliant new projects." C.L.

BOOKS BY C.L. BLUESTEIN

Political Thriller
SEDUCTION SERIES

#1 SEDUCTION – Love, Loss, Leverage, Murder
#2 PERCEPTION – Love, Loss, Leverage, Murder
#3 ISOLATION – Love, Loss, Leverage, Murder
#4 DECEPTION – Love, Loss, Leverage, Murder

You Want Me To Do What? is available now. Walk in the sandals of our ancestors through this engaging interactive contemporary scripted Story of the Exodus/Passover for Jewish and Interfaith Families. Targeted but not limited to tweens.

REVIEW: "You Want Me To Do What" is the most innovative addition to the Passover literature I've seen. This is not just another pretty Haggadah....these interactive mini-dramas will make ANY Seder using any Haggadah come alive for all ages." Cantor Charles Bergman, Los Angeles, CA

Free download at http://carolbluestein.com/

DEDICATION

With my love and gratitude to and for
my late husband, Michael R. Bluestein,
our children Sandra, Mark, and Lisa,
and their families

They are my inspiration.

ACKNOWLEDGEMENTS

First and foremost, I'd like to thank my family for their unwavering support.

Also, I want to note those who have passed but, in their own way, made my journey possible: Michael Bluestein, Roslyn and Noah Levine, Alynne Levine Sharp, Jack D. Main, Abraham and Selma Bluestein, Daniel Bluestein, and Ilse Bluestein Vanderpot.

As I worked on each chapter and phase of the book, I shared my words with my monthly writing group, Women Who Write. They listened and critiqued chapters with open hearts, frank critiques, and generous suggestions that contributed to the overall process and book.

In particular, my appreciations go out to the following people to my professional editors, Paula Chaffee Scardamalia for story and Anne Fraiser Walradt for language.

My readers: Carol Marchewka, who keyed into the emotional connection; Barbara Traynor, who caught the non-essential passages and pacing; and William Petell, who identified the logic breaks.

The creative Judith Prest for allowing the use of her poem.

Thank you to my teachers and friends at The International Women's Writing Guild (IWWG) who continue to replenish my soul and offer insights into to the wonderful world of expression. It takes a village to support an author and the IWWG is all about encouraging writers and sharing stories.

Finally, the patience awards go to Cooper and Kelly, my rescued schnoodles. They fill the exalted positions of snugglers, walkers, jesters, kissers, listeners, and protectors.

Table of Contents

ISOLATION

Chapter 01 ▶ Damir, Tawanda

Monday, 30 March
Under the morning African sun, a small boy jumped to his feet and ran, zigzagging around home-made tents, leaping over troughs of human waste, and avoiding refugees, old and young, in his path. He slid to a stop in front of the sector mayor. Arm outstretched, he pointed and said, sucking air between each word, "Four. Buses. Coming."

The mayor left the shade of his makeshift office in a corner of his elaborate six-foot square home, four wooden posts supporting a corrugated steel roof and walls of faded fabrics. He stepped out into the morning light as the buses braked at bottom of his section.

The vehicles had been whitewashed for continuity, but it didn't hide the multiple paint jobs applied over the years. Wind and sand stripped away layers in patches, burnishing exposed metal and the edges of color. Shadows under the thin overcoat gave the appearance of camouflage which fooled no one. These buses had been around a long, long time.

Doors on the first bus squeaked open and the driver stepped out, cleared his throat, and pulled a paper out of his coat pocket. He whipped it open and read the announcement.

"Refugees, your new home is Hope City. It will have food, shelter, schools, work, and medicine.

"Mayors must keep extended families within their sector together.

"You may bring what you can carry. The first groups leave in three hours."

The mayor approached the man. In a quiet voice, he said, "May I ask if there is a choice? For many, it's home or here. Relocation is not an option."

The man said, "We will take the willing first. If necessary, the army will encourage the resistors."

The mayor nodded and returned to his home, trailed by the elders. They gathered around a small table, and he said, "This is a chance to better our lives."

"Just like that," an elder said, snapping his fingers, "the government cares about us." He shook his head. "I don't believe a word of it."

Another said, "Maybe we go look first."

Noises outside rose to a crescendo. The men emerged and saw the lead bus draped with a poster showing Hope City's crisp white tents against the African landscape.

"Pick us." Refugees crowded the elders. "Pick us."

Someone found a wooden box, and the mayor stood on it. "Please quiet down and form a line. We will need your family members' names and their original village." He pointed to a man, "One." Then another. "Two." And another. "Three. That's it for now. I will come around to get everyone's information."

By ten that morning, families filled the buses and began their journey to Hope City. Their excitement vented in singing and conversation. No one heard or saw the drone flying high above the caravan.

<~<~|~>~>

Lucy Kilmer watched the first evacuation from the drone's feed. The buses crowded with people. Children leaned out the windows to catch the breeze. Possessions, strapped to the roof, were tied down with ropes and fraying bungee cords.

She felt a shiver of excitement. This ambitious and intricate operation, her biggest yet, would save thousands from the agony of starvation and disease.

The Hope City initiative also saved Lucy from excruciating boredom. She'd been under FBI scrutiny, capture, and questioning, ever since they found a photograph of a woman who looked like her on a missing person's phone.

The late Theodore Donovan, mastermind vigilante and her mentor, had taught her well. Together they had arranged disappearances for a number of deranged psychopaths. After he died, the FBI tried to pin the disappearances on her. The photo did not prove she had anything to do with anything. Still, they persisted and requested more time to complete their investigation.

Lucy looked down at her ankle-bracelet. She was out of one prison and in another, her home in Harrison, New York. She smiled. Fortunately, the precautions she had taken to hide a complete computer center now served her well. While the FBI kept tabs on the main set-up in her office, she worked under an invisible cloak of electronic wizardry hidden behind her bedroom closet.

Her keen mathematical mind and her penchant for details put her at the top of a small but competitive industry—first choice for those who could afford her.

Her new contract came from Tawanda's President, Kwanh Ebu, via James Vanderhagen. Ebu needed to clean-up the refugee problem if his country intended to comply with human rights initiatives put forth by the United Nations and an even stronger declaration expected from the United States.

Lucy checked her watch. The buses' ETA to Hope City's receiving tent gave her two hours of free time. She checked in with her ground crew, worked out, and showered. She returned to her monitor in time to observe the first group of refugees.

Cameras, positioned outside and inside the main tent, started sending a live feed to the site manager and Lucy at the moment the first bus entered the unpaved road.

Pristine white tents lined the drive leading up to the large receiving tent. In the distance, heavy equipment prepped the ground behind a sign—"Hope City Mines." A large white truck, positioned next to the tent, housed command central and sported a large banner, "WELCOME."

Refugees spilled from the buses in a matter of seconds. They formed lines to check in, use the portable restrooms, and enter the air-conditioned tent with a canvas floor mat. The travelers found food and drink on tables along the far wall.

After the receiving agents checked in the last family, the site manager welcomed everyone. He explained their tents would be ready and assigned in a few hours. They were to relax and get some rest until his return.

After everyone ate and used the rest rooms, the journey's tension evaporated, and the refugees dozed. The cameras stopped recording. Command central released nitrous oxide into the filtration system, sending all into a deep sleep, followed by the potent anesthetic, sevoflurane. The coup de' grace, in the form of carbon monoxide, killed them in less than thirty minutes. No pain. No sound.

Lucy watched as her team removed the tent top and, by means of ropes, gathered the corners of the canvas floor and offered them to the crane claws. The bundle of bodies and belongings rose in the air, swung over and placed in an over-sized dump truck.

She switched her view to the drone the semi-crew had launched. Lucy saw the vehicle travel to a prepared burial site, empty its load into the deep hole, and leave. The earth mover filled the pit and tamped the dirt. The operators swept the area and removed any tell-tale signs of a major disturbance—save the top of a small pipe inserted into the pit to release the gases.

Lucy smiled, stood, and stretched. She looked at the time. She had four hours before the final preparations for the next group arrived. She decided to have lunch on the porch, play a few expert Sudoku games, and, if her head cleared, take a short nap.

This was turning out to be a great day.

Chapter 02 ▶ West Wing, Washington D.C.

Wednesday, 29 April – a month later
Vice President Dani Mitchell walked over to the bar in her West Wing office, prepared a vodka on the rocks, returned to her desk, sat down, and contemplated her exclusion from the Oval Office.

She sipped her drink. It'd been over two weeks since she'd had any contact with President Franklin Taylor Sandford. Wendell Waters, the president's Chief of Staff, acted as a go-between. He advised her on all actions she needed to take on the President's behalf, from personal appearances to pushing bills in the Senate as its presiding officer.

But why doesn't Sandford deal with me directly?

Another sip. This wasn't the first time she'd experienced dominant-male dismissive silence. Like it or not, the Oval Office crew were in for a shock because she never, ever, let it stand in her way. She'd get over it, under it, or around it, any way she could, and reach her objective despite duplicitous efforts to derail her.

Another sip. *What is that objective, exactly?*

She turned her head to stare at the two framed documents on her office wall: The preambles to the United States' Constitution and the United Nations Universal Declaration of Human Rights.

She sucked an ice cube into her mouth and rolled it around with her tongue. *I want to make a difference on a monumental level, have a broader reach than one person at a time. Use my knowledge, skills, and experience to offer people the chance to enhance their lives and achieve their definition of success and happiness.*

That's what she told the Senate Review Committee. However, at times, she questioned herself. Was she, the former Sarah Daniels (Dani) Vanderhagen who married Terence Mitchell, in fact, just chasing power, recognition, status, or all three? Was she determined to prove to her father, James, that he and her late grandfather, Philip Vanderhagen, wrongfully devalued the women in their lives? Their misogyny sent her Aunt Sybil on the path of philanthropic social justice and herself on the path of legal justice.

She crunched the last bit of ice.

Maybe, she decided, *she just wanted to prove to her father and the world, once and for all, that she never bowed to their ambition, physically or emotionally. First step, Senator. Now, Vice President. Next? Who knows, maybe President.*

She rolled her bottom lip in between her teeth as she considered her last thought. It wasn't going to happen overnight. Sandford's presidency had high ratings and he'd likely get the party's nomination for a second term. That gave her six years to work her magic.

Her phone rang. She looked at the ID and answered, her voice hard. "Father."

James Vanderhagen said, "Sarah, you don't have to be so formal."

"Dani, and you know it."

He ignored the correction. "How are you doing in your new position?"

"Fine, thank you."

"Is there anything I can do for you?"

"Do for me? That's a joke. You mean bribe, threaten, browbeat, undermine, overthrow, and terrorize anyone who stands in my way?"

He chuckled. "You've always had a way with words, my dear. It is, and has always been, family policy to seduce those who stand in the way of progress—make them advocates or encourage them to get out of the way."

"A rose by any other name...."

"I'll take that as a 'no' for now," Vanderhagen said. "However, do not think for one minute that you've been appointed without some very powerful people pushing your nomination through."

Dani set her jaw. The thought of this man screwing with her life again made her furious. "What are you saying?"

"We're partners."

"Never."

"Don't kid yourself. You're in a position to support the cartel's global economic policies to equalize wealth and prevent a devastating world-wide market collapse."

"I'm not anyone's puppet."

"Your words, not mine. However, you are a Vanderhagen and, as such, invested in our common goal."

Dani gritted her teeth. "Not your puppet," and pressed END.

With eyes closed and deep breaths, she willed herself into stillness, silently repeating her favorite stanza from the Judith Prest poem, "Stillness Is Like Water":

> Stillness blankets me

cushions me against my own
sharp edges
wraps me in her protective shawl
keeps my tender heart
from ripping
on the thorns
of the world

Dani sat back and pondered her father's assertion. It couldn't be ignored. Everything she did, going forward, had to take it into consideration, but she wasn't going to let it deter her from her agenda. My father's going to find out that I'm a Vanderhagen too!

Chapter 03 ▶ East Side, N.Y.C.

Sunday, 3 May

Rachel Allen and her service dog, Zeus, a Staffordshire Terrier-American Bulldog mix, stood outside Sybil Powell's penthouse apartment. She knocked again. "Come on, Sybil. Let us in." She heard shuffling beyond the door. It got closer. The security chain rattled. The latch clicked.

"Okay, Okay. I'm here," Sybil said as she opened the door. "I didn't realize we had an appointment."

The once indomitable, smartly dressed, impeccably coiffed woman now looked listless, puffy, and unkempt. Her robe, covering her nightgown, sat askew on her shoulders and the belt's half-knot drooped. She'd finger-combed her boyish hair, but it refused to lie flat and orderly.

Rachel said, "We don't and that's the problem."

Sybil gave Zeus a pat on the head and shuffled over to the bar. "Want a drink?"

"It's eleven o'clock in the morning. I think I'll pass."

"Suit yourself," Sybil said, pouring a bourbon, neat, and walking it over to the couch. She sat down. "So, are you here to check up on me?"

"I called you at the PRAISE offices. Seems you haven't been in for quite a while."

"A couple of days."

"Try a couple of weeks."

Sybil looked at the drink in her hand. "Really? Time evaporates without Lidia."

"I'm so sorry."

"I loved her, you know. Still do even though she's dead."

"Yes."

"Lidia was a good person." Sybil sipped her drink. "Kind."

Rachel said, "And full of life."

Sybil swirled the bourbon. "She had an artistic soul." A sip. "You know what I miss the most?"

"Tell me."

"Lidia loved me unconditionally." Sybil let out a wail, muting the sound by covering her mouth with her hand.

Rachel picked up the tissue box and offered it to Sybil who pulled out a few. She put her glass down, blew her nose, and wiped her eyes. "How dare they kill her for her art and stuff her in a box? How dare they?" The tissues dropped to the floor, and she took another drink. "My father, and I spit on his memory," she spat three times, "was a greedy, tyrannical, murderous-control freak. I'd kill him again and again if I could." She finished her drink and got up to make another.

Rachel remembered Sybil's lethal attack on her father. Philip Vanderhagen had taunted her with his deniability in Lidia's murder. "I spoke to my friend at the FBI. Dylan Garret, the man who actually killed her, is in jail without bail."

"I knew he'd be trouble the first time I saw him."

"You've got good instincts. They got him for at least three murders and maybe more."

Sybil returned with her refill. "My father put out the contract on Lidia. I hope he rots in hell." Sybil took a gulp of liquor. "He took her from me without a second thought."

"Sybil, you do know you're not going to stand trial for his murder, right?"

Sybil looked at Rachel and nodded. "Of course. I wouldn't have this apartment if you hadn't offered. Still, none of it matters without Lidia. She was my life and now I'm…nothing. Empty. Hopeless."

"You have Peter."

"Right, except my son's made himself scarce. Tells me he's taking care of PRAISE while I'm recovering. Who knows?" A sip.

"He is," Rachel said. "I've talked to him. He's at his wits end trying to figure out how to help you."

"Can Peter bring back Lidia?" Tears welled in Sybil's eyes and slid down her cheeks. "Can he love me unconditionally like she did?" She reached in her pocket for a tissue. Finding none, she wiped her nose with her sleeve.

Rachel offered the tissue box again, and said, "No one can take Lidia's place."

Sybil pulled several tissues out at once and used them to cover her face as she sobbed. "I'm so alone."

Rachel shifted closer to her, put her arms around Sybil's shoulders, and waited.

Zeus sat on the floor between the women and rested his head on Sybil's lap. She didn't respond. He nudged her and waited. Still nothing. Demanding to be of service, Zeus placed his paws on her lap and raised himself just high enough to lick her hands. That did it.

Sybil uncovered her face and focused her attention to Zeus. "Good boy, Zeus. Thank you for your concern."

Zeus sat, his tail thumping on the floor.

"You're quite a dog, young man."

Rachel watched. "I think he smiled."

Sybil wiped her eyes and blew her nose. "There. Done for now. Sorry I put you through that. My emotions are on a hair trigger."

"You don't have to apologize."

"I do. I feel like I'm letting everyone down. I want to be back at work, but I can't concentrate. I can't even make simple decisions like what to wear or eat."

"Perhaps I can take your mind off your problems and pick your brain about our Human Rights agenda."

"Sure. I'm game, although I don't know how much use I can be right now."

Rachel pulled out her ePad and brought up a headline: "Tawandian War Refugees Missing."

"What?"

"It seems there are rumors that whole villages within the encampment have disappeared. Buses came and went, transporting the refugees to a place called Hope City. An investigation couldn't find the city, the vehicles, or the drivers."

"You mean no one knows anything?"

Rachel shook her head. "All gone. Not a trace—that is, if the reports are to be believed." She swiped the screen several times. "Now, look at this." She read the text. "Plague ravaging encampment."

Sybil said, "With so many people living in such poor conditions, I'm surprised something like this hasn't happened before."

"People have died over the years, but not in these concentrated numbers."

"What do you know?"

"Nothing for sure. I just find it a little unsettling that these two stories have surfaced after Peter's debriefing and after we sent our Human Rights proposal to the White House."

"That's crazy," Sybil said. "It has got to be a coincidence."

Rachel shrugged. "No such thing."

Sybil shook her head. "We can't hypothesize about this, Rachel. The ramifications are huge."

"Regardless, do you agree it has to be investigated by an impartial observer?"

"Are you suggesting PRAISE?" Sybil sipped her drink. "Because if you are, I'm not up to it."

"People are dying." Rachel jumped up, put one hand on her hip, and used the other to shake her fore finger at Sybil. "You've got to be up for it. We have to stop the genocide."

Sybil took another sip. "You don't know that."

Rachel walked over to the windows. The East River and the Brooklyn Bridge were a constant in a world of turmoil. She turned to Sybil. "You're right. I don't know that, but I do know PRAISE can find out."

"No. I can't."

Rachel returned to the couch. "Sybil, this has to get done. How about I take over as acting Executive Director while you're in recovery. As soon as you're able to come back, I'll step down."

"What about Peter? Isn't that what he's doing?"

"I've talked to him, and he wants to go back to Tawanda and be our boots-on-the-ground. He knows the people, speaks the language, and has the contacts."

"My father put him there."

"He worked for the State Department."

"Peter worked for the cartel. He investigated a problem with the raw diamond output from the dig site and figured it out. That's why they tried to kill him."

"He never said anything to me."

Sybil wrung her hands. "I can't. I can't let him go, Rachel. He's all I have left."

Rachel sat next to Sybil and joined hands with her. "This is his idea. I couldn't talk him out of it. He feels he's the best man for the job. All I, we, can do is provide him with the support he needs."

Sybil nodded. Tears. Big globules of watery pain dropped on their hands.

Rachel gave her a hug and said, "He'll be okay."

Sybil composed herself. "I have to believe that's true."

"Believe it. With time, you'll be okay too."

Chapter 04 ▶ Gramercy Avenue, N.Y.C.

Sunday, 3 May

Rachel entered the lobby for 215, 217, and 219 Gramercy Avenue. At the reception desk, Nikolai and a younger man were deep in conversation. She said, "What's going on?"

Nikolai looked up and smiled. "My nephew, Tareek, is officially my new assistant."

She smiled in return and looked at Tareek. "Congratulations. Welcome to the team."

Zeus barked.

Rachel patted his head. "I think he wants to meet you."

Tareek walked over and started to place his hand on Zeus's head. The dog shied away. "I don't think he likes me."

"Try extending your hand so he can smell you. When he's good with that, pat him on his side or under his chin."

Tareek followed the instructions and got a lick on his hand for his efforts.

Nikolai laughed. "I predict they will become fast friends. In fact, leave him with us. I'll make sure he gets walked."

Rachel handed him the leash. "Thanks. I'm going up to see Chris."

Nikolai said, "Third floor."

<~<~|~>~>

Rachel's fiancé, Christopher Gregory, founded the very successful ICU, Inc. computer security firm. She knocked on the door to his third-floor office and walked in. She heard him tap the keyboard and saw his monitor revert to his company's logo. Without missing a beat, he got up and gave her a welcome hug and a kiss, which she returned.

She said, "Hi. What's going on?"

He said, "What do you mean?"

"I don't remember you ever hiding your work from me." She looked past him to the logo on his monitor.

"It's nothing," he said. "Just playing around with some conceptual stuff."

"Okay…." She nodded toward the refrigerator. "Got some ice cream in there?"

He smiled. "Always." He prepared two cups of confection, and they sat down on the couch. "All right. Tell me about your visit with Sybil."

She ate a spoonful first. "I'm planning to accept the job as acting director of PRAISE until Sybil is ready to come back. The board offered Peter the job, but he wants to go back to Tawanda and address the human rights issues."

"Isn't PRAISE supposed to be a world-wide funding operation for other people's projects?"

"PRAISE stands for Positive Response with Action to Insure a Safe Environment. That means everywhere. It has the resources to do specific projects as well as develop an international initiative, using Tawanda as a template. Once we have it, we can put together a list of areas where war refugees need help and implement proven strategies."

Chris said, "Are you sure this is what you want to do? It could keep you busy for, I don't know, the rest of your natural life."

"Not too busy for you." She smiled and kissed him. "I'll always make time for you. Besides, it's only until Sybil gets back on her feet."

"That's a pretty public position for a woman who tends to be a recluse."

"I know. I know. I am frightened."

Chris collected their bowls and put them on the coffee table. He put his arms around her. "I hear a 'but' coming."

"This is important. I've written books and articles about these issues and it's time to step up. Sybil is in no shape to do it and Tawanda is in critical need. Disappearances followed by plague sounds fishy to me. The refugees need help."

"You're making too much out of this."

"Maybe. While I can't believe I'm the only one who suspects a growing extermination problem, I must address it."

"Even if it means giving up your writing?"

"This isn't permanent. Sybil will be back. My work can wait a couple of weeks."

"If that's what you need to do, you've got my support."

Rachel looked at Chris and lifted her chin. They kissed. "I love you," she said.

He said, "Don't forget, we've also got our wedding on the radar."

"Speaking of which, Mom and Dad will be back in Scarsdale next week. They'll spend a couple of weeks getting settled and arrive here by the end of the month.

That's when the fun begins. I'm going to 'yes' her to death unless she crosses some insane boundary."

"Sounds like your mind is made up."

"You're okay with it, right?"

"You bet."

They kissed in agreement.

Rachel stood. With a good-bye wave, she said, "I'm going to PRAISE for some folders." She dangled the keys. "I'll be back before dinner.

Chapter 05 ▶ Philadelphia, PA

Monday, 4 May
James Vanderhagen, the third generation to own the stately Vanderhagen home, sat in the formal dining room. Mahogany wainscoting and flocked striped wallpaper provided a richly textured backdrop to ornate mirrors and valuable paintings.

He sat alone at the long, polished cherry-wood table. Since his father, Philip, passed, he occupied the comfortable high-back chair at the head of the table. From this position, he had a view of the room and, through the French doors, the manicured lawn and gardens beyond the veranda.

In this chair, his father had presided over family meals enlivened by conversation, humor, and appreciation for all they had. When Sybil left, things changed. When Dani left, the darkness descended. He missed his family. Friends disappeared. The Vanderhagen business required he meet people on their turf, if at all. James sighed. Only his nephew, Peter, appreciated him.

"Your breakfast, Sir," the housekeeper said, and laid the tray on the placemat. A stainless-steel cover rested on the food plate and the carafe held hot coffee.

"It's not the same, you know," James said. He looked up. The housekeeper had a hockey player's physique, a ninja's presence and capabilities, a Native American facial structure, and a stoic expression. The individual's presentation offered little information as to gender. If the trusted housekeeper ever had a name, it had long been lost. "H" sufficed if necessary. The house ran like a Swiss watch by an invisible staff. "Since Sybil murdered Father."

"I'm sorry, Sir."

"He was a difficult and complex man."

"Yes, Sir."

"People thought he loved them. Family and friends flocked to this table for Sunday dinner. Until each found out his largesse came with unspeakable strings attached -- refusal not an option. One by one, they left and never came back."

"Yes, Sir."

"He had a philosophy and vision, which fit together like a gigantic puzzle. Each piece so crucial that it far outweighed the collateral damage."

"Yes, Sir."

"The women—his wife, daughter, and granddaughter—hated him. He tried to run their lives like he ran the business. Everyone had to play her part."

"Yes, Sir."

"And where did their opposition get them? My mother committed suicide, my sister's husband got sanctioned, and then her wife got killed. None of that was my fault, yet my wife and son died in childbirth and my daughter left without a good-bye."

"Yes, Sir."

James drank the small orange juice and said, "Coffee." The housekeeper stepped forward, raised the carafe, turned the lid to reveal the spout, and poured. James took a sip. "Father dedicated his life to overseeing the cartel's vision of global economic equality. He made sure those who compromised the cartel's program received lethal repercussions."

"Yes, Sir."

"Father's bold and swift moves excised cancers before they had a chance to spread. He did what he had to do. No qualms. No regrets. A man of action. You know, now that I see this all so clearly, my father should have received the Nobel Peace Prize."

"Yes, Sir."

"Now, I'm in charge of implementing the cartel's global initiatives by using any means necessary to eliminate any and all obstacles."

"Yes, Sir," the housekeeper said, stepping forward and uncovering the plate filled with eggs, toast, and sausage. "Will there be anything else?"

"A small glass of sherry."

Chapter 06 ▶ West Wing, Washington, D.C.

Monday, 4 May

President Sandford rolled his pen around between his hands as he watched an on-line news report covering the Tawandian refugees' problems. At the end, he turned away from his computer and looked at his Chief of Staff.

"Sir?"

"We're going to have to do something." Sandford put his pen down and leaned forward, elbows on the desk, hands clasped. "Have the final touches been put on our Human Rights statement?"

"Secretary of State Uriah Henderson told me it's almost ready."

"Good. I want to see it as soon as possible."

"It may be something you'd best put on a back burner for now."

"Why?"

"If we take a forward position on the refugee issues, we'll have to open our borders to boat-loads of people that we are unprepared to absorb."

"We?"

"The American people, Sir."

"The people or the Congress?"

"Does it matter? It's a touchy subject and likely to put your presidency in jeopardy."

Sandford stood and gazed out the windows. "It would seem out of sync to put out a strong Human Rights policy without being prepared to follow it."

"My point exactly," Wendell said.

"Nevertheless, if I act responsibly, do the right thing, I might rob myself of a second term."

"Not just you, Sir. You'll risk the support and careers of the senators and representatives who made it possible for your jobs initiative to move forward."

The president turned to face Wendell. "I can't allow the deaths of all those people to rest on my conscience."

"We have some time, Sir, before we can physically do anything. Let's wait until the medical teams have assessed the situation. If it is indeed a plague, there has to be some kind of plague antidote to insure anyone leaving the encampment is healthy."

"That could be as much as several months. More than enough time for President Kwanh Ebu to come up with Tawanda's strategy on his own. Still, it won't ultimately solve the problem."

Wendell pulled out his phone. "Sir, I've received an email from Peter Powell."

"Our consular agent who isn't."

"Not exactly. He took a leave of absence. Currently, he's working for PRAISE. He's contacted me and asked to be reposted to Tawanda. He wants to find out what's really going on."

"I like the idea of sending Peter. He already has a relationship with President Ebu, and he uncovered the human rights violations in the first place."

"Shall we send him as a U.S. agent or give him our blessing as a PRAISE emissary?"

"Both. Keep him on leave and approve his PRAISE mission. If those refugees are truly in an untenable situation, we're going to have to make sure they get help."

"They are not our problem, Sir."

"Unfortunately, refugees will always be a problem and the Senate has tied our hands."

"The Senate has done you a favor."

"I think humanitarian help trumps internal politics."

Wendell shook his head. "I don't think so. We can't do anything until we're pushed to the wall. No need angering our big donors with speculative forays."

"What if it wasn't me?"

"What if what wasn't you?"

Sandford smiled. "I think I've just come up with a job for my new vice president."

"Dani Mitchell?"

"Exactly. I think we should let her do all the footwork and head investigations into the refugee problem as it relates to our ability to absorb those seeking asylum."

"Are you kidding? She's Vanderhagen's daughter. He's likely to influence her findings."

"Exactly. It will keep him off my back, and she can deal with his input and innuendos."

Wendell rubbed his chin. "I like it. Any public concerns or outrage will fall on her shoulders, and you'll remain squeaky clean."

Sandford returned to his desk and sat down. "Not to mention that if the negative press even approaches what you think it will, Dani will never be President.

Vanderhagen can kiss that plan good-bye." He pushed the intercom and spoke to Nancy, his secretary. "Schedule Dani Mitchell in for tomorrow." To Wendell he said, "Get Peter Powell to Tawanda as soon as possible."

Chapter 07 ▶ Observatory Circle, Washington, D.C.

Monday, 4 May

Dani finished her last staff meeting, packed her briefcase, and headed home. She settled in the back seat, her security team, ever watchful, in the front seats. During the drive to Number One Observatory Circle, she used her ePad to review and edit her schedule. Her concentration broke when the phone rang. She looked at the ID and answered. "Hi, Nancy."

"Madame Vice President, President Sandford requests a meeting at ten AM in the Oval Office. Will you be available?"

"Of course." About damn time.

"Thank you, I'll tell him it's confirmed."

After the call ended, Dani added the appointment to her calendar as the SUV pulled up to her front door. She entered, placed her briefcase on the entry table, and looked for signs of life. Seeing none, she listened and heard the TV in the small lounge. Walking past the formal staircase, through the sitting room, and up a short flight, she paused in the doorway. Her sixteen-year-old-twins, Ivan and Isaac, slouched on the couch, playing a video game.

They came with her marriage to Terence. She'd loved them from the start. Cute, beguiling, and mischievous, the three-year-old boys made her heart skip a beat for ten years. Then, at thirteen, they stopped interacting with her. No communication. Mono-syllabic sentences. Dismissive. Disinterested. All her efforts to break the wall met with indifference. She'd almost learned to live with it, them—almost.

Dani entered the room. The TV monitor flickered with a video game and the twins were engaged on their ePads. To get their attention, she said, "Hi."

No response.

"Did you boys have a good day?"

Two quick nods as their fingers flew over the virtual keys.

"Where's your father?"

No response. No sideways glances. No shrugs. No finger pointing.

Dani felt a flush start to spread. Something was up and it wasn't good. She glanced at the security guard. He looked at her and said, "He'll be home for cocktails."

She recognized the code. He had a date. Jesus, he fucking promised to give it a rest at least for a month until I got settled. She went to the bar, filled a glass with ice and wine, and went upstairs to soak in the tub.

The drink and heat relaxed her. Dani closed her eyes and remembered when she found out Terence had a lover.

<~<~|~>~>

It was the afternoon of her swearing-in. The family dressed in the fifth-floor suite at the Sofitel Lafayette Square. Terence announced he had to go out and would be right back. Forty-five minutes passed and he hadn't returned and didn't answer his phone.

Dani checked with the head of her security team. He made a call and reported back. "Mr. Mitchell had entered a seventh-floor room."

"For what?"

The man's eyes went to the floor.

"Come with me and tell the manager I want that door opened," Dani said. "I'll take care of this once and for all." As they rode up, she called Terence again. No answer.

Dani went to the door where the manager stood. She knocked. Nothing. She said, "Unlock it." He did.

She told the agent to wait and marched into the room. "Terence. I'm done with this shit. Who's the bitch you're screwing?"

Dani paused on the threshold to the bedroom. Terence stood, naked. "Dani...."

"Don't." She walked toward the bed. Terence tried to stop her. With his hand on her left arm, she reached for the covers with her right. "Show yourself this minute, or I'm going to rip your eyes out."

Terence said, "Dani, wait."

"Wait for what?" She ripped her arm free.

"Stop."

Something in his voice made her pause. She looked at him and then at the figure emerging from under the sheets. Her fury dissipated, replaced by surprise, followed by shock. Terence's lover was his administrative assistant, Bruce. Her gaze shifted back and forth between the two men as reality sunk in.

Terence said, "Dani."

"No." She raised her arm, palm outward. "I can't deal with this right now." She walked to the doorway, paused, and turned chin held high. "Terence, you will not ruin this afternoon for me. Get your ass downstairs in five minutes, suited, and ready to walk with me and the boys."

Terence said, "Dani, I...."

"Four minutes." Dani pivoted and stormed out.

Back in her suite, she blocked the large TV monitor and addressed the twins. "This afternoon is my formal swearing in as Vice President. It's important."

Ivan and Isaac gave her a blank stare.

"Stand up."

They did.

Dani got into their faces—her voice hard, her body stiff. "I expect you to smile through the entire ceremony."

They broke eye contact.

"Look at me," she said.

They did.

"Smile or you'll never own another piece of electronic equipment—phone or otherwise—unless it's battery wired to your very expensive braces."

Their eyes widened. She fixed their ties and straightened their jackets. By the time she finished, Terence sauntered in, in his usual casual manner. Their eyes met. Business as usual.

He approached the twins and grinned. "You boys look great. He put his arms around them. "Dani, we're very proud of you."

On the eleven o'clock news, the cameras showed the Mitchell family united. The boys smiled for the cameras, resembling cardboard cutouts. Upon exiting the arena and entering the car's back seat, Dani thanked them. Dismissing her, Ivan and Isaac lost their smiles and pulled out their mobile phones. She shook her head and looked at Terrance.

He gave her a shrug, a half-hearted smile, and pulled out his phone. For once, Dani took comfort in the silence. She turned off the ringer on her mobile phone and kept her eye on the incoming calls, texts, and emails. Her mother, Aunt Sybil, Peter, friends, and colleagues all wished her well. Her father texted one word, "Congratulations."

When they arrived at One Observation Circle, their new home, Ivan and Isaac ran into the kitchen and returned with arms full of sandwiches and water bottles. They ran upstairs. Seconds later, music blasted from their room.

Terrance took off his jacket and laid it on a chair. He walked over to the stairs, yelled "Turn it down," and went to the bar in the sitting room. He poured two glasses of wine and returned to the entry where Dani stood. Handing her a drink, he said, "Let's talk." He loosened his tie and opened his shirt's top button as he walked back to the sitting room.

She followed him.

Terrance stood by the fireplace and put one elbow on the mantle. "I'm sorry you found out the way you did. I wanted to wait until after the ceremony and things had calmed down."

"How supportive and understanding of you," Dani said, sitting on the arm of the couch—her eyes hard and her lips tight. "Where did you hide all this compassion when you accused me of indifference and called me a frigid workaholic?"

"Your work always came before me and the kids."

"Our work, Terence. We. Together. We fell in love, created our law firm, raised the children, and planned our future—together."

"I never expected you'd go political on me."

"Sure, you did. We talked about us entering public life, about making our world a better place."

"You talked. I listened, but never agreed."

"What are you saying? It's my fault that you're fucking Bruce?"

"I didn't say that."

Eyes narrowing, Dani said, "When did you know? The first time you turned your back on me—too tired for sex? When you made me feel undesirable? When you accused me of cheating?"

Terence averted his eyes and stared at his wine glass.

"Did you know when you said my sexual aggressiveness emasculated you?"

He glanced at her. "You're blowing this out of proportion."

Dani stood up and walked over to Terence. "Look at me."

He shifted his weight and removed his arm from the mantle.

"Look at me, Terence."

He did.

"Did you know you were gay when you married me?"

He shook his head. "I swear."

Dani took a long sip of wine, threw the remaining liquid in his face before smashing the glass in the fireplace. "You bastard." She spun on her heels and walked toward the stairs. "I'm going up now. We'll talk in the morning about new arrangements. Use the guest room for now."

She made it to the bedroom before the tears started. She stood in the shower, the rain of hot water embracing her and drowning out the explosion of wrenching sobs. How dare he dump his problems on me, make me doubt who I am and how I feel. In time, she lifted her face from her hands, raised her chin, and let the cleansing happen. By the time she stepped out of the shower, she had a plan.

<~<~|~>~>

Since the night of discovery, Dani and Terence agreed to be civil, friends even, live together in separate rooms, and parent Ivan and Isaac. After she left public office, they'd get a divorce. Until then, Terence would keep his romance with Bruce out of their lives and out of public view.

The family assembled for dinner at seven. The twins sat across from each other, and each switched his cell phone to his left hand. Dani noted they had become ambidextrous. Terrance took his seat at the head of the table.

Dani cleared her throat. "Before we begin our meal, I have a few things I'd like to clarify."

Three pairs of shoulders sagged followed by three groans.

Dani watched the performance and laughed. "You know it can't be that bad, we haven't used the guillotine in this country for years." The boys didn't move but Terrance sat up.

"What's up, Honey?"

Dani raised an eyebrow but let it go. She said, "I understand driver's licenses have been mentioned around here. Is that true?"

That got their attention. They sat up and stared at her.

"I shall take your actions as a 'yes.'"

Ivan and Isaac nodded.

"No one more than I would love to see you get your wish."

Partial smiles accompanied by narrowing eyes. They'd been here before.

"Here's my wish. No more electronics while I am in the room—no phones, ePads, games, or media …unless it's movie night."

The twins looked at each other and shrugged.

"And…."

In unison, the twins said, "There's more?"

"Our conversations, going forward, have to be verbal, in English, with no less than five words per sentence until you get your licenses. That includes answering questions and returning greetings."

The boys' faces lost color. They looked like they were going to pass out.

"Failure to adhere to these new rules closes 'The Bank of Mom.'"

Shoulders fell.

Terence said, "Dani, don't you think you're being a little harsh on the kids."

"I'm their mother and I love them." She looked at the boys. "I love you. I don't relish the job of disciplinarian, but someone has to do it." She glanced at Terence. "Perhaps you'd like to say something?"

"No," he said. "I think you've said it all."

"Don't bet on it."

Chapter 08 ▶ Damir, Tawanda, Africa

Tuesday, May
The taxi driver sailed down the highway, windows down. He wanted to make the airport before all the other cabs commandeered the passengers. The car radio screamed rock and roll. He had one elbow resting on the window ledge, while the hand of that same arm managed the wheel. With the other hand, he managed his breakfast—coffee and a meat roll-up. He felt good and anticipated a busy, successful day.

The clear morning sky had clouded over. If it rained, his rides would triple.

As he popped the last of the meal into his mouth, he spied a person, crouching on a rock, between the road and the refugee camp. He became concerned. People had long ceased trying to thumb a ride. Years of trying had proven fruitless. The solitary figure piqued his interest.

He applied his foot to the break and slowed until he stopped next to figure, an old man. He got out and approached. The man's leathery skin stretched over bone—muscles absorbed by his body. His hair blew in the breeze. Reddened eyes followed the driver as he approached. "Grandfather, may I help?"

Parched lips rolled back and forth over gums. "No."

"Grandfather, can you tell me why you sit here?"

"The wind speaks."

The taxi driver sat on the wall next to the old man. "What does it say?"

"Many souls have taken flight."

"How does the wind tell you this?"

The old man raised his chin. "Their scent rides the air stream."

The taxi driver imitated the position of the old man and took a deep breath. "I don't smell anything."

"Wait. It comes and goes—dancing on nose hairs."

"Grandfather, can you tell from where?"

"Hope City.

"What's that?"

"Hundreds sought life and found death."

The old man held up a hand to silence his interrogator, took a deep breath, and pointed Northwest. "It is there that spirits rise to meet the ancestors and bodies seep into the earth.

The driver looked skyward. "Grandfather, can you show me?"

"As close as I can." The old man turned to look at the taxi driver. "What is your name?"

"Just call me Taxi," said the driver with a big grin.

With the old man sitting cross legged on the passenger seat, Taxi drove north. After a while, a skeletal hand gripped his arm. "Stop. Out."

Taxi pulled over and stopped the car. He ran around the vehicle to assist the old man. He guided the frail man to top of a rock formation. Leaning on Taxi, the old one sniffed the wind. By the fifth breath, he knew and pointed.

Taxi said, "Beyond the curve, past the trees, after the grass?"

"Yesssss," rode the old man's last breath before he passed out.

Taxi carried him back to the car, placing him gently on the passenger seat. Circling the vehicle, he got into the driver's seat and followed the directions—past the curve, through the trees, beyond the grass—and parked. Taxi sniffed the air and shivered. The odor brought back war memories he thought he'd forgotten. It smelled like decaying flesh.

With no visible source on the ground, Taxi left the car and walked the area, turning his head and body this way and that, zeroing in on the stench. He saw no tracks, no graves, and no indication human intervention. Still, the odor persisted, stronger with every step.

He pulled out a handkerchief to cover his nose and tripped. Sitting on his ass, he spied a small pipe sticking out of the ground. He crawled over to it, coughing and gagging as he got closer. He'd found the source.

He backed away and pulled out his receipt book. Pencil in hand, he sketched the area, noting the position of the pipe. Finished with mapping the area, he pulled out his phone, took pictures, and returned to his car. He could tell someone had taken great pains to hide whatever happened here.

All the way back to the refugee encampment, to return the grandfather to his people, Taxi contemplated his options.

<~<~|~>~>

Figuring the grandfather hadn't strayed far from his place in the encampment, Taxi drove to that area of the refugee village. The stench of garbage and zero sanitation saturated the air. He tried to keep his breathing shallow as he carried the old man from his car to the mayor's hut.

The three men sitting at the makeshift table stared at him.

Taxi said, "This man has passed out from the heat. I would like to return him to his family."

One of the sitters said, "He is, perhaps, with them already."

Taxi said, "He's a wind listener. I want to show him respect."

A sitter stood. "I will take him."

Taxi transferred the old man to the carrier and watched them disappear into the crowded village. Turning to the only sitter that hadn't spoken, he said, "Are you the mayor?"

The man nodded. "I am Arvada."

"What can you tell me about Hope City?"

Mayor Yar'Adua waved the other man away and beckoned Taxi to sit next to him. "Why?"

"The wind reader said many died there and I think he is right."

Yar'Adua nodded. "Many have gone, and none have returned, or sent word."

Taxi said, "Tell me."

Chapter 09 ▶ West Wing, Washington, D.C.

Tuesday, 5 May

Dani arrived at the Oval Office on time. Sandford kept her waiting. Nancy offered her tea or coffee which she refused. She heard a low buzzer followed by Nancy's voice. "You may go in."

President Sandford greeted her. "I'm sorry for the wait."

"Not a problem, Sir," Dani said. The President looked older than his fifty-two years, but elegant, with his graying temples adding a bit of dash. She shook hands with Wendell Waters, who was built like a linebacker, and Uriah Henderson, who reminded her of Ichabod Crane with glasses.

The men sat down on the facing couches. She took the balancing seat next to the President, who said, "We have a situation simmering in Africa that needs more attention than I have available. After much thought, I've decided to ask you, Dani, to take it over. Wendell and Uriah are here to let you know you have their full support and will provide you with anything you need to develop an operational plan."

The door opened and the president stood. "I'm sorry. I've another appointment. Wendell will fill you in." He extended his hand. Dani stood, shook it, and watched as the president disappeared. Turning to Wendell and Uriah, she said, "What's going on?"

Wendell said, "Tawanda has a refugee problem."

Dani said, "It's not the only country."

"True, but there are reports that someone may be killing them off."

"Genocide?"

"Possibly," Uriah said. "And we have reports of pockets of cholera escalating and spreading. It may be part of the same effort."

She said, "Someone is taking care of the refugee problem by eliminating the population?"

"Possibly."

"Is it us?"

"No."

Dani said, "Then I'm not sure what you want or need from me."

Wendell said, "The refugees are afraid and getting restless. It is more than possible that they will flee for their lives. The problem is they are landlocked and there is no place for them to go."

"Why would we get involved?" Dani said. "We don't even recognize Tawanda."

Uriah said, "The President is preparing a human rights initiative and is considering using Tawanda's refugee crisis as an example to the rest of the world."

Dani said, "Because Europe is still absorbing all the refugees crossing the Mediterranean and escaping from the Mideast while the United States has been able to pick and choose?"

"No," Wendell said. "Because President Sandford wants to take a firm stand on genocide and human rights to send a message that the United States will take measures against all who don't."

Dani opened her mouth. "I...."

Wendell said, "Enough." He got up and stood in front of her. "President Sandford would like you to draw up two operational plans for his consideration. One, how do we ease the suffering in Tawanda and, two, how can we handle future immigration issues more efficiently."

She rose from the couch and looked Wendell in the eye. "First, I will need his position on human rights and all status reports on Tawanda. Second, will any of your staff be assigned for this project or do I use my own?"

Wendell said, "Let me see what I can do."

Dani nodded. "Before I go, does the President have a deadline for my reports?"

"We'll be having update meetings with you on a regular basis. However, in general, the sooner the better."

When she left the Oval Office, Dani marched right out onto the street, Secret Service right behind her. She strode around the block to cool off and to get her breath back. The President had thrown her under the bus before it even left the depot.

The whole immigration issue would challenge the Senate's referendum, making her, not Sandford, the target of mistrust. Then, the human rights issue, if strong enough, would create problems with current international trade agreements since not all partners complied with current standards. Including the United States, if truth be told.

By putting her in charge of these two areas, Dani would take the heat from the government and the corporations who depended on product globalization.

She'd be the most hated Vice President in history and would never make it, at the end of Sandford's term, to the Presidency.

<~<~|~>~>

Dani returned to her office ready to tackle the problem. She sent aides scurrying to dig up anything and everything on Tawanda's economics, government, climate, and history, including its ongoing war with the Democratic Republic of the Congo—the DRC.

Engrossed in research, she didn't realize anyone had entered the room until she heard a throat clear. Looking up, she encountered a dark-eyed man with a great smile, standing at attention, holding a folder in one hand.

He said, "I'm Yosef Hassan, a gift bearing a gift from Wendell Waters." He offered her the file, which she accepted. "I've been working on the Tawanda issue since it became an issue. Mr. Waters has temporarily assigned me to you."

"Relax, Mr. Hassan…."

"Yosef, please."

"Yes. Yosef, please sit down while I look over these papers."

"Shall I summarize for you?"

Dani smiled and put the folder down. "Sure."

Yosef began at the beginning. "The Tawandian war with the DRC started when the DRC revoked legal nomadic status to the Menanandu Tribe on a technicality that could have easily been overlooked. The clerk wouldn't budge and those higher up didn't care. The nomadic tribes in the area joined forces, usurped a piece of DRC land, and called the new state, Tawanda."

"The cause of all the fighting."

"It might have ended sooner if the land hadn't been filled with exportable minerals, especially diamonds."

"Let me guess," Dani said. "Too poor to mine themselves, they allowed foreign companies who paid for the privilege."

"And still do. The new tariff laws will, over the next ten years, more than double this source of government income."

"What does this have to do with human rights and refugees?"

"War refugees are piled into a massive village. The men who couldn't be conscripted into the army must work for the mining companies, which value profit over people. Hence, they treat the workers no better than the refugees."

"I understand, but why now?"

Yosef leaned toward Dani, who mirrored his action. "An international human rights foundation, PRAISE, wants the President to approve this." He reached out and opened the folder in front of her. He pulled out a piece of paper. "Would you like me to read it?"

"Yes."

"PRAISE believes all lives matter. Classifying any human being as 'them,' 'collateral damage,' 'those people,' 'not-our-problem,' or any term which removes concern and recognition for an individual's humanity is neither acceptable nor tolerable.

"Let it be known any and all incidents of genocide—internment without representation and due process, denial of basic needs including, but not limited to, clean water, proper waste disposal, food, and housing—will invoke an immediate export boycott and suspension of trade with any government supporting the above behavior, excluding non-profit monies and services that directly support individuals in need.

"PRAISE demands that governments direct attention and monies into programs that feed, house, clothe, educate, and care for their poor, indigent, and refugee populations. In the absence of effective positive action, a large group of dedicated humanists will electronically cripple communications, financial and otherwise, of offending governments.

"PRAISE is dedicated to supporting and encouraging those more fortunate to end starvation, dehydration, hygienic diseases, false imprisonment, kidnapping, disappearances, and human trafficking. Our programs, as stated above, start the first of June."

Dani said, "There's nothing wrong with that, except it is more like a declaration of war, backed by a threat to disable world-wide communications."

Yosef said, "It is my understanding it is meant to encourage the President to take the stand he's been promising, sooner rather than later."

Dani said, "It sounds extreme." She thought for a minute. "Why PRAISE?"

Yosef said, "President Sandford has had a special relationship with that foundation, its founder, Theodore Donovan, and several board members, including your grandfather, were major donors to his campaign. Your aunt, Sybil Powell, is now at the helm. She's the one who sent this."

Dani controlled her surprise. "Of course. I've been out of touch with her business interests."

Yosef put the paper back in the folder and said, "The President wants to be the lead on this, not PRAISE."

"Yes. I'll take care of it. What about Tawanda?"

"The President is currently getting ongoing reports from a state department operative, Peter Powell."

"My cousin?"

"Yes. His interview is in this folder as well. Mr. Waters believes, based on Mr. Powell's findings, the President will take an aggressive lead on this issue."

"I see," she said, and leaned back in her chair. "Give me some time to study the material before I comment on strategies."

Yosef nodded, stood, and excused himself.

Dani pitched forward, elbows on the desk, her head fell into her hands, fingers splayed into her hair. The Vanderhagen men had bought into the White House. Sybil and Peter were connected to PRAISE and the dreaded human rights initiative. No wonder Sandford, surrounded by Vanderhagens, didn't want her around.

With this realization, the political fog around her cleared. Her careful and deliberate disassociation from her family carried no weight. Her grandfather's death did not end the cartel's grip. Her father, James, now represented it. Sandford must consider her the enemy as well, by association. Hence, her political isolation. Great.

Dani decided she'd get through this and her family issues by burying her frustration in work. All she had to do was focus—because screaming was out of the question.

Chapter 10 ▶ Gramercy Avenue, N.Y.C.

Tuesday, 5 May

Rachel lay fast asleep on the couch in Chris's apartment. Folders were tucked into the space between her and the couch. Another one, open across her stomach, lost all its papers to the floor, partially covering Zeus.

The dog jumped to his feet, stretched and shook, sending documents even further afield. Rachel woke and saw Zeus greet Chris. In return, Chris scratched behind the dog's ears with more than his usual energy and went to his knees. Play time. She smiled at the roughhousing. It didn't take long for man and beast to collapse on their backs and rest. She pulled out her phone and took a picture of their pure bliss before gathering up all the papers.

"Come on, you two. Wash up for dinner. I ordered in."

Chris got up as the front desk buzzed. He said, "I'll make drinks while you go with Zeus, the delivery dog."

Rachel and Zeus disappeared and seemed to reap-
pear within seconds, the dog carrying a bag in his
mouth.

"That was fast."

"We had some help." Rachel said, releasing the bag
from the huge jaws. "Tareek."

"Nice young man."

"Yes. I like him a lot and he's made astounding
progress with Zeus."

<~<~|~>~>

After dinner and a movie, while still on the couch,
Chris maneuvered their bodies so that Rachel lay in his
arms, her body alongside his. He said, "How do you
like working for a living?"

Rachel said, "Very funny. Writing is solitary. Running an organization and being responsible for all that
entails is a whole other story. Not to mention having to
get dressed every day I go in. I'll be glad when Sybil is
well enough to be back in charge."

"How's she doing?"

"Not well. She doesn't go out. Not eating. In fact, I
think she's in her PJ's all day."

"Maybe she needs to go back into the hospital."

"Peter's not talking, and he's the one taking care of
her," Rachel said. "I hope he's got a psychiatrist on
call. Depression sucks. I know."

"I know you do."

They kissed.

Rachel said, "Now you. What have you been working on?"

He said, "Me? You know, the usual stuff."

"Really? Then, why are you hiding it from me?"

"I'm not. It's a work in progress which will become
another module in ICU Inc.'s security system. I'll show
you when I've got it to a point where I can talk about it

with clarity." Chris changed the subject. "What's with all the folders on the table?"

"Monthly applications for grants, board meeting alerts and agendas, and the human rights declaration which is on hold pending notification from the White House. Once Sybil returns to PRAISE, I'm back to crazy normal."

"Good. I love you crazy normal."

Rachel lifted her chin for his kiss.

"Speaking of crazy, you know my parents are coming," She paused. "But there's a problem."

"I can't imagine." Chris smiled and gave her a squeeze.

"Hey. I'm being serious," Rachel said and kissed him. "There's only one bed in my apartment."

"As I recall, that's true."

"So, we have two options."

"I'm listening."

"One, my parents stay here with you in the second bedroom."

"Sounds like a hotel is out of the question."

Rachel ignored his wisecrack. "Two, they stay in my apartment, and I move in with you."

Chris pushed her away with a shocked look on his face. "You mean before we're married?"

"What…." Before she could finish, Chris embraced her. Kissed her. Kissed her again. Their busy hands attacked zippers, buttons, and hooks.

"Come on." Chris got up and led Rachel into the bedroom. They peeled off their final pieces of clothing seconds before collapsing on the bed. There, under the skylight, in full view of the star-filled-sky, they made love.

Chapter 11 ▶ Damir, Tawanda, Africa

Wednesday, 6 May

President Kwanh Ebu sat before his cabinet ministers. He stared at them in turn, and they kept their eyes down.

"So, that is it. No one can tell me what is going on?"

Silence.

"Where did these headlines come from? Disappearing refugees. Dying refugees." He waited. Slapping his hand on the table, he roared, "Tell me."

Shaking heads did not produce answers.

Ebu sat down. "Then tell me what you suggest we do now?"

The tension relaxed.

One minister said, "I suggest we announce a special investigative committee to look into these matters."

Ebu said, "Do you not think that is the same as admitting the issues exist?"

"Sorry, Mr. President."

The Minister of Information said, "If you wish, Mr. President, I can have an announcement prepared in less than an hour that says we categorically deny any such allegations."

"Yes. And include our outrage." Ebu paused and turned to the Chief of Security on his left. "General, find the source and make sure there is no further incendiary remarks leaked to the press."

The man nodded.

Ebu said, "Now clear the room. Not you." He looked at Oliver Odili, his Counsel to the President. "You stay and follow me."

Ebu led his friend into the garden. "I know this is where our last President died, but it remains one of the most secure spaces in the complex, and we must talk."

"I am not afraid."

"We have to find a way out of our refugee situation. You must have given it some thought once the reports emerged. I would like to know what you think." Ebu ducked into a benched alcove. "Come sit out of the sun where drones cannot monitor our words."

Odili sat and said, "To be truthful, as disturbed as I was, it did mean fewer people to be concerned about."

Ebu nodded.

Odili continued. "The sickness is spreading, also reducing numbers."

Ebu said, "In short, not a bad thing but not a solution. The world is watching, and I have several requests from medical teams who want to treat the refugees." He looked at Odili. "I have said 'yes' to all. Because if the sickness leaves the refugee encampment and infects Damir, we are all at risk."

"Do you want me to handle them?"

"Yes. To the world, next to our winning the war with the Democratic Republic of the Congo, our citizens are our first priority."

Ebu watched the man leave the garden and pulled out an undocumented phone. He called the only number in the contact list. "Do it."

Chapter 12 ▶ N.Y.C. - Washington, D.C.

Wednesday, 6 May
The next morning, Rachel, accompanied by Zeus, arrived at PRAISE offices and saw the secretary on the phone. She caught Rachel's eye and began gesturing and mouthing words in between answering the caller.

Rachel understood. She rushed into her office, sat down at her desk, took a deep breath, and let it out slowly. When the console on her desk buzzed, she picked up the phone. "Rachel Allen."

"Miss Allen, this is Dani Mitchell."

"Good morning, Madam Vice President."

"I'm calling this morning because your human rights declaration has become my responsibility for the moment. I'm interested in the background that prompted such a sweeping statement and no-holds-barred illegal enforcement."

Rachel said, "We, Sybil Powell and I, had a firsthand account from Peter Powell, her son. He had just returned from Tawanda, Africa. His report on the war refugee encampment abuses spurred us into action, and we drafted a statement.

"However, the more we thought about it, we realized it would take just as much effort to address one instance as it would to address the worldwide issue. If we were going to do that, it had to have teeth.

"We revised and sent the document you have to President Sandford before we released it. We didn't want to interfere with any initiatives being developed by the White House."

"I see," Dani said. "Do you realize that it is unenforceable as written? The United States can't have any part in electronic attacks on another country."

"Neither could we," Rachel said. "It's a confirmed statement from human rights allies who have access to the dark web, Madam Vice President."

"If you see, hear, or find it again, please stop that particular conversation."

"Of course. Consider it done."

"On my part, I'll undertake a thorough review and get back to you."

"Thank you."

"May I ask if you are the author Rachel Allen?"

"I am."

"Would you be able to come to Washington D.C. and meet with me? I've read your books, and I think Communication Strategies for Peace of Mind, Country and Global Safekeeping is a seminal work. I'd like to discuss it with you, in person, at your earliest convenience."

<~<~|~>~>

Dani ended the call and returned to the folders Yosef brought. She spread the information out on her desk and grabbed a highlighter. She discovered Peter had talked with the Counsel to the President, Kwanh Ebu, now the new president. He had been Vanderhagen's eyes at the mines. However, he observed the war refugee encampment on his own time.

Dani got up and walked. There had to be a way to turn this career-killing assignment upside down and use it to her advantage. Before she had a chance to start planning, her phone rang.

"Madam Vice President, this is the General Administration Office. We have just received a set of plans to alter the top floor of your residence."

"From my husband. Yes, I know. I agreed to his turning the third floor into a private office."

"Our problem is that you live in an historic house. Changes like these must go through many layers of approval. I wanted to let you know that we will start the process immediately, but work won't begin before next spring."

After the phone call, Dani knew alternate plans had to be put in place. She checked her little black book and made a few phone calls. In less than ten minutes, she'd rented an office suite for Terence in a building with keyed elevator entry and security scans.

She leaned back in her chair. Crisis Averted.

Another call. The security detail assigned to the twins. "Ma'am, the boys were found drunk in the school locker-room."

"Where are they now?"

"We brought them home."

"Hold them there and don't do anything. I'll be right home." She put on her jacket, grabbed her purse, and scooped the folders on her desk into her briefcase along with her laptop. She alerted her security detail and said, "Let's go."

In the car, Dani made several phone calls. The boys were about to crash into reality.

She instructed her team to drive around to the back of the house. She asked one to take her bag and briefcase inside and have the boy's security bring them outside. Then, she went for the hose.

The agent came out holding each twin by the arm. "It seems they had cans of beer stocked in their backpacks. Sorry Ma'am."

The boys were giggling and texting.

"It's okay," she said to the agent. "Stand them over there and get out of the way."

By the time Ivan noticed the hose in her hand, the pressured stream of water had hit him in the chest. "Whaaa...."

Isaac laughed. The cold water soaked his groin. "Ma...."

She had just wanted to get their attention, but her frustrations poured out. She'd had it up to here with taking and dealing with shit, standing-up for herself at every turn, and being disrespected and ignored by her own sons. Where was Terence? The perpetual good guy? Why do I have to be the disciplinarian when all I want is for them to acknowledge me, include me, love me?

She walked toward them, using the hose like a weaponized snake, biting Ivan and Isaac all over their bodies. They tried to run only to be turned back by the secret service agents. She saw the twins fall to the ground, soaked to the bone, and heard their pleas. "Stop. Stop already. Mom!" Her reason returned.

Dani handed the hose to the agent who offered to take it. She thanked him and turned to her forlorn sons. "You have disgraced yourselves. Despite all efforts to keep this prank out of the papers, I'm sure some tabloid is running the headline, complete with front page photos your friends took, 'Veep's Sons Caught in Drunken Orgy." The boys looked at each other and cast their eyes down to the wet, matted grass. "Great job screwing up."

<~<~|~>~>

Dani relaxed in the tub. The glass of wine and the hot water did the job. With her head resting on a pillow, she closed her eyes and drifted into a dream state.

She saw a younger version of herself. The girl had dark wavy hair gathered into a ponytail, wore a blue striped shirt, belted jeans, and sandals. She sat on a farmhouse's front porch steps. The sunbathed the landscape in gold, with crisp and dark shadows punctuated by glistening highlights. A movement in the distance.

Two men emerged from the barn, exchanged a few words, and separated. One, Terry, before he insisted on Terence, walked toward her. As he approached, the tall, broad shouldered, muscular, blue-eyed Adonis made her heart race, her lips ache, and her body arch with desire.

A door slammed. Dani's eyes flew open, and she sat up. Angry voices. She scrambled out of the tub and threw on her robe, tying the belt as she entered the bedroom. An angry pound on the door and it flew open.

Terence, red-faced, stepped into the room, and pointed a finger at her. "What did you do to my children?"

Calm, Dani's practiced defense against anger, she said, "They're our children and they were drunk."

"You humiliated them. Demeaned them. In front of the secret service."

Dani stood in front of him. With clarity and precision, she said, "They were drunk. Thrown out of school. They humiliated themselves."

"You did nothing," Terence said through clenched teeth. "You let the coach throw them off the team." Terence turned to the door and then, returned to her. "How could you?"

"This is my fault, is it? Where were you?"

"Busy. Where were you?"

"Busy."

Dani ignored his hulking bluster, crossed to her dressing table, and sat down on the bench. She picked up a brush and stroked her hair. She spoke to his reflection in the mirror. "What are you still doing here? Your bedroom is next door."

Terence marched to her side. "I want those boys back on the team."

"Not happening," Dani said, still doing her hair. "I've other plans for them."

"Are you going to mess with them like you've messed with me?"

"I don't know what you're talking about." Dani got up and walked into the closet to pick out her clothes and dress for dinner.

Terence moved into the center of the room to maintain visual contact. "Did you visit the office suite you rented for me?"

"I didn't have time. The agent assured me it's in a prime location."

"For what?"

"I'm sorry, Terence. What does that mean?"

"The building is prestigious but the suite's a disaster. There's no view, no light, and no height. It's a fucking hole."

"I made sure the address impressed and," she emerged, dressed to face him, "you had all the privacy you needed to do whatever you wanted." He started to say something, but she stopped him. "Before you continue your hissy fit, did you notice you had a private back door and a fire escape?"

The energy left Terence's body. "No."

"You're welcome. I'll see you at dinner."

<~<~|~>~>

The twins looked confident when Dani and Terence took their places. She nodded to staff to begin serving.

Terence cleared his throat and addressed the boys. "I'm sorry, guys, your suspension stands."

Their disappointed faces turned to Dani.

"Your father is right. However, I know how you need to be busy and active. I've found two volunteer positions that are available and will take you. One's with people and the other with animals. You may decide who wants which."

Ivan said, "I'll take people."

"Good. You will be volunteering at the veteran's hospital and you, Isaac, will report to the DC animal rescue center."

Isaac said, "For how long? There's only four weeks left in the season."

Dani said, "From now until fall. You'll both be starting at the janitorial level. While there will be opportunities for advancement, they must be earned. Slacking off is not an option. Any negative reports will land you in Summer Boot Camp for Teens."

Three male jaws dropped. Boot Camp had a rough reputation—for the program's extreme difficulty and the kids who get sent there.

Dani said, "I see we've reached an understanding. Good." She looked down at the food on her plate, put her napkin on her lap, and said, "This looks delicious."

They ate in silence.

Chapter 13 ▶ Damir, Tawanda, Africa

Thursday, 7 May

Taxi spent another restless night thinking about the grandfather, his visit to Hope City, and the mayor's story. He had been a soldier, trained to fight for the rights of his people. The wound in his chest sent him home. He'd survived for a reason—maybe for this.

That morning, before starting his daily runs, Taxi went to the Damir police station. "I'd like to speak to the officer in charge." He waited for close to thirty minutes before seeing the inspector on duty.

"How may I help you?" the inspector said, leaning back in his chair.

"I have come to report a travesty of justice."

"I am listening."

"Many people were killed in a place called Hope City, which has since disappeared, and buried deep beneath the surface."

"Do you have proof of this atrocity?"

Taxi pulled out the names of the missing villagers. "These represent close to two hundred people who travelled on the buses to Hope City."

The inspector took the list, scanned it, and placed it on his desk. "This means nothing to me."

Taxi leaned forward. "Sir, I found where the people are buried. Small pipes sit in the ground, emitting the unmistakable odor of decay." He reached into his pocket for his phone and receipt pad. "I have a map and pictures."

The inspector looked at Taxi's evidence, scribbled on a piece of paper, and handed it to an officer. "We will wait." Not three minutes later, the officer returned and shook his head. "It appears we have no information on a place called Hope City. Nor do we have any report of missing war refugees."

Taxi said, "I'm here making the report. I'm telling you I was there. I know. I've talked to various sector mayors who witnessed the buses. You must listen. A genocide happened right under your nose."

The inspector stood. "I am sorry, Mr. Taxi. I must attend to other matters."

Taxi got out of his chair. "May I bring in other witnesses?"

"From the encampment?"

"Yes. They will verify these people are missing."

The inspector glanced at the officer who shrugged. "Go with the officer. He will give you a permit to bring your witnesses."

<~<~|~>~>

Taxi took a picture of the permit with his phone before he went to the grandfather's sector within the encampment. Familiar with the location, he found the mayor without any problem. "Sir, I have been to the police and explained about the missing people."

The mayor said, "I did not expect you to do that."

"I have a permit," Taxi showed him the piece of paper, "that will allow witnesses to accompany me to the police station where they can verify that the people who went to Hope City are now missing."

"No one will go," the mayor said. "This encampment is filled with the old and the young. Dismissed and forgotten. The healthiest men go to the mines. The children are bought or stolen for the sex trade. No one has any energy left to complain, much less travel to the government building."

Taxi looked around and saw the truth in the man's words. "If anything changes, here is my card."

The mayor put his hand up. "I have no phone."

"Leave a flag on the wall near where I found the grandfather. I pass by there every morning. If I see it, I will know to come to you."

Chapter 14 ▶ Harrison, NY

Thursday, 7 May

Lucy Kilmer poured over the reports from Damir. The Hope City genocide went better than expected for six days. She stopped the operation at the encampment's first sign of distrust. As a result, the operation received no push-back from the sector mayors or the government.

The spike in cholera cases attracted no attention either. More people gone. The health inspectors never checked the trucked-in water for contamination and none of the refugees raised an alarm. Still, she'd stopped that initiative to be on the safe side. No need to press her luck. Lucy had an arsenal of episodic lethal disruptions. Her plan depended on frequency creating fear as motivation for movement—get the refugees to leave the encampment and live somewhere, anywhere, else. So far, it wasn't working.

Her phone buzzed. A text. "In place." Her engineers had completed a grid of core samples, identified the stress areas, and planted improvised explosive devices, known as a IEDs, where they could do the most damage. No one had bothered them. Their paperwork indicated they were testing the ground for contamination to eliminate further cholera outbreaks.

Lucy checked her watch and texted. "test #5 @ 3 AM ACT"

Tomorrow morning at ten she'd know whether to proceed or not.

Chapter 15 ▶ Gramercy Avenue, N.Y.C.

Thursday, 7 May
Rachel walked into the living room--her body covered by a translucent nightgown.

Chris tore his eyes from the computer monitor and looked up.

She said, "Are you coming to bed?"

He smiled. "You bet."

She returned the smile and put her hands on his shoulders. "Did you book the helicopter flight for to-morrow?"

"I did. I also hired a car for the day."

She kissed him on the neck, right near his ear. She felt him quiver as her breath entered his body. "You're my hero."

He turned, looked up at her, and encircled her body with his arms. In mid kiss, her phone rang.

"Leave it," he said.

"I can't. It's late. It may be important." She ran into the bedroom. The ID said, "Sybil." She answered.

"Rachel. Rachel. I don't know what I'm going to do."

"Sybil, what's going on?"

She heard sobbing followed by hiccupping for breath as Sybil struggled to speak.

Under control, Sybil said, "He's leaving me. Peter is going away tomorrow. He promised he'd stay with me for at least two more weeks." Sybil's sniffling went on for about a minute. "I need him here. It's the anniversary of Lidia's death."

"It's been four weeks, Sybil."

"See. You know too. Why can't Peter see?"

Rachel said, "Is Peter there? May I speak to him?" She heard Sybil call him to the phone.

"Hi, Rachel. Sorry Mom dragged you into this."

"Peter, are you going to Damir?"

"Yes. There's been some refugee activity and the State Department wants me to go over there earlier than expected. Since I already know President Ebu, they think I'll be more effective than any other person they could send."

"Makes sense. When are you leaving?"

"In the morning. I'll catch a flight out to DC and then Damir."

"Want to come down with us? Chris hired a helicopter and driver."

"Sure. Thanks. Have him text me time and place. Anything's better than battling the airport."

Rachel said, "In the meantime, Sybil needs attention."

"I've taken care of it. The nurse who was with her at the hospital has agreed to come and stay while I'm gone."

"Good move."

"I think her anxiety is fueled by her fear of losing me."

Rachel heard more sobbing in the background. "You're probably right." She paused. "Okay. See you in the morning. Let me say good-bye to Sybil."

Sybil didn't give her a chance to talk. "Rachel, what am I going to do?"

"You're going to be fine. The nurse will be there with you. I promise I'll stop in after I return from Washington."

"Oh, no. You're leaving too?"

Peter's voice. "I'll take care of this, Rachel. Don't worry. It's time for her meds."

Chapter 16 ▶ Damir, Tawanda, Africa

Friday, 8 May
At three AM, the ground trembled beneath the encampment's far end. Meager kitchenware pitched and toppled, unstable supports collapsed, and shrieks pierced the air. People scurried to help and calm each other. By dawn, all those affected gathered in the main thoroughfare. Section Mayor Yar'Adua listened to his people and sent a child, with a strip of cloth on a stick, to sit on the wall.

<~<~|~>~>

The refugees who had the strength and energy agreed to follow Yar'Adua and Taxi to the police station. By seven AM, the group of fifteen set off at a slow shuffle. As the rag-tag line of elders and youngsters passed through their first encampment intersection, others joined them.

When Taxi turned around to check for stragglers, he couldn't believe how many had joined the contingent. They were now forty strong. As the group snaked their way to the main road, their number increased to hundreds. The refugees wanted to have their voices heard. Their simple foray turned into a march—a slow march, but a march never-the-less.

By the third hour, the front of the line made it to the first traffic light between the encampment and the government building.

Taxi looked at Yar'Adua. "Do you think we'll make it?"

The mayor shrugged his shoulders. "We can only try."

Without waiting for traffic, Taxi led the way across the street. Angry drivers honked and shouted to no avail. The refugees kept eyes forward. Those accosted by screaming, appalled, and inconvenienced storekeepers and shoppers, did nothing except turn a blank stare without breaking their forward motion. The enormity of their effort—their snail's pace, their unclean odor, their rags on bone, and their endless numbers wound up silencing the city. A reporter called it, "The march of the undead."

People got out of cars. Many watched and some stepped forward to help those faltering. Locals offered water or bread. Police responded, prepared to use force to stop the invasion. Instead, they lined the route.

Taxi and Yar'Adua rounded the corner to the Presidential Palace and government offices well past noon.

President Kwanh Ebu watched the march on his large screen TV monitor. As the leaders emerged at the bottom of the hill, he screamed for Oliver Odili, his chief counsel, who entered breathless.

Ebu pointed to the TV, "I don't want those people in here. Get rid of them. Send them back."

"Sir, you know that would be looked upon as bad faith."

"What do they want?"

"I understand they believe some of their family and friends have been, um, executed and buried."

"And why do they think that?"

"An ancient wind listener."

"You mean this assault on my home and office is on the word of a crazy old man?"

"The police inspector I spoke to said someone, a Mr. Taxi, had been to the site and confirmed the strong possibility of the grandfather's words."

"Ridiculous. I would have known. Turn these people away."

Odili didn't move.

"Why are you not on your way?"

"My President, from what I understand, once they got moving, they inspired others to join them. Therefore, Sir, before you do anything rash, there are hundreds of mobile phones out there recording this phenomenon, besides the TV cameras. I suggest you let the police inspector handle it or be very temperate in your own approach."

Ebu grunted. They watched the procession while the President received periodic texted updates from the police inspector.

The marchers started to fill the large entranceway and, sooner than expected, overflowed into the roadway and parking areas. The sea of humanity spread before Ebu's eyes.

Odili said, "Sir, I think you should speak to these people."

"I will not respond to a mob."

"Sir, I see reporters moving among them. This is not going away."

"Fine," Ebu said. "Write something and I will look at it."

Odili nodded and left the room.

A knock at the door and Olidi entered. "The police inspector would like to have a word."

Ebu nodded. The inspector came in. Odili left.

"Mr. President," the inspector said, "I have come to you for advice."

"How can I help?"

"I am going to meet with a few representatives about Hope City and what transpired there. I have denied knowledge of such a place since there is nothing in our files. Is there anything you wish me to know?"

"Take down the information and send it to me."

"I have a request. It has taken these people almost all day to get here. May I ask that military vehicles be employed to transport them back to their shelters?"

"Mr. Odili, get in here."

The man flew into the room, a paper in his hand flapping in the wind. "Here, Sir. A speech for your approval."

Ebu accepted the document, scanned it, and said, "Good. Get the military to take all these people back to where they came from."

"Where they came from originally?"

Ebu looked up. "What?"

"Did you want to send them home?"

"You know I can't do that. That's enemy territory now."

"Sorry, Sir, I misunderstood." Odili pulled out his phone. As he tapped the extension required, he confirmed his orders. "You meant back to the refugee encampment."

Ebu glared in response. While Odili made the call, he marked-up the speech, read it aloud, made a few more notes, and said, "Ready. Get me some cabinet members to stand with us so it looks like the whole government supports this action."

He paced while he waited. Without a glance at the time, he went out to the open balcony that overlooked the mass of people. It wasn't, but it felt like the whole country had decided to descend on his office.

Quickly the balcony filled with officials who stood at attention.

Ebu opened the leather portfolio and read his speech.

"Welcome to the good people of Ta-wanda. While I am surprised at this spontaneous gathering, I am glad to have the opportunity to speak to you today.

"I know your journey has been hard. The war has taken a toll on our country, diverting much needed currency to our determination to retain our lands. My sole goal is for you to have a home and live in peace.

"To that end, I will work with the cabinet to develop and implement new systems to benefit every citizen through job opportunities, land, and education.

"Thank you all for coming today to register your concerns. I am heartened by your participation and will continue to give your plight my undivided attention."

Ebu raised his hands above his head and shouted, "Tawanda, my home," three times.

The crowd responded. "Tawanda, my home!" after each.

Ebu left the balcony and Odili stepped forward. "Ladies and gentlemen, for those who have made the long journey today, President Ebu is providing military vehicles to transport you back to the encampment. He wishes you well. Thank you for your show of support."

<~<~|~>~>

Taxi didn't hear the President's announcement. He, Mayor Yar'Adua, and seven members of the community were in with the inspector. In turn, they described what they saw and knew about the disappearances. The problem was that no one had any firsthand knowledge about what happened after the buses left the encampment.

After listening to everyone's account, the Chief Inspector said, "Thank you for testifying. We have taken all your statements. I believe you saw what you saw. I must now turn it over to a special detail of officers who will try to put together what happened and find your friends."

Taxi said, "That is it?"

"Until I find out more, it is all I can do."

"Do you want me to take you to the site?"

"When it is time, if we need help, I will contact you." The inspector stood. "I have a special van to take you back. Inside are provisions provided by local churches for you to distribute. Again, thank you for coming."

As the van pulled away, Taxi heard the inspector say, "Fumigate the office."

<~<~|~>~>

They hadn't moved more than one-hundred yards before they had to stop. A wall of people blocked their way and encircled the van.

Taxi said, "Open the window."

The policeman on the passenger side open his about two inches.

The crowd chanted the same indistinct words over and over.

Taxi said, "A little more. I want to hear what they are saying."

Another inch lower. Taxi moved to put his ear close to the opening and heard, "We want go home," over and over. He turned to the mayor and said, "The refugees, who were ready to join their ancestors by the time they arrived here, have now found the strength to demand a return to their homes."

"Impossible."

Taxi said, "We have to get out of here."

The driver said, "We can't go anywhere."

"No, out of the van."

The old woman by the door used two hands and pulled the levered handle toward her. The door opened and all nine got out with Taxi in the lead. People seemed to know him and moved aside. He and the mayor took a position on the government building's steps, facing the sea of humanity spread before him. To the right stood buses and army transports ready to take the people back to the camp.

Taxi asked the man standing to his left, "What is going on?"

The man said, "The refugees won't get on and the soldiers won't touch them."

"When did the chanting start?"

"At the end of President Ebu's speech."

The next person over leaned forward and said to Taxi, "It was not much of a speech."

Taxi looked at the mayor and opened his mouth to speak. Before he could get a word out, he saw a change happening within the crowd. The old ones, who could stand no more, sat down. It started to his left about one-third of the way down. The standers sat, in a domino effect, which turned the sea of swaying bodies, into a massive field.

The chanting stopped. The day done. Energy gone.

Taxi turned to the mayor only to be interrupted again, this time by a policeman. "Excuse me, Mr. Taxi. Will you please come with me?"

"And Mayor Yar'Adua?"

"Yes. Bring him, too."

A guide let the two men through the building's hallway maze and into the office of the Counsel to the President.

"Good evening, gentlemen. I am Oliver Odili. I have asked you here to determine if there is a way to diffuse the civil action outside. I fear for the safety of the refugees, and the demonstration's ramifications with respect to government operations and traffic patterns throughout Damir."

Yar'Adua tugged on Taxi's arm. "We must go. We are in the wrong place."

Odili said, "No, you are in the right place."

Yar'Adua said, "You want to discuss civil action, is this true?"

Odili nodded.

Yar'Adua said, "I will only discuss the rights of every displaced refugee here and in the encampment."

"I see."

Taxi looked back and forth between the men and said, "Perhaps the two goals are not mutually exclusive. The encampment is unsafe and unhealthy. These people want to go back to their villages and a way of life that made them happy. If you want them to disburse, you must offer them relief from the hell hole where they now live."

Odili looked at Yar'Adua. "Will you give me some time to prepare a plan?"

Taxi said, "You've had almost twenty years."

Odili said, "Two weeks."

Yar'Adua said, "In exchange for what?"

Odili paused, looking back and forth between the two men standing before him. "Food and medical supplies to get everyone healthy and ready for the next phase."

Yar'Adua said, "Food, medical supplies, and sanitation until the last person leaves for home."

"Done. Move them."

Yar'Adua said, "We start at dawn with the help of your transports. Food, medical supplies, and sanitation

must be available upon their return to the encampment."

Taxi said, "I'll go back tonight and wait for the
supplies to arrive. As soon as they do, I'll let the mayor
know. He'll make sure everyone boards the transports."

"Gentlemen," Odili said, "thank you for your
help."

<~<~|~>~>

Ebu saw Odili's ID and answered his phone. "I hope
this is good news."

"Mr. President, the refugees will move at dawn."

"Excellent."

"Sir, we still have a problem."

"Tell me."

Odili said, "We have two weeks to figure out how
to get the refugees home to their villages."

Ebu said, "Their homes are destroyed, and their
land is war zone."

"Sir, two weeks or they return for another sit-
in…unless…you want to negotiate an extension."

"It's late. Let us talk in the morning." Ebu ended
the call as the private phone in his back pocket, buzzed.
A text.

Chapter 17 ▶ Washington, D.C.

Friday, 8 May

The next morning at eight-thirty, Rachel, Zeus, Chris, and Peter sat in the helicopter, clicked their seat belts, and leaned back for fifty-minute ride.

Chris closed his eyes.

Rachel looked at Peter. "How is Sybil this morning?"

Peter said, "Subdued."

"I guess that's good," Rachel said. "It's been hard for her."

"She's tough and I've got good people taking care of her."

"I know. And she loves having you close."

Peter's phone buzzed. He pulled it out and checked the screen. "Seems there's a refugees' march to protest conditions. A friend of mine, a guy named Sam, sent me this."

Chris opened one eye to watch over Rachel's shoulder, resuming disinterest by the end.

Rachel said, "Peter, this is no uprising."

"I know," Peter said. "It took hours for them to get from the camp to the government offices—two, maybe three miles away." He shook his head. "I've no idea what I'm walking into."

"Are these the people that need PRAISE's help?"

"Yes. Something must have scared them into action."

"Any clues?"

"Not yet. Everything I know is second or third hand. I hope my relationship with the former Counsel to the President, Kwanh Ebu, who's now President, is intact. At least, that's what Washington's betting on."

"Peter, stay in touch. Let me know if you need anything like money, supplies, or guidance. I'll even represent our interests to President Sandford, if necessary."

"Thanks, Rachel. I just might."

<~<~|~>~>

At ten AM, Rachel and Zeus entered the Vice President's office. Dani rose and walked around her desk to great her guests.

"Welcome."

"Thank you. I have to say it's very exciting to be invited to a meeting in the White House."

"Who is your companion?"

"Dani, this is Zeus." At the mention of his name, his tail wagged.

Dani said to the dog, "You're my very first canine visitor."

Rachel said, "He's not unfriendly, he's working."

Dani went to her intercom and said, "Ready." An aide brought in a tea service and set it on the coffee table. "Let's sit and get to know each other before we get down to some serious brainstorming."

The Vice President poured tea and offered Rachel a cup. "These cookies are from the best bakery in town. Take one now and put the rest in your pocket."

Rachel laughed. "For Chris, my fiancé, if they last that long."

"Before we get down to business, I want you to know that I've recently spoken to my Aunt Sybil for the first time in over fifteen years, and I want to thank you for being there for her during that awful time in New York."

Rachel froze, cup at her lips. She swallowed. "Your aunt?"

Dani nodded. "I'm the black sheep. I left the family, went to college, and haven't been back since."

"Is that why you weren't at the funeral?"

"Yes," Dani said. "I've already started to repair some of those relationships. For now, though, please tell me about Aunt Sybil and Lidia."

Rachel said, "I happened to arrive at Sybil's when she realized Lidia was missing. Two hours later, the police verified that Lidia was dead. Murdered. By order of her father."

"After which, she murdered him."

"Dani, that happened so fast no one could have stopped it. Sybil's emotions exploded—her sorrow at Lidia's death, anger at the killer, and fury at your grandfather, who had ordered the hit. If he'd just said, 'I'm sorry,' he might still be alive."

"He'd never do that. He always justified everything he ever did."

"He told her he'd get off scot-free, and Sybil snapped."

Dani said, "Afterward, you took care of her."

"I helped where I could."

"Rachel, you did way more than that." Dani put her cup down. "Thank you. I'm so glad and grateful you were there for my family. How is Sybil doing now?"

Rachel put her cup down. "She is working her way through her losses. I'm here as her temporary surrogate."

Dani smiled. "No explanations necessary. I think we're going to get along fine." She got up, picked the laptop off her desk, and brought it to the coffee table. She hit a few keys and said, "Take a look at this footage from the refugee protest. President Ebu double-talked his way through a speech. The Tawandians sat down in protest. They're not leaving until tomorrow morning. We have no inkling as to why this protest happened. Hopefully, we'll hear something soon."

Rachel said, "These people are in terrible shape. It's a wonder they could walk at all."

"I agree. Whatever it was, it's the first time in almost twenty years that they've left the encampment," Dani said. "Did you bring the report?"

Rachel reached into her brief case and pulled out Peter's report.

Dani took the report. "Is this a copy?"

"Yes. You may keep it."

A knock on the door jam. Both women looked up. Dani folded the report and stuck it behind her. "Yosef."

"Yes, Ma'am. I have a communiqué from Tawanda regarding the uprising. One of our operatives spoke with a police department inspector."

Dani held out her hand. Yosef gave her the folder and paused. Dani said, "Is someone specific waiting for my input?"

"No, Ma'am."

"Then, thank you."

Yosef looked at Rachel.

"That will be all, Yosef."

Dani opened the folder and scanned the report. "Here, I want you to read this so we are on the same page." She handed it to Rachel while she collected folders from her desk and put them in her briefcase.

Rachel reviewed the information and handed the report back to Dani, who placed it in the briefcase. After closing it, she put on her jacket, turned to Rachel, and said, "Let's go."

<~<~|~>~>

After a brief stint as tour guide for Massachusetts Avenue, Dani said, "This is my official residence for the rest of my term. I thought it best to be in a more creative space for our discussions. Follow me."

Once inside, Dani said, "Put your things here, including your cell phone. I'd like to make sure we aren't being monitored." She turned to an agent. "Have the garden room and veranda been scanned today?"

He nodded. "All done and good to go."

Dani turned to Rachel. "Inside or out?"

She looked at Zeus and said, "Out."

"Then the veranda it is."

<~<~|~>~>

"Dani, you have my complete attention. What is going on?"

"I've been assigned a task and could use your help."

"What task?"

"Solving the Tawandian refugee problem through relocation."

"In Tawanda?"

"No. In the United States."

"I'm speechless."

Dani said, "I believe the President wants a plan to announce that backs up his human rights initiative, but any pushback, and there'll be plenty, that's on me."

"How soon do you need this plan?"

"I suspect that with these new developments in Tawanda, he's going to want to see something in the next few days."

Rachel said, "It's not going to be easy. The refugees don't want to leave Africa. They want to go home."

"How do you know?"

"Your cousin, Peter. He's been there. I trust his judgment on this."

"Do you have his personal mobile phone number? They've been keeping me in the dark regarding his activities, and I'd like to talk to him one-on-one."

"It's on my phone. I'll give it to you inside."

"Good. I'll call him and confirm the situation," Dani said. "For now, though, let's assume we have to evacuate. As I see it, we have three broad main issues—getting the refugees to agree to leave, transportation, and settlement in this country."

Rachel said, "What about large convoy planes? Can they use the runways at Tawanda's Okoro Airport?"

"That's a DOD question," Dani said. "I'll find out."

"Where will they land over here? I don't think you'll hit a lot of immigration problems if you bring refugees through a U.S. base."

"I'm way ahead of you," Dani said. "I already have a list of possible sites."

"How many people are we talking about?"

Dani said, "According to my information, about five-thousand, if they all come."

"Where will the refugees go once they're here?"

"I'm thinking we can renovate and use vacant buildings throughout various cities."

Rachel said, "That'd be easy for shelter. Stove, refrigerator, and washer-dryer would run about fifteen hundred to two thousand dollars per family. Do you have that kind of budget?"

"Not yet. However, I've been thinking of an idea. It's so crazy that I need to hear it out loud."

"Tell me, Dani. Nothing's worse than dumping five thousand refugees in the middle of an unsuspecting city."

"I want to target towns throughout the middle of the country that need an economic boost. Create refugee villages on bank-owned deserted land. Give them the seeds and support to develop sustainable organic farms or vertical hydroponic gardens."

Rachel said, "Not so crazy. As immigrants granted asylum, they'd get a monthly government check to spend in their new location. In turn, that would generate currency circulation, which would invigorate the entire area."

Dani nodded and said, "The main problem, as I see it, is selling the idea to the President and the designated areas."

"How could anyone say 'no'?" Rachel said. "You're bringing industry to their towns. That's good, right?"

"An industry for immigrants."

"I see your point," Rachel said. "Wait. What if you create Jobs Centers?"

Dani shook her head. "No one's going to get excited about a Jobs Center for people of color."

Rachel got up and walked to the railing. Looking at the lawn and spring flowers, she smelled the lilacs. She turned back to Dani. "The main faith in middle America is Christian Fundamentalism. Go to the church Elders for the naming of the jobs centers. They'll be able to tap into their congregation's imagination and goodness. You know, something like The Garden of Eden Project."

Dani said, "Good idea. That'll give the towns a vested interest from the beginning."

Rachel sat down and said, "It's not going to be as easy as we've made it out to be. The success or failure is in the details."

"Including the advanced ages of the incoming."

"Dani, they might not live through the flight."

"Or the internment."

"Or the resettlement."

"So much to think about," Dani said. "Let's take a break and have lunch."

Rachel said, "One more thing before we do. I know this may be too forward of me, but I'd like to know who's threatening this project. I talk to a lot of people, and I don't want to take a chance of ruining your plans."

Dani didn't say anything right away. She shifted in her seat so she could look directly at Rachel. "I think it's my father."

"James Vanderhagen?"

"He's inherited my late grandfather's position with the cartel and wields a lot of power. Sandford has been very cool. Giving me this project is the first time he's talked to me since I took office. At first, I thought he didn't like women. But after watching him in cabinet meetings, I knew it wasn't true. It had to be something else. I think my father has his hooks into him."

"And because you're Vanderhagen's daughter, you're also the devil."

"Exactly. What Sandford doesn't know is that my father and I are estranged. I've got nothing to do with him."

"Why don't you tell him that?"

"Because, Rachel, there's something else. I feel like someone's watching, spying on, and interfering with my work. My briefings always seem to be missing vital information. The result is my assessment is incomplete, and I look like a fool in front the President."

"That's not Sandford's doing?"

"No, I don't think so."

"Then, there's a mole."

Dani said, "Yes, who may be working for my father, who's instrumental in financing elections and controlling global actions."

"Peter said your family had something to do with Tawanda's mining industry."

Dani said, "I work for the people of the United States, not my father.

Rachel said, "There'll be repercussions."

"I know," Dani said. "I have to do it anyway."

Chapter 18 ▶ Observatory Circle, Washington, D.C.

Friday, 8 May

Dani and Rachel lingered over lunch in the garden room and managed to finish a bottle of white wine. The grandfather clock in the living room chimed four.

Dani said, "Let's call it a day. Who's picking you up?"

"My fiancée. I think he's meeting with DOD, but I'm not sure. I'll give him a call."

"Before you do, how about having dinner with me and my family?"

"Here?"

"Why not?"

"I don't want to put you out."

Dani said, "One minute." She walked out and returned a few minutes later. "I checked with the kitchen. Two more for dinner is not a problem. We dine at six."

<~<~|~>~>

Dani brought Rachel and Zeus up to the master bedroom so the women could freshen up before dinner.

As they stood side by side in front of the double-wide bathroom mirror, Dani said, "I want to thank you for today. It's the first time since I've been Vice President that I've truly enjoyed my job. Nothing and no one hanging over my head, no furtive glances to ignore, no busywork to make me feel like I'm doing something."

"My pleasure."

"I'd like to think the trust goes both ways."

Rachel said, "Of course."

"In return…."

"Not necessary. You don't…."

Dani disregarded Rachel. "In return, I'm going to work with you on making the human rights declaration powerful and impactful without the threats. In fact, I plan to attach it to any deal I wind up proposing."

Rachel smiled. "Now that's an offer I can't refuse."

<~<~|~>~>

Dani's phone buzzed. "My family is gathered for cocktails in the sitting room, and Chris is coming up the driveway. Let's go down and meet him before my family tears him to pieces."

"You're kidding."

"I am. That statement couldn't be further from the truth. The twins transform into mono-syllabic automations in my presence."

"Oh, wait," Rachel said. "Let me give you Peter's number before I forget."

Dani entered the contact and led the way. They intercepted Chris at the door. Rachel gave him a hug and a kiss hello, and said, "Madam Vice President Dani Mitchell, this is my fiancé, Christopher Gregory."

Dani extended her hand.

Chris reciprocated and said, "I'm honored to meet you, Ma'am."

"Call me Dani, or it's going to be a very long evening."

Chris smiled and nodded. "Chris." Then he looked down at Zeus, who was so excited he could barely sit. "Good to see you too, boy." He spent a few seconds acknowledging the dog.

Rachel said, "I need to feed Zeus. I'll be right back. Meanwhile, you two can get to know each other."

Dani motioned for Chris to follow her. She led him into the sitting room where the twins and Terence were attacking the hors d'oeuvres. She formally introduced Chris. Terence shook Chris's hand and asked what he would like to drink.

Dani glanced over at the boys—no phones, no slouching, no sleeping. To her surprise, they were sitting up straight and watching Chris's every move.

Rachel entered, Zeus by her side. She met Dani's family and asked for a vodka tonic. After twenty minutes, the dog stood. Rachel put her drink down. "I…"

Chris said, "I'll walk him."

Ivan and Isaac stood and grinned. "We'll show you around."

Dani's jaw dropped as she watched them leave.

<~<~|~>~>

At dinner, Rachel sat on Dani's left, with Zeus by her side, and Chris sat on Terence's left. After the grown-up chatter had subsided a bit, Ivan said, "Are you the Christopher Gregory who started his multi-billion-dollar security business in high school?"

Dani almost choked on her salmon. She hadn't heard either one of them speak in sentences for years. She looked at Terence who shrugged and listened as the boys quizzed Chris.

As a mother, her heart leapt with joy. Her handsome sons were bright, articulate, funny, and inquisitive. They exchanged puns, sarcasm, and information about science, business, problem solving, and girls. She saw Chris look at Rachel before he advised the teenagers. "Date whomever you want but marry the spirited smart one." Dani nodded before she realized he'd said, "Like your mother," and all eyes were on her.

She bowed her head and said, "Thank you."

Chris said, "Dani, I've been wondering all night, how's security around here? Are you on the DOD system?"

"I believe so."

Chris looked at the boys and Terence. "So, you three, and possibly you, Dani, are the weak links in the system."

The twins started talking, both at once.

Dani raised her eyebrows. They'd gotten the "security" talk when the family moved in and never said a word. She had no idea what, if anything, registered. Apparently, it all did.

Chris put his hands up to quiet them down. "All good. Now let me explain. Your mother is Vice President of the United States. If anything happened to the President, she'd have to step in and take over."

Heads nodded.

"If anyone breaches security here or anywhere, they would have information that would make it impossible for your mom, as Vice President or President, to do her job."

Everyone turned toward her. She said, "Yes, Chris's right."

Attention back to Chris. "Ideally, if you're not using your phone, pull the SIM card. For your password, I'll send the file. Email please." Chris typed it in. "This is the same sheet I give all my clients. Share it among you. And one more thing. Your biggest threat to the security of this country is…your mouth. What goes on in this house, stays in this house. No texting, emails, social media, or complaining to anyone, including family."

"You mean like cousins or grandparents?"

"I do. Especially them. They can all brag that they know what's going on."

"So, they don't live anywhere around here."

"You never know who they know and…."

Then Isaac said, "You never know who's listening."

Chris smiled. "That's the drill. Do you think you're up to it?"

Ivan looked at Isaac, and they both said, "Yes, sir."

"Please tell either your mother or me if security is broken. There is no penalty here. The leak has to be plugged on the other end."

Ivan said, "You mean actually call you? Direct?"

"I do." Chris pulled out his business cards. "Here's one for each of you and your parents. Put me on your phone as a friend, uncle or cousin with nothing else but the number. Then put the card in a safe place."

The twins nodded. Isaac said, "Thank you, Chris. It's been a pleasure meeting you." They looked at Dani, she nodded, and they ran upstairs.

The ensuing silence in the dining room made them laugh.

Dani said, "I just can't believe how animated they were."

"I agree," Terence said. "Normally, they sit through dinner without a word. We were getting ready to have a doctor check them out."

Rachel said to Chris, "It's fun to see you interact with kids."

"Whoa," Chris said. "We're not even married yet." He laughed.

"And I have Zeus, so no push here."

Dani said, "You guessed about the twins, didn't you?"

Chris smiled.

"How did you know?"

"I was once sixteen and a smug smartass. I hardly spoke to anyone and lived in the room over the garage. My parents dropped food off at my door because my attitude ruined family gatherings."

Rachel said, "You're kidding."

"Maybe, just a little. I observed the boys never looked or talked to anyone else but me. I figured it couldn't be good because I acted the same way, and my parents hated it."

Terence said, "What about the security?"

"Oh, that issue is real. I wasn't kidding. However, the boys are potentially the biggest leak you'll ever have here unless guests manage to access your information."

Dani smiled. "Very cagey, Mr. Gregory. By getting Ivan and Isaac to invest in the process, even monitor it, you've given them a responsibility to share with us."

"No Oscars yet, please. I simply shared real information and gave them the tools. What happens next is anyone's guess. I may have opened a Pandora's box of hyper-sleuths. I suggest you let them show you what they've figured out and go with it as a unique common bond—even if gets tedious. The rest will come."

Rachel glanced at the time and then at Chris. "It's time to go."

Chris thanked the Mitchells for the dinner invitation. To Dani he said, "I hope you ladies enjoyed your day."

Dani said, "Yes. I think our projects made big strides today." She saw Rachel extend her hand, waved it away, and offered a hug. Rachel accepted. As they parted, they agreed to talk the next day.

Dani walked out onto the entrance landing to watch Rachel and Chris leave with Zeus. Terence came up behind her and put his arm around her waist. She smiled and teared at the same time. This is the way it used to feel. Good times. Tender touches…only for her. The smile faded and she turned, forcing his arm to drop. "Good night."

Dani climbed the stairs. Alone. Living the lie.

Chapter 19 ▶ Damir, Tawanda, Africa

Saturday, 9 May

Peter arrived in Damir and sailed through customs. In the terminal, he saw a fortyish tanned man, wearing a native shirt, a straw hat, and a big smile. Peter smiled back. "Good to see you again, Sam. You can't imagine my relief upon hearing you survived our little adventure."

Sam laughed. "Good. Because it was all your fault."

Peter feigned hurt. "I…."

"Don't even try. If you hadn't uncovered the scam at the diamond mine, no one would have blown up the hotel or tried to kill you."

"You saved my life."

"From what I heard," Sam said, "you didn't do so badly on your own."

Peter stopped smiling. "I'm not proud of killing Wembe. I had no choice."

"Bakama's still around and running the open dig operation."

"By now, he knows I didn't give him up."

"Don't worry. I still have your back."

"I feel better already."

Sam lowered his voice. "As I understand it, you're under Ebu's protection. Be careful what you do and who you piss off this time."

"I consider myself warned," Peter said. "Can you bring me up to date?"

Sam said, "There's been some sort of shake-up, and my sources are mum on details."

"You want to tell me about your sources this time or hide under your triple-agent spy story."

"I have to stay with the story. However, my orders are to keep you alive and get you home safe. So, never doubt I'm on your side."

Peter smiled. "I'm good with that."

"Come on," Sam said. "Let's get a beer and I'll catch you up on what I do know."

The two men walked out to Sam's car. Next to it a tall bald broad-shouldered man leaned against a taxi and smiled at Peter. "Hello, do you remember me?"

Peter's eyebrows pinched and then smiled. "You're the driver who took me around the refugee camp, right?"

"Yes, my friend. My name is Taxi."

"And mine is Peter." He nodded to Sam and introduced him."

Sam stared at Taxi. "Do I know you?"

Taxi shook his head. "I do not think we have met before."

"I don't forget," Sam said, stroking his chin. "I got it. You walked with the refugee protesters."

"Yes. That was me."

Peter said, "You were involved?"

Taxi said, "Perhaps a quieter place for this discussion would be more appropriate."

Peter said, "Is there any place we won't be noticed?"

Sam laughed. "I don't think so."

Peter looked at Taxi and said, "Then, join us at the Damir Hotel Hawa bar. I'll cover your trip fare."

"Perhaps you will consider taking my taxi."

Peter looked at Sam.

Sam said, "I'll be fine. Meet you there."

Peter let Taxi take his bags as he addressed Sam. "Good. I'll see you in a few."

<~<~|~>~>

During the ride, Taxi told Peter about the refugees' predicament and how he got involved.

"You're telling me that hundreds of people were murdered, buried, and forgotten?"

"I am not sure of how many. I am told all the people from ten villages are missing. I believe they are buried because I have smelled the decay."

"That's unbelievable."

"After that, new outbreaks of cholera showed up in specific areas within the encampment. The sector mayors believe the trucked-in water carried the disease. They are convinced someone tampered with the supply to further reduce the numbers of refugees. By the time the health inspectors arrived, they found no contamination."

"You're implying there's a plot to systematically reduce the size of the refugee population."

"I am simply connecting the dots. People are dying at an unprecedented rate. The night before the march, we had maybe fifteen people who were going to come with me to report the suspected genocide to the police inspector. After the ground shook, many marched."

"Was it an earthquake?"

Taxi shrugged. "It has never happened before, and it has not happened since."

"What did the government do?"

"They have promised to present a plan in one week and six days."

"How can I help?"

"Make sure it happens. The refugees want to go home."

<~<~|~>~>

Peter checked in to the hotel. He unpacked his clothes but kept his electronics in his ever-present messenger bag. Then he showered and changed, looking forward to a cold beer. As he approached the door, his phone rang—an unfamiliar number. "Hello."

"Peter, this is Dani."

"Madam Vice President," Peter said. "This is a surprise."

"Dani to my favorite cousin."

"Only cousin," Peter said.

Dani laughed. "Family aside, I called to tell you that I am now responsible for our refugee initiative prompted by your report from your last trip."

Peter said, "That gives me hope."

"I would like us to make a difference. Please keep me abreast of activity in Damir. Anything of significance will affect time frames and urgency."

"No problem."

"By the way, Peter, I have touched base with Rachel Allen. She's taken over PRAISE, temporarily, until Sybil gets back on her feet."

"Yes, I know. I'm glad you two talked. She'll be a strong ally."

"Good to hear."

Peter said, "You're in good hands. If you need anything from me, call."

"Note this number," Dani said. "It's my private phone.

"Done. You'll be my first call."

<~<~|~>~>

Peter found Sam in the bar at their favorite table—in the back corner.

"No Taxi?"

Peter said, "He thought it best to maintain distance."

Sam said, "What are we up against?"

"Taxi told me the refugees believe they're being systematically murdered."

Sam said, "You can't believe that's true?"

"He believes the refugees think it's true."

Sam took two long sips of his beer. "My people don't want to make Tawanda's problems the target of global attention. If what you heard is true, we need to find a way to take care of it, quietly and efficiently—whatever that takes."

Peter stared at Sam. "Your people? What the hell does that mean?"

"We need to make this go away. It's in the best interests of all concerned." As Sam finished his sentence, his phone rang. He took the call. Listened. Nodded. Put the phone down. "You've got a meeting with President Ebu in one hour."

<~<~|~>~>

"My friend," President Ebu said. "It is good to see you again. Please sit down, we have much to discuss."

Peter nodded. "Mr. President, I'm happy to be here."

Ebu went to his desk and pressed a button. Peter watched. The man's distinguishing features were his blue eyes and his wide girth, which had expanded since last time they met. He wore a military uniform decorated with medals and a beret with a red "T" on a round beige-filled circle insignia. Peter decided Ebu wore it to minimize the outward angle of his ears.

Seconds later, a man, the same height as Ebu but slimmer, entered the room. "Mr. Peter Powell, this is Oliver Odili, my counsel."

The men shook hands.

Ebu continued. "Come let us sit down. We must go over the current situation and our needs. Oliver, would you please summarize."

Odili said, "Yesterday, without warning, a swarm of refugees besieged the Presidential Palace and government offices. In getting here, they held up traffic, stopped commerce, fouled the air, and caused the government much bad publicity. We met with their representatives and what they want is to return to their homes."

Peter said, "Is that a problem?"

Odili said, "Their homes, which are in the middle of our conflict with the DRC, are decimated."

"So, there's nothing to go home to."

"It seems it doesn't matter. Therefore, in order to solve one problem, we must solve another."

Peter said, "I see. You must end the war."

Ebu spoke. "Never. If I give up, Tawanda will be absorbed into the DRC. We must maintain our independence."

"Mr. President," Peter said. "I don't see what I can do."

Ebu said, "You, Mr. Powell, can broker a truce."

Peter looked at the two men. "I have neither the diplomatic standing nor the authority to do such a thing."

Ebu said, "I think you underestimate your importance."

"How's that?"

"You are the cartel's representative. That carries much weight."

Peter said, "You're misinformed. I'm unofficially representing U.S. interests."

"What about your uncle?"

"Not this trip."

Ebu held out his hand in Odili's direction. The man got up, retrieved a document from the President's desk, and gave it to Ebu who offered it to Peter.

Peter took the paper and read it. Peter Powell is our agent and under our protection. Please extend him the same courtesy as you do to us. He looked up. "Do you really think this will carry weight with the DRC?"

"The cartel is heavily invested throughout Africa. To dismiss you would not turn out well for them."

"On your word, I'm willing to try."

"Excellent." Ebu started to get up.

"Wait," Peter said. "What are your terms?"

The President sat down. "Terms? I'll stop shooting at them if they stop shooting at me."

"Have you not taken over land that belongs to them?"

"Did not their callous indifference take away our right to our historic nomadic life? We had to have somewhere to live."

Peter said, "Why do you think they care so much about Tawanda?"

"To save face."

"Really? Saving face will require huge gifts and abject humility on your part. Is that what you're prepared to do?"

Ebu shifted in his seat and glanced at Odili before re-engaging with Peter. "Perhaps," he said, "they will mention the mining rights."

"In other words, you have something they want."

"A tiny fraction of their total operation."

Peter sat forward, elbows on knees, and said, "Regardless, this war is all about money. Am I right?"

"It is possible."

"How much money?"

Ebu hesitated before answering. "A pittance compared to the DRC's holdings."

"Mr. President think like the DRC. What will be enough money for them to save face, stop the war, and recognize Tawanda as a separate country?"

"Anything I offer will never be enough. They will bleed us dry."

Peter said, "Come on, Sir, you have to give me some idea of what the stakes are. I can't go talk to them without a reasonable first offer."

Ebu stood and went to his desk. Odili followed. Ebu opened his computer and began typing. Odili stood behind his shoulder and watched.

Peter waited as they discussed their options. Closing the laptop, Ebu said, "I will authorize one-tenth-of-one-percent of the annual gross mining tariffs."

Peter said. "A start. I will need documentation to confirm a number. What kind of wiggle room do I have?"

"You may go up to one-half of one percent without calling me."

<~<~|~>~>

The next morning, in the DRC government offices in the capital city of Kinshasa, Peter spoke with the President's appointed negotiator, employing the same strategy he used with Ebu.

At first, the negotiator insisted on total and complete Tawandian surrender, with all lands returned to DRC control.

Peter said, "If you were Tawanda, what would you want?"

"For us to go away and let them have their state, such as it is."

"Are you willing to do that?"

"Absolutely not," the DRC negotiator said. "Tawanda's land-grab is prime real estate that is worth a fortune to us. Besides, they started this damn war and it has cost us dearly. Any leniency would show us as weak."

Peter said, "How much would it take to stop the war and move forward? Remember ending this war would save many lives and redirect precious resources. War is expensive."

"Come back in two hours."

<~<~|~>~>

Peter returned early. He sat and waited until the appointed time.

The negotiator sat behind his desk and nodded to the visitor's chair. Peter sat down. The negotiator leaned back in his chair and said, "We are aware Tawanda is imposing new tariffs similar to ours."

"Yes, that's true."

"We will take twenty percent."

Peter remained calm at the outrageous demand. "That will bankrupt Tawanda. It is war on a different battlefield. Can't we figure out a win-win situation?"

"Twenty percent," the DRC negotiator said.

"Are you telling me that the teeny tiny little country of Tawanda is mining twenty percent of your resources?"

"That's my offer."

Peter said, "That is robbery. No way do Tawanda's holdings come close to representing twenty percent loss."

"The uprising has cost us far above anything we expected."

"Sir, with your permission, may I have a moment?"

"Take fifteen." The man got up and walked out.

Peter grabbed his computer out of his messenger bag. His phone buzzed. A text from Sam. "How's it going?"

He replied. "Researching. Later."

Peter found the information he needed. The DRC's revenues before and after Tawanda's existence. It confirmed the offer on the table far exceeded actual loss.

The negotiator returned and sat behind the desk.

"Are you ready to accept?"

"As you are no doubt aware, Tawanda can't meet your demand. Post war, they'll have to initiate and fund a huge jobs program to employ all the out-of-work soldiers."

"Not my problem."

"It is if there is a mass exodus to DRC looking for jobs."

The negotiator frowned. "We will not accept Tawanda's jobless or its refugees."

"The refugees lived here before the war."

"They made their choice."

Peter cleared his throat. "I have researched Tawanda's economic impact on your gross income and your figure is nowhere close to your actual loss."

"I see. Do you have an offer for me?"

Peter said, "I am authorized to offer one-tenth-of-one-percent of the annual gross mining tariffs, divided into equal monthly payments. It is a fair offer based on your published revenues."

The negotiator pulled out his phone, did the calculation, made a phone call, walked outside the room, and returned. He countered with, "My President won't take less than a half."

Peter had the authority to go that high, but he didn't want to look weak. The DRC would have to work for that number to be satisfied with it. He pulled out his phone and pretended to call Ebu. Holding the phone to his chest, Peter looked at the negotiator and said, "Counter of point 3."

"A half or nothing."

Peter rose out of the chair and walked away. He put the phone to his ear and became very animated—his free hand gesturing and his head bobbing. A minute later, he turned to the negotiator, "Point 4.75."

The negotiator let the number echo in the air before responding. "Accepted. With the addendum that no jobless or refugees cross our border."

Peter turned, phone to his ear, nodded. Faced the negotiator and said, "Agreed. Now, we need to get this agreement drafted and officially signed so we can declare peace. This is President Ebu's Chief of Staff." Peter handed the man a business card. "He will work with you to get this done."

"You do not want something signed now?"

Peter said, "I recorded our verbal agreement, but you're right." He asked for a piece of paper, wrote down the percentage, and signed it. He offered the pen to the negotiator, who took it and also signed. Both took phone pictures of the document and sealed the deal.

Chapter 20 ▶ Harrison, NY

Sunday, 10 May

Reports from the refugee camp made Lucy's eyes shine and her groin tingle. The charge worked better than she had expected. The natives were restless. Time for the next phase. She picked up her phone to text the order. She hesitated. Put the phone in her pocket.

Hesitation meant an issue remained unresolved. Lucy always trusted her gut and this particular sign. In her experience, those who didn't, died.

She sat down at her computer and ran the stats again. Using the data from the core samples, she rendered a three-dimensional diagram of the refugee encampment's subsurface.

The monitor showed a relatively flat surface covering layers of subsoil which formed the ceiling of a cavernous space sans centered stabilizing structures. Next, she added the layer corresponding to the placement of the charges.

Lucy ran the simulation. She wanted to create a sink hole with as few charges as possible. She placed four on the floor to take out the walls and four above them to rupture the ceiling. If all went off at the same time, there would be a huge explosion.

If she went with the four on the top exclusively, the surface would tremble. Based on the radiating blast waves, some people would wake but probably not sound the alarm. Still, she couldn't take the chance the sinkhole would fill before it had done its job.

She ran the modeling program again and again. She had to be one-hundred percent sure. In less than an hour, she had the bomb sequence that would do the most damage.

Lucy texted President Kwanh Ebu's throwaway phone. "1-2nite or 2-2mrw nite." His people. His call.

His text, "wait5days."

Chapter 21 ▶ Washington, DC

Monday, 11 May
Dani went down for breakfast at her usual time, 7 AM.
The house was quiet. As always, the sound the boys
had left for school, and Terence didn't get up before
nine. It gave her time for peace and contemplation over
two poached eggs, one slice of toast, one ounce of
cheddar cheese, and a strong cup of coffee. The ritual
prepared her for the day.

This morning, unlike the others, on the table, she
saw a big floral bouquet, filled with hydrangea, roses,
and lilacs, accompanied by a basket of wine, all sent by
Rachel and Chris. Dani smiled and sat down.

Half-way through her meal, the sound of a buffalo
stampede startled her. She turned to see the boys' four
big feet thumping on each stair tread. They rounded the
banister and took two seats at the table to her left.

"What are you two still doing home. Don't you
have school today?"

Isaac said, "This is more important. We'll go later."

She opened her mouth to protest but Ivan shut her down. "Mom, can we have your phone?"

"Why? What for?"

Ivan said, "We checked with the guys," nodding toward the secret service agents, "and they said you have two phones. One is for POTUS, you know White House business, and the other is personal."

"Yes. I don't think that's a secret."

Isaac said, "It's not. So, we've spent a good part of the night going over personal security measures like, um, Chris suggested, and we've clean-up and cleared out our phones and computers. We've installed Chris's suggestions for passwords and initiated a schedule for testing for malware and back-up."

"I have to say I am impressed."

Ivan said, "We want yours and Dad's phone to include in our security checks."

"How long will it take?"

Isaac said, "Fifteen minutes."

She handed him her phone and they took off. Halfway up the stairs, Ivan called down to her. "Your laptop is cleared through the White House security so should be okay." Then they were gone.

Dani shook her head and looked at the agent. "Tell me you checked this all out."

"I did, Ma'am. I observed them and Mr. Gregory through the whole process. I also checked with DOD. The modifications they're making are approved upgrade procedures."

By the time Dani finished breakfast, the boys presented her with her "clean" phone. "Here it is, Mom. Good to go," said Isaac.

"We found an electronic tag," Ivan said. "It means someone is trying to listen to your conversations. But don't worry, we took it off."

"Yeah," said Isaac. "It'll help a little if you keep it out of sight. But if someone really want to get into it, they can."

Ivan said, "We'll check it every day or more often if you want. Just ask."

"Sure," Dani said. "Thanks. I'm amazed."

"Just part of the team," Isaac said, and they left for school.

<~<~|~>~>

On the way to her office, Dani wondered who could be listening through her phone. She congratulated herself for meeting with Rachel in an electronic free zone. She'd have to be more vigilant, even though she only used that phone for personal calls.

She stopped at her Senate office and took care of business before going to her West Wing office where she had more privacy.

Deep into the transcription of her meeting with Rachel, she didn't hear the rap on her door. Her secretary stepped in. "Secretary of State Henderson to see you."

Dani nodded and Uriah walked in and took a seat. "I've heard from Mr. Powell."

"Peter, Uriah. He's my cousin."

Uriah cleared his throat. "Yes, Peter just contacted me. His connection with the new President of Tawanda paved the way for his participation in negotiating a peace treaty." He stood. "Crisis averted. Anything else?"

"Peter's there for a couple of days and now there's a peace treaty?"

"I admit I was surprised as well. I must have been the right time."

"Or, something else is going on," Dani said. "Do you know the specifics?"

"In general, Tawanda is paying the DRC a percentage of mining profits so they can redirect their limited resources to support their own people."

"President Ebu has suddenly become a humanist?"

"Hardly. He wants to become part of the United Nations. To do that, he must solve his human rights issues. The war is a distraction. He needs his limited manpower on his own soil, not engaged in war."

Dani shook her head. "I guess we should be thankful the conflict will end and not second guess Ebu's motives."

"Yes, Ma'am."

"Thank you, Uriah, for the personal update."

"No problem." He turned and left.

She returned to her immigration plan. If not this wave of refugees, there'd be another, and another after that. She paused. No word about the mine workers. She'd deal with that.

Using the White House phone system, she called Rachel.

"Thank you for the wine and flowers."

"We had a wonderful time, and Chris is cherishing his first groupies."

"They boys are very excited. We even had a conversation. A big deal in my home."

"Glad we inspired them," Rachel said. "What's going on?"

"It looks like the refugee problem in Tawanda is settled. President Ebu, through Peter, has negotiated a peace with the DRC. He expects the agreement will be ready to announce in the next ten days or so. The only hitch is that the DRC will not permit refugee re-entry for any reason."

"That can't be good," Rachel said. "Any news regarding the mine workers?"

"Not that I know of. I'll talk to Uriah Henderson and see what he suggests."

Rachel said, "Does this mean the relocation scenarios are on hold?"

"That depends on President Ebu. If he doesn't make good on his promise to the refugees, we have to be ready to handle our part in any rescue operation. By tackling this now, we'll be pro-active."

"I like that," Rachel said. "It can also be a model to other countries who are now just trying to figure out what to do with the influx of immigrants from the Mideast and Mediterranean areas."

Dani said, "I'll finish framing it and send you a copy. We'll go from there."

"Can't wait. Thank you, Dani, for including PRAISE."

Dani ended the phone call and heard a commotion outside her door. Her secretary ran in, followed by Yosef, who waved a newspaper over his head. He overtook the woman, who backed off, hovering in the doorway.

Yosef laid the paper on Dani's desk. "Breaking news."

Dani looked at him and then at the picture front and center above the fold. Without a doubt, someone caught Terence and Bruce kissing. A window shot. Terence's office.

Yosef said, "What are we going to do about this?"

"About what?"

"You're going to have to respond to this."

"And say what?"

"Madam Vice President, are you being dense? Your husband is two-timing you with a man."

"Terence is bi-sexual, a fact I've known for a long time. It's not unusual for the spouse of a busy public official to have dalliances."

Yosef crossed his arms and tapped his toe. "Really? Is that what you're going to say?"

"I'm not going to say anything. It's a picture framed in suppositions."

Yosef reached for the paper. Dani pulled it out of his reach. He straightened and said, "I'll talk to Wendell and see if he wants me to prepare a statement for you to release."

Dani said, "No matter what, no apologies and no recriminations."

"As you wish." Yosef left and shut the door behind him.

Dani took a deep breath and called Terence.

He answered her call with, "Don't."

She said, "Are you crazy? Messing around with no curtains? You must be out of your mind."

"I thought we were surrounded by brick walls."

"With windows, apparently."

"I know. I know. Decorators are already here correcting the problem."

Dani said, "The White House wants me to issue a statement. I've told them you're bi-sexual and we are comfortable with that. Do not say anything else."

"I want to tell everyone that this has nothing to do with you."

"Don't say anything, but if you must, don't be defensive or we'll be victimized by the press forever. Our position is we are aware and accepting."

"Okay. Got it. Private matter. Bi-sexual."

"Be sure to tell Bruce no interviews. If I hear he's said anything other than 'no comment,' I will personally see to it he is banished to a cave in Afghanistan."

"He's not going to like that."

"I don't care," Dani said. "Do you want to alert the boys, or shall I?"

"Umm."

"Okay. I'll have their agents pull them out of school. You go meet them when they arrive. They're going to have to deal with this."

"I'll handle it."

"Good. We'll talk later."

"Dani," Terence said. "I'm really sorry."

<~<~|~>~>

Dani put the phone in her pocket, got up, and fixed herself a vodka on the rocks. She took a sip. First the boys get caught drunk at school, and now Terence is outed. Egad. What's going on? Two damaging situations, one after the other. Coincidence? Her gut said no.

Another sip.

A knock on the door. Yosef came in. "Here is the statement we'd like to issue on your behalf."

Dani went to her desk. She wanted to feel official as she read out loud. "Vice President Dani Mitchell appreciates the concern that has flooded the White House on her behalf. Her marriage and her family are a private matter. They'll face this issue together, supporting each other as unique individuals, and moving forward. Thank you all for your continued support."

Yosef said, "Well? What do you think?"

She took a pen and signed off.

<~<~|~>~>

When she got home, Terence met her with two drinks in hand. He offered her one.

"Let me put my stuff down." She did and took the drink. Walking around him, she went into the living room.

He followed, showering her with apologies. "I'm so sorry. I had no idea. I never meant to hurt you."

Dani said, "I know. How did your talk with Ivan and Isaac go?"

Terence smiled. "It went well. Surprisingly, better than I expected. They're good boys." His face turned serious. "I'm so sorry I hurt you, Dani. I would never do such a thing."

She said, "I believe you."

Terence's eyes open wide. "You do?"

"Of course. You were targeted to hurt me."

"You?"

She nodded and sat down.

Terence said, "Your father?"

"Maybe. Or someone in the White House."

"I don't understand."

Dani said, "I may be seen as a threat…for myself or because of my Vanderhagen connection."

"Jesus." Terence downed his drink and poured himself another.

She said, "What I can't understand is why and why now?"

The thunder of feet descending the stairs announced the twins' arrival. They raced in and skidded to a stop.

"Hi, Mom," said Ivan.

"Hi, Dad," said Isaac.

She said, "What's going on?"

Isaac said, "Nothing. Just initiating our evening security check."

Terence sat down. "Didn't we do this at breakfast?"

Ivan said, "We're following protocol."

Dani said, "Explain."

Ivan said, "Remember we said we found something on your personal phone?"

"Yes."

Isaac said, "When we got home, we ran Dad's info and we think we found one on his."

Terence said, "Someone's tracking my movements?"

"We don't know," said Ivan.

Isaac motioned to his ear and his mouth as his eyes scanned the ceiling. He looked at each parent, his forefinger bisecting his lips. "We're just learning this stuff."

Ivan said, "It's our science project." He motioned to Terence for his phone and did the same to Dani. Devices in hand, the twins left.

Dani called out, "Dinner in a half-an-hour."

Chapter 22 ▶ Gramercy Avenue, N.Y.C.

Monday, 11 May
Rachel and Zeus returned home after several hours at PRAISE. She dropped her bag and briefcase off with Nikolai for safe keeping while they went on their afternoon walk.

Her phone buzzed on her way back. Chris texted. "Aft cocktails ready." She smiled. Every day, it seemed, she loved him more.

She walked into the lobby. Nikolai grinned as he handed her things back to her. She said, "What's making you so happy?"

"I am always happy to see you."

"Yeah, not this happy. What's going on?"

Nikolai shrugged his shoulders. "What has to be going on for me to be happy?"

"You're not going to tell me, are you?"

"There is nothing to tell."

"Really." Rachel narrowed her eyes and leaned in toward the big man. "Where's Tareek. I'll get it out of him."

Nikolai raised his hands and took a step back. "Nothing to get out of anybody."

Rachel said, "Okay." She looked down at Zeus. "We'll see, won't we?" The dog looked up at her to confirm. Rachel scratched him behind his ear, and he closed his eyes. "Enough. Let's go see what Chris has for us."

<~<~|~>~>

She entered the living room and Chris got up. Rachel unleashed Zeus and walked over to Chris.

He picked up two champagne flutes and gave her one. "This is a toast to us."

They sipped and kissed.

She said, "This is nice. What's going on?"

"Nothing. Can't a guy toast the love of his life?"

Rachel started walking around the room.

He said, "Looking for something?"

"Yes. Nikolai and you are both acting way out of character, and I want to know why."

"I see," Chris said. "Well, you're not going to find anything in here."

She pivoted to face him. "Show me."

"Close your eyes."

With one hand around her waist and the other holding her hand, Chris led her into the bedroom. He positioned her in front of the sliding door closet, released her, and opened the one of the doors. "Okay," he said. "Open your eyes."

"Your clothes closet?"

Chris stood grinning ear-to-ear. "Yes."

Rachel cocked her head. "This is significant?"

"Uh-huh."

"Because…." Then it dawned on her. Her eyes widened and her mouth dropped open. "Because they're not in the walk-in." She ran to the big closet and threw open the door. "Oh my God. You and Nikolai moved my stuff in here today."

"Yes, we did."

She threw her arms around him, gave him a long kiss, and whispered, "You are the best!"

They did a slow-motion dance to the bed—opening buttons, removing clothing, and touching bared skin. Zeus watched and dropped to the floor, resting his head on his front paws.

They landed on the mattress, arched their entwined bodies, and made love with abandon.

Afterwards, they showered, put on sweats, and returned to the living room to enjoy the cocktails Chris had prepared.

Rachel said, "Now this is the way to end a hard day at the office."

Chris said, "I agree."

"Oh, I spoke to Dani Mitchell today. She said the boys were in touch with you."

"They are. I can tell you, they're very bright and eager to learn."

"She said they instituted new security procedures on the family's personal equipment."

"Easy stuff. Gives them some practice."

"I didn't get that impression."

"It's all good, Rachel. I promise. I ran it through the DOD since it's their security. The boys are not operating in a vacuum. Everything is checked and double checked before it goes live."

"Like what?"

"Why are you interrogating me like some CIA operative?"

"I'm not," she said.

"Feels like it."

"It's just that…." Rachel decided to skip her explanation. Chris made it clear he didn't want to discuss her concern. She went to safer ground. "What's for dinner?"

Chris jumped up. "I totally forgot. It's been heating in the oven." He hurried into the kitchen. He pulled out the pizza. "It's crisp." He removed a slice and tasted it. "Still good." Zeus whined. "Sorry, buddy. Guess I forgot you, too." He served Zeus and then brought dinner out to Rachel.

After a few slices, she stood. "I'm going to walk Zeus. Coming?"

Chris got up and stretched. "I'm tired. It's been a long day. You go. I'll finish up a few details."

She didn't move.

He said, "What's the matter?"

"That's what I'd like to know."

"Nothing."

"No walk. No ice cream."

"Huh?"

"Chris, I know something's off because you're forgetting the little endearing things that have always been a part of you, of us."

"You're paranoid and I'm tired. Let's do this another time."

"Really? You're shutting me down?"

"Don't do this."

Rachel stared at him. "You go ahead. Zeus and I will be back soon."

Chris shook his head and left the room.

Rachel and Zeus went out and returned a half hour later. She gave him a treat and made herself a sundae, vanilla with a ton of hot chocolate sauce. Zeus whined. She smiled and put some vanilla in a dish for him. Carrying both, she collapsed on the couch and put the dog's dish on the floor. Zeus's happy slurping made her chuckle.

She turned on the TV and watched the news—anything to keep her mind off Chris. It wasn't working so Rachel flipped channels, hoping something would catch her eye or attention. Either one would work. A couple more flips and there it was—the demonstration in Tawanda.

She had seen it on a computer screen, but the impact on the large TV monitor took her by surprise. The magnitude of the refugees' distress showed in their deteriorated physical condition—their muscle mass gone, faces gaunt with hunger, bodies pocked with sores. She put down her half-finished ice cream and picked up her phone. She couldn't wait for the huge wheels of government. She had to act now.

Rachel dialed Peter without looking at the time. She didn't care.

"What are you doing?"

She looked up. "Um, calling Peter." She pointed to the TV.

Chris positioned himself so he could see what she meant. "Come on. You can do this in the morning."

Rachel said, "No. I'll lose a whole day. It'll only take a…." Her attention shifted to the phone. "Peter, are you okay?"

"Yes, fine."

"I just saw the video of the uprising."

Peter said, "More a march then an uprising. Have to say, the refugees did themselves proud. I'm ready to board—leaving Kinshasa for Damir."

"Let me know what you need and where to send it. Right now, you are my top priority."

"Good to know, Rachel. I'll talk to you after I land."

Rachel put her phone down and looked up at Chris. "The war is over."

Chris said, "You must be relieved."

"For now. Tomorrow's another day."

He walked over to her and offered both hands. "Come to bed."

She nodded. As she followed Chris, she heard slurping. "Zeus is still washing dishes."

"Let him. We can do other things."

Chapter 23 ▶ Harrison, NY

Tuesday, 12 May

Lucy Kilmer prided herself on her self-control, thoroughness, and patience. Those traits combined with a photographic memory, a degree in actuarial science, and a genius I.Q. made her worth her exorbitant fee. Although as a youngster she drove her plodding middle class parents to their emotional and financial limits.

Within their home, they forced her to comply with their mundane ways. Out in the world, they scrimped and saved to provide her with training that befitted her talents and interests.

She felt she deserved everything she got and praised herself for putting up with them. When she left home, it was for good. She never contacted them again—except for the reimbursement check. She calculated the amount to the penny. It cancelled all their debt and if the rest were invested in a conservative fund, it would afford them the means to maintain their lifestyle. That settled any outstanding score and wiped them from her memory.

Today, approaching the cave-in launch, she felt uncharacteristically edgy, despite going over every detail five times. She spent an extra thirty minutes on floor exercises and did an additional two miles on the treadmill. After her cool down and shower, she laid down on her bed. Eyes closed, she reviewed her plan...again.

After fifteen minutes, her eyes flew open. and she ran to her laptop. Lucy engaged the computer model of the catastrophe about to befall the refugee encampment...two times. The results never varied—she'd nailed it. Still, maybe she could improve her numbers.

She ran the simulations again. Tested several new hypothesizes. Once she was satisfied, she amended the launch.

She smiled as she took pride in the expanded effectiveness of her plan. She checked the time. Not yet, but soon. That's when she noticed—no hesitation anxiety. She felt calm and centered.

Chapter 24 ▶ Damir, Tawanda, Africa

Wednesday, 13 May

At three AM, Peter's eyes flew open. He sat up. Looked around. Listened. Nothing stirred in his room. No sound interrupted the air-conditioner's drone. Uneasy, he got up and opened the door to the hotel corridor. The halls were empty. He went to the window. The street was deserted. In any other place it might be normal, but in Damir, people worked or hung out twenty-four hours a day.

Peter got dressed, put his phone in his pocket, took the stairs down to the lobby, and spoke to the desk clerk. "Where is everyone?"

The clerk raised his eyebrows. "I don't know what you mean, Sir."

"Yes, you do. Tell me."

"It does not concern our guests."

"I'm different."

"Please, Sir, go back to your room. Everything will be fine."

Peter grabbed the counter, his muscles flexed, ready to launch himself at the smug clerk. A hand on his shoulder stopped him. He turned.

Sam said, "Come. I'll show you."

The two men rushed outside. Sam said, "Get in the car. There's been a cave-in. I can get us half-way there. After that, we run." He drove to the business district, pulled into a side street, and parked. "Follow me."

The men raced through the streets which were filling up with people looking confused. After three blocks, Peter heard shouts and screams coming from the encampment.

They slowed to a trot as people filled the roadways—some running toward the chaos and others running away. Suddenly, everyone froze. No motion. No sound. One heartbeat. Two. A rumble. The ground shook beneath their feet. A screaming, stampeding crowd surged toward them, propelling the men backwards. "Run. Run for your life."

Peter and Sam did just that and swept up small children in danger of being trampled to death. Behind them, the earth opened for the second time. A huge sinkhole sucked people, huts, possessions, and roads into its depths. The deafening noise stopped. The earth settled. An eerie silence hung in the air.

The crowd stopped and turned. Peter and Sam each had a child sitting on his shoulder, and four in his arms. They put the children down and made their way to the collapse to help in any way they could. At the edge, they saw a saucer-shaped barren gouge on the African plain where part of the encampment used to be.

"Jesus," said Peter. "One minute that whole area supported thousands of refugees, and now, nothing."

Sam shook his head. "Un-fucking-believable."

Peter stood dumbfounded by the enormity of the catastrophe. Sirens and flashing lights preceded the swarm of police cars, army vehicles, and ambulances. Officers cordoned off the area and moved everyone, including Peter and Sam, away from the site. Squads equipped with floodlights encircled the sinkhole. Light beams crisscrossed over the entire area. No survivors.

"Come."

Peter and Sam turned to the voice behind them. Taxi said, "Follow me."

A half-a-block away, refugees huddled in a large vacant parking lot.

Peter said, "This can't be all…."

Taxi's eyes watered. "I hope not."

<~<~|~>~>

Lucy watched the drone's images on her monitor. The evacuation worked as planned. From the fly-over, she estimated maybe two-thousand refugees, twenty percent, had survived the blast and instant burial. She figured another two hundred wouldn't survive the stress of the next twenty-four hours.

She shut her laptop and went for a shower.

<~<~|~>~>

President Ebu watched on his monitor.

Odili raced in, wringing his hands. "This is a tragedy. So many people. All gone. Dead. You have to say something. The city is in chaos."

Ebu said, "At least the end was swift and the dead no longer suffer."

"I will draw up a plan to care for the survivors."

"In and out of Tawanda. Perhaps other countries will take them."

"Sir, you want to send them away?"

"It would be best for Tawanda," Ebu said. Odili's jaw dropped. Ebu had gone too far and decided to retreat. "Ignore that. I am in shock and talking foolishness. Of course, we will do all we can to help the city and the refugees get through this. Go make your plans."

"Yes, Mr. President. Right away." Odili left the room. Ebu rubbed his hands together and smiled. He pulled his chair closer to the desk so he could type. In a new document, he typed a letter to the United Nations which would accompany his application for membership. Without a refugee problem and its accompanying human rights issues, Tawanda would become a recognized world power.

<~<~|~>~>

The two hours dragged at the rim. Officers and soldiers checked every crevasse for signs of life. Finding none, they prepared to leave. Splitting their circle on the far side, each half walked to the front where their vehicles waited. An officer from the left side, sixth from last, stopped. "Sir."

His superior stepped forward. "Yes, officer."

The young man pointed to the ground at the rim's edge, "See that, Sir. A fissure, not eight inches long. It is one of many in this area closest to the city."

The superior officer glanced down and around the rim. There were others, some smaller, and one or two longer. "I see no reason to be concerned. The earth is dry."

A small force remained to insure no one else got hurt. They put up a caution tape to separate the sinkhole from the main road and the marketplace beyond. Throughout the day, people came to hold vigils by the devastation. By mid-afternoon, the vendors sold out, packed up, folded their tents, and left.

<~<~|~>~>

On the far side of town, the government commandeered large event tents and set them up behind the Damir Hotel Hawa for the refugees. The hotel staff set up long food tables and served the frightened people. The army set up water stations and portable toilets and showers. City churches distributed clothing, blankets, and personal items.

Peter, Sam, and Taxi helped the refugees settle in the tents. For the first time since the second sinkhole collapse, Peter felt the phone vibrate in his pocket. He pulled it out and answered. "Wait, I need to get to a quiet spot." He made his way through the tents and into the bar.

"Okay. I'm here." He signaled the bartender for a beer.

"Peter, this is Dani. What happened over there? I've seen the images. It's looks surreal."

"Around three this morning, Damir time, the ground shook and half the sinkhole dropped. People disappeared. I'm told the earth just swallowed everything on the surface. Then, about fifteen to twenty minutes later, the second half collapsed. It eradicated almost the entire refugee encampment. Dani, that's almost eight thousand people gone. It's beyond horrific." Holding his beer, he walked to his favorite table in the bar's far corner.

Dani said, "What about the survivors?"

Peter explained the situation. "It's bad. I don't know what's going to happen."

Dani said, "Is there anything we can do from our end?"

"I can't say for sure. I haven't talked to anyone from President Ebu's office. I will make my way there right now. In the meantime, would you contact Rachel and see if she can get…." Peter felt the vibration. "Something's happening. Got to go." He ran out the bar's side entrance, to the intersection of hotel's entrance and the main thoroughfare.

From his position, half-way up the hill, he could see the city below and the government buildings above. People who had gathered to see the catastrophe scattered in every direction, like a human starburst. He watched as the ground beneath the marketplace at the city's edge gave way.

Peter heard glass windows popping before shattering, wood squealing as joints pulled apart, and people screaming. The new sinkhole swallowed people and storefronts. Only the roadway between the encampment and the marketplace remained intact.

Sam appeared next to Peter. "What…." He couldn't complete his sentence as he stared at the far end of the city. "Oh, my God."

Like the first two collapses, there were no survivors. Witnesses wailed. Others scrambled in a frenzy, grabbing anything they could, and leaving the city with whatever they could carry. Cars, bikes, and pedestrians filled the roadways. Everything and everybody moved west, past the hotel, away from the sinkholes.

Peter said, "Come on," and started running up the hill. Sam followed. "We've got to get to Ebu." Taxi joined them. They made it to the stairs as the rumble started, and to the building's entrance as the next jolt hit. Seconds later, they watched another sinkhole claim more lives and buildings. Damir's entire downtown— gone.

<~<~|~>~>

Peter, Sam, and Taxi entered President Ebu's office. They found him staring out the window, Odili by his side.

Ebu said, "The Tawandian people are leaving in panic. It breaks my heart. My vision for my country included it being a haven for all. A place the disenfranchised could call home, put down roots, and feel secure. Damir's random destruction has killed many and ruined many more lives and livelihoods. I am bereft beyond words. As President of this great country, I pledge my time and resources to help my countrymen."

Odili said, "Anything else?"

Ebu turned to him. "No. Release that to the world press."

Odili raced out.

Ebu sat down and offered the men a seat. He said, "Do you think it will reach the government offices?"

The three men looked at each other, dumfounded at the question. Taxi found his voice, "Did you ask so you could offer a safe place for those fleeing?"

Ebu cleared his throat. "Of course, but only if you think it will stand."

A knock on the door and an aide appeared. "We are ready, Sir."

"Excellent." Ebu stood and the men followed suit. "I have made arrangements to guard the integrity of my government at an undisclosed location until Damir is stable, at which time, I will return."

Peter said, "You're leaving your people?"

"An act of God. I must save the leadership."

Taxi stepped in front of Ebu. "You must show your people strength and protection. Organize the police and the army for their protection."

"You are right," Ebu said. He called out, "Odili." The man arrived, breathless. "Mr. Oliver Odili, I appoint you President Pro-Tem. Do what you must. I must leave to safeguard this government."

Odili's eyes bulged with surprise.

Peter said, "You can't just walk away."

Ebu said, "I must, for now. I will be back." With that he swept out of the room and disappeared.

Peter said, "Mr. Odili, your orders, Sir."

Odili cleared his throat. "Do what you do best. Let me know what you need and if I can supply it, I will."

The three men walked out of the office, down the steps and toward the hotel.

Sam said, "I feel like I'm in a movie in an alternate universe."

Chapter 25 ▶ West Wing, Washington, D.C.

Wednesday, 13 May
Dani called Nancy and asked to see the President.

Nancy said, "I'll call you back with a time."

"Tell him it's important. It's about the disaster in Tawanda."

"He has a very full schedule. I'll get back to you."

Dani heard the click-off and looked at the phone. "Fuck."

She grabbed some papers and marched out of her office, almost running over Yosef. "Sorry." She tried to get around him, but he didn't move.

"Maybe I can help," he said.

"You can get out of my way."

In the ensuing stare-down, Dani won, and Yosef stepped aside and walked with her. "Are you sure this is what you want to do?"

She stopped. Looked at him without blinking as she knocked on the door to the oval office and walked in, closing the door behind her.

"I'm sorry to barge in, Mr. President. There is a crisis in Tawanda." She nodded acknowledgement to Wendell, sitting in the visitor's chair by Sandford's desk. Thousands of people have died in the last twenty-four hours, and they our need help."

Sandford said, "I understood a sinkhole all but eliminated the refugee situation."

"I've spoken to Peter Powell. The Damir's central business center is gone. He fears the city is collapsing beyond repair." She placed the folders on the President's desk. "Sir, we're not just talking about a refugee encampment anymore."

"People are resilient," the President said. "They'll move."

"To where?" Dani said. "Damir is Tawanda's only city. The rest of the country's populated with villages. There is no place equipped to take a whole city."

"So, they migrate to the DRC or adjacent countries. We don't have to get involved."

Dani handed him several papers from the top folder. "The surrounding countries have reinforced their borders. They are not accepting refugees."

Sandford looked at the information and at Wendell Waters.

Wendell said, "We have not crafted the final human rights declaration, nor put into place a safe and secure port of entry for a mass intake of refugees."

"You're right. That assignment is mine." She retrieved another piece of paper from the folder and held out her hand. "Here's the plan."

Sandford took it.

Dani said, "With your say so, I'll begin initiating the transportation and setting up receiving stations at the named airports in my report."

"Let me go over this with Wendell and Uriah. We'll get back to you."

"Sir, as you are aware, this is a humanitarian action, and we can't wait too long to start."

Sandford nodded.

Dani started to say something but thought better of it. She collected the folders and left the room.

Yosef met her in the hall. "How'd it go?"

Dani didn't bother to answer. He followed her. Her phone rang. She pulled it out. Saw the ID and said, "What's going on?" she said.

Peter said, "The place is in panic mode, and President Ebu's abandoned the city for higher ground."

"Bailed."

"Yup. He's left Odili in charge."

"Of the city?"

"Who knows? Maybe the whole country."

"The country?"

Peter said, "What's left. Wait. Another tremble. Gotta go."

Dani looked at her phone and spun on her heels. Face to face with Yosef, she said, "Stop following me and get out of my way."

He stepped aside and she returned to the Oval Office.

Sandford stood, hands on his desk. "Stop. I am in the middle of another crisis. You must schedule…."

Dani didn't stop until she stood in front of Sandford's desk. "Sir, I am fully aware that you keep me at arm's length from the boys' club in here." She looked at Wendell and Uriah, who had arrived before her dramatic entrance.

She returned her gaze to Sandford. "However, right now, I am the most informed individual in the room about Tawanda. Making decisions behind my back, that is, without including me, is not in the best interests of Tawanda or our country."

She didn't wait for affirmation. "That said, I've just heard from Peter. President Ebu left the capital and abandoned his people in this time of crisis. Mr. Odili is in charge, which is not necessarily good news. Peter's assessing the damage and will get back to me."

Wendell stood up. "When did Powell start reporting to you?"

She swiveled her head about thirty degrees and met his eyes. "I'm sure you're aware we're cousins and he's comfortable talking to me. Furthermore, you know the President assigned me to the refugee project. If you have a problem, we can discuss it another time."

Sandford, motioning for Wendell to sit, said, "What do you expect from me? We are seven hours away from Damir."

Wendell, seated, said, "It's an African problem, unless the refugees make it to Europe."

Dani said, "You mean trek to and cross the Mediterranean like the Syrian refugees did some years back?"

"Yes. Exactly."

Dani stared at Wendell. "The refugees from the encampment look like they couldn't negotiate a five-mile hike. As for the others, anything is possible if they've got enough food and water."

He said, "Then that's the answer. Survival of the fittest."

"Would you say that if, say, Ireland collapsed?"

"That's different. We have a cultural link."

Dani blood-pressure soared. She pointed her finger at Wendell. "You racist. We have a human link and can have planes in the air in a matter of hours."

Sandford put both hands out. "Calm down, everyone." He sat. Let's discuss this rationally. We need to figure out if we need to choose an extreme or can find middle ground that serves the refugees and us." He slapped the desk and stood. "Let's break for an hour to refresh our minds. Each of you come back with inter-mediate steps we could take." He exited through a side door.

Dani left next. She didn't think she could talk to either Wendell or Uriah without exploding. She marched down the hallway to her office, threw on a jacket, and pulled some bills from her purse. With agents by her side, she walked to the Potomac River, buying a chili dog and a can of iced tea from a vendor along the route.

On the bench, in the sunshine, surrounded by cherry trees, and calmed by the river's motion, Dani found her breath. She closed her eyes and listened to life all around—people, kids, dogs, birds, planes overhead, even a helicopter. Normal.

She ate in peace and enjoyed every bit. Then, she stood, stretched, and ran her fingers through her hair. I must walk back in there smiling. Otherwise, they'll rip me to shreds instead of working with me. Fuckers.

Chapter 26 ▶ Gramercy Ave, N.Y.C.

Wednesday, 13 May

Rachel overslept. She found Chris and Zeus in the living room. Zeus bounded over to her, licking her hand and begging for his morning attention. She gave him scratches behind his ears and under his chin, and pats on his side and head.

Out of the corner of her eye, she observed Chris on the phone, speaking too soft for her to hear, and keeping his back to her. The phone in her pocket buzzed. She pulled it out. A text from her mother. She'd be arriving on the 25th to begin the wedding plans. Rachel sent her a "thumbs up."

She gave Zeus his final pat for the moment and went into the kitchen for her first cup of coffee. Chris had made a whole carafe. She liked his thoughtfulness. He did make her feel special. Rachel filled her coffee cup and topped it off with a tablespoon of frozen yogurt.

She took her first sip and pondered what else she might like. Before she compiled a definitive list, Chris arrived. He pulled a plate of French toast out of the microwave. "Just for you," he said.

She gave him a kiss. "Thank you."

"A heads-up. I just got off the phone with Washington. Have to run down."

"Let me see if Dani can schedule time for me."

"I'm leaving in," Chris looked at his watch, "two hours."

"Not a problem."

Chris hesitated.

She said, "You don't want me to come?"

"I didn't say that."

"Your body said it."

"I'm avoiding a fight."

"Really? We never fight."

"We're going to fight over this because I know how you feel."

"How could you if we've never talked about it?"

"Rachel, you're making too much of this."

"Of what? If I'm going to be mad, I want to know why."

Chris leaned back and crossed his arms across his body. He said, "I'm working on a project that's about ready to be tested. I'm going down to the DOD to clarify the scope."

"And the project is…."

Chris ran his fingers through his hair and paced the room. He pulled out his phone and put it away. He sat on the couch and patted the cushion next to him. "Come here. Sit down and I'll tell you."

She sat. "I'm ready. Tell me."

"Promise you'll hear me out before jumping to any conclusions."

"I'd never…."

Chris held up his hand. "In this case, you might. Promise?"

"I'll try."

He leaned forward, elbows on knees, and said, "I've developed an ultra-thin microchip tracker for incoming foreign nationals entering this country to stay, whether for asylum or student visa, green card, or whatever."

Rachel's hands locked, knuckles white.

He said, "It's been in the works for several years, but there has been no policy in place that justified using such a tool."

Rachel said, "Profiling. You're talking about profiling people."

"No, not exactly. It's more about personal information such as name, from where, reason, family, blood type, issues. Mainly, it's for the government to keep tabs on mass immigration."

"You're planning on testing this system on the Tawadanian refugees."

"Wow, honey, that's a big jump."

"It's true, isn't it? That's why you didn't want to tell me."

"I have no idea. Maybe that's what today's meeting is about."

Rachel bit her bottom lip, released it and said, "It didn't have to be you. You knew this had horrible overtones. First this group. Then that group. Pretty soon, it's all of us. It'll never end until everyone has one."

"If not me…."

"Chris, you've got enough money to keep you off bread lines during your next three lifetimes. You're enabling the government's violation of a person's right to privacy."

"It has nothing to do with money." Chris sat back and looked at her. "I did understand the ramifications. I took the job because I felt that if I had control, I'd be able to judge if it got out of hand and stop it or at least minimize any problems the project might cause."

"Designer, implementer, and adjudicator."

Chris looked at the time. "Yes." He stood. "Now I've got some work to do before we leave, that is, if you're coming."

Rachel stood. "I'll be ready." She took a step toward him. He left without looking back. Pulling out her phone, she called the Vice President. "Hi, Dani. Chris and I are coming to Washington. We expect to land around noon. Can we meet?"

"Yes. I'll make time. Call me at touchdown."

Chapter 27 ▶ Philadelphia, PA

Wednesday, 13 May

Vanderhagen made the call. "Peter, tell me what's happening."

"Uncle James, I'm in Damir. Your authorization letter got me in to see the DRC. There is a peace treaty in the works."

"Between Tawanda and the DRC?"

"Yes. It has to go through the whole legal review, but the terms are firm."

"Excellent. Good job, Peter."

"Listen, I can't talk for long. The city is in chaos. The refugee camp and main thoroughfare have collapsed into enormous sinkholes. Thousands have died and the city is in a panic."

"Wait," Vanderhagen said. "What about the mines?"

"No word. But be prepared. If food runs out, the stores at the mine's warehouse will be impounded."

"Peter," Vanderhagen said, "you make sure that doesn't happen."

"I can't promise."

"Block the road."

"Not a good idea. Confinement will only make the situation worse. Look, I've got to go. I'll get back to you."

Vanderhagen scowled. Uprisings were common enough and a royal pain in his ass. He had to save the mines.

<~<~|~>~>

Less than an hour later, to Vanderhagen's grave disappointment, none of his contacts in the surrounding countries could assure him of aid to Tawanda.

A throwaway phone in his top drawer rang. Vanderhagen fetched it. "Yes."

"It is I," Ebu said.

"Where are you?"

"In the north."

"You must get back to Damir and take charge."

"What if I am swallowed by the devil?"

"You mean if the cartel doesn't kill you first."

Ebu said, "I am not afraid of ghosts."

"You should be," Vanderhagen said. "The mines are as much the cartel's as yours."

"I have reports. The mines are safe."

"If anything happens, it's on you."

Vanderhagen cut the connection and returned to his computer screen. Lucy had given him access to a drone camera which sent back images in real time. Peter's phoned in report did not do justice to the devastation. He saw the deep holes flecked with debris—a cover for the dead below. He tried the controls and found they worked. A few taps later, the drone captured the cartel's holdings and the workers' camp.

Here the ground remained firm. Vanderhagen breathed a sigh of relief and watched the screen. The camps were calm. Too calm. He leaned forward in his chair. He changed the drone's pattern. Nothing altered the fact that the camps were empty. The open mines unattended. The main gate… appeared closed, and he hoped, locked, with the fence electrified.

Positioned his cursor in the comment field. "VIP guard assets."

The answer came back. "Checking."

Minutes later, Vanderhagen watched two jeeps roll into view and eight men got out. Four remained at the gate and four went inside the management building. They returned shaking their heads. The mines were deserted and, as he feared, putting the cartel's holding at high risk.

<~<~|~>~>

Vanderhagen's stress triggered his acid reflux. He retrieved his medication from the desk's middle drawer and drank it straight from the bottle. Leaning back in his chair and closing his eyes, he gave the thickened liquid time to do its job while he considered his next move.

He picked up his phone, chose his contact, and texted, "Assets require action."

The White House had to earn its keep.

Chapter 28 ▶ Washington D.C.

Wednesday, 13 May

Dani's phone buzzed. It was a text. "Research in progress. Oval Office in 90." She checked the time. They'd reconvene at two. Another buzz. "Be there in 15." Rachel. Good. Dani got up, tossed her garbage in the can, and walked back to her office.

A half a block from the White House, she saw people arguing. Her Secret Service agents stopped her and took their positions as two figures broke away and ran towards her. In the next instant, the agents relaxed.

"Mom. Mom." The twins slid to a stop in front of her. Ivan said, "We have to talk to you."

They looked from agent to agent. Isaac said, "Alone."

Dani said, "Okay. Let's go to my office."

The boys glanced at each other and shook their heads.

"Then where?"

They looked around and pointed to a park bench across the street.

<~<~|~>~>

The agents cleared the area and the three sat down. Ivan put his forefinger on his lips. Dani nodded. Isaac held out his hand for her phone. She gave it to him. He opened the back and removed the sim card. Ivan said, "Any others?"

Dani shook her head. "Now, what's this about?"

Ivan said, "You know we found tracking on your phone, right?"

She nodded.

"We keep taking off the code," Isaac said, "and it keeps coming back."

Ivan said, "We wiped it off this morning and it returned around eleven."

Dani knew she had been in the Oval Office at that time. She said, "Does it matter where I am?"

The boys shook their heads.

Dani said, "Someone's listening?"

The twins nodded.

"Do I need to keep my phone off?"

Ivan said, "It doesn't make a difference once the sim card is back in place."

She said, "I understand. You did great. We'll take care of this at dinner."

They stood and Dani threw her arms around the boys' shoulders. "Love you. See you later."

Isaac returned her reassembled phone, and the boys took off. She watched them get into the car and walked to her office. She arrived at the same time as Rachel.

Dani said, "I have until my two o'clock meeting with the President."

Rachel said, "This will only take a few minutes."

"I'm all ears." Dani pulled out her phone and extracted the sim card. "The walls have ears."

Rachel nodded. "I understand."

"Okay, tell me."

"I found out this morning that Chris is working on a technology for the DOD to imbed subcutaneous trackers in all incoming foreign nationals. I think they're planning to use it on Tawandian refugees as a test."

"Interesting."

"That's it? Don't the implications horrify you? First the immigrants. Next the Blacks. Then the Jews. And the Muslims. Mexicans. On and on, until the government can pull any targeted group off the streets."

"Possibly. However, it also gives us a database so we can track potential terrorists."

"Dani, I can't believe you're saying this. This whole idea is an affront to individual freedom."

"I'm just exploring the positive applications."

Rachel pushed to her feet as Dani put her hand out in a "stop" position and then used her index finger to circle the room.

Sitting down, Rachel nodded and said, "Yes, that's a good idea."

Dani said, "I'm going to meet Sandford to talk about Tawanda."

A knock on the door. Yosef appeared. "Oval Office in fifteen."

Dani gave him a dismissive wave. "Rachel, you'll come for dinner?"

Rachel texted Chris, waited for an answer, and said, "Of course."

"Good. The boys can't wait to talk to Chris."

"We'll be there at 5:30."

<~<~|~>~>

President Sandford felt the vibration. He retrieved his private phone from his pants pocket and noted the ID. A call from Vanderhagen was the last thing he needed right now. He answered anyway. "James."

"Franklin," Vanderhagen said. "Good to hear your voice. I hope you're well."

"Yes."

"I'm sure you've heard about the catastrophe in Tawanda."

"Yes. I have a meeting on that very issue in twelve minutes."

"I suspected as much. I won't keep you."

"Good."

"However, I do have in interest in the region, as you well know. It's imperative that the mining operations are not impaired by Damir's inner city collapse."

"I have no way of assuring that, James. We don't have troops there. We don't even recognize the country. Tawanda is land locked. We would have to get approval on a humanitarian level to consider operations over there."

"I have it on good intel that Kwanh Ebu is returning to Damir and will oversee the recovery. I suggest you negotiate with him to secure the best outcome for the cartel properties and, thus, your second term election."

"James, you put me in an awkward position."

"I'll text you Ebu's private number. Use it."

"James."

"Good talking to you, Franklin. We'll be in touch."

Sandford returned the phone to his pocket and walked over to the bar. He poured one-finger of Scotch and downed it in one gulp. After checking the time, he decided his call to Ebu would have to wait.

He heard a knock on the door and walked into the center of the room. Wendell, Uriah, and Dani entered and sat down in the same configuration as earlier.

Sandford sat on the same side as Dani, and said, "Let me hear your ideas."

Dani said, "This is a humanitarian discussion. We can't ignore people in distress. Many have lost their homes as well as their families. We have to do something."

Uriah said, "This is not a government induced problem. It is an act of God. We can't be held responsible."

Dani said, "That's a copout. We are responsible. We've known about the conditions since two-thousand one. The refugee problem has been on our radar for years and we never addressed it. If we had, maybe they would have been spared this total devastation."

Wendell said, "We are not responsible for the way a sovereign power treats its citizens."

Dani blurted out, "Are you kidding me?"

Sandford put his hand up. "We are looking for solutions for this current situation. Rehashing the past is not going to be productive."

Uriah used his ePad as a reference. "None of the surrounding countries are willing to accept the refugees. Aerial surveillance shows that more cave-ins are possible."

Dani said, "So the whole area is unstable and must be evacuated."

Wendell said, "Evacuated to where? Europe is flooded with evacuees from the Middle East, Turkey, and Albania. There is no space."

"My plan," Dani said, "shows how we can bring them here with little disruption to our citizens, economy, or our housing market."

Wendell dismissed her. "Don't be ridiculous. The strain on our healthcare will be outrageous and expensive. Uriah, did you have an estimate per person?"

Uriah said, "Our previous experience shows that we spend close to five thousand dollars per person to situate them in appropriate housing and, thereafter, about a thousand per month until they are on our social welfare rolls."

Dani said, "You know we can cut those costs if we use existing government facilities and train the refugees to be self-sufficient."

Wendell said, "It's not that easy to open closed facilities or find interpreters for hordes of people who can't speak English."

Sandford said, "But it can be done, right?"

"Uh, yes, of course," Wendell said.

"What would be the best evacuation strategy?"

Wendell said, "Sir, you can't seriously be considering...."

"I am. Tell me about a possible evacuation scenario."

Dani said, "We can utilize our aircraft carriers in the Indian Ocean and ferry people by plane and helicopter. Then we could transfer them to a troop transport for their trip to the United States."

Wendell leaned forward. "Sir, our discussion on immigration policy did not include Tawanda. It's not in our country's best interest to accept and relocate the greater population of an African country. We are simply not equipped to handle the huge differences in cultural expectations."

Uriah said, "Before we go there, we've only surveyed adjacent countries. There are many more which may be willing to accept the refugees."

Sandford rubbed his chin. "Maybe, but it will cost us either way." He looked at the time. "It's two-thirty now. I've got a call in to President Ebu. Uriah, you check possible African evacuation sites. Wendell, you find out about the status of American and Foreign investments in Tawanda—in particular, the mining industry. We have nationals concerned with their operations and they want our protection."

Wendell and Uriah left the room.

Sandford stood. "Dani, find out if there are any food shortages. We can make drops. Come back in forty-five and let's see if we can develop a working plan."

As she got up to leave, her phone buzzed. A text from Ivan. An angry emoji. The bug was back. Frowning, she turned. "Sir."

"Not now, Dani."

"I think…."

"Another time," he turned away.

She stood there unsure whether to let it go or tell him what she knew. If he ordered the bugging, no problem. If not, every word reached another's ears.

Sandford sat down in his desk chair and pulled out his phone.

Dani tapped on the desk.

Sandford looked up and his face went dark.

Before he could say anything, Dani raised her hand, circled it above her head, and then pointed to her ear.

The President's face morphed into surprise. His eyebrows shot up and his jaw dropped. He put the phone down and walked her to the door. After opening it, he sent her through with a loud admonishment. "Enough of that. Go get me the info on the supply situation. I don't care what you have to do to get it." The door shut behind her.

The trip to her office seemed twice as long, every step plagued by whispers and side glances. Still, she held her head high and smiled at each offender. "Taking names," her grandfather would say.

Once she settled into her office, she called Peter. His voice was groggy. "Sorry, Peter. Did I wake you?"

"It's okay. Grabbing naps as I can. What's going on?"

"That's what I want to know."

"No new sinkholes. Panic has subsided. Human scavengers are sifting through the above-ground rubble, saving what they can for rebuilding or sale. The sinkholes' surfaces are a good twenty to thirty feet below ground level. People stay away from the edge. It is eerily quiet. No movement. No noise. A mass grave. Under the caution tape, residents are placing stones representing those they lost. Occasionally, there is a picture, or a piece of clothing, or a flower. Others leave notes."

"Twin Towers."

"Yes, like that."

"How is the food supply?"

"Rationing it for now, but it will run out unless truckers take the chance of getting through."

"President Sandford is considering a supply drop. We have ships in the Indian Ocean. Can you give me an idea of what the people need? I'll try to get as much to you as I can as soon as I can."

"I've been making a list. I'll copy it and send it."

"What else can I do?"

"Let Mom know I'm okay. I tried calling but she's not picking up."

"I'll have someone check on her," Dani said. "Is Odili still in charge?"

"No. President Ebu has returned. He's reassembling the police force and army to help maintain order and assist people. It's slow going."

"Okay. I won't keep you. Send me your lists and I'll check on Sybil."

Chapter 29 ▶ Washington, D.C.

Wednesday, 13 May

Sandford waited until the Vice President left the office before summoning his Chief of Staff.

Wendell raced in, "Sorry, Sir. I've not had time…."

Sandford held his hand up. "How did Dani Mitchell know we recorded sessions in here?"

Wendell's face went blank. "I have no idea, Sir. That's strictly on a need-to-know basis."

"Find out."

"Now?"

"No. First, I want you to talk to Ebu and find out what's happening on behalf of our U.S. companies operating in Tawanda. Make it informal. A courtesy. If I do it, it's another step toward recognition, and this would be a bad time to have him think we're his saviors in any way."

Wendell said, "Anything specific?"

"Find out if the industrial area is safe—mines and workers, a refugee count, and the status of the city. If that city goes, Tawanda is just a gas station by the side of the road. Not sure that will upset anyone." The President paused and rubbed his chin. "Don't offer anything if he asks. Tell him we'll take it under consideration."

Nancy's voice interrupted their conversation. "President Ebu on the line, Mr. President."

Sandford got out of his chair and offered it to Wendell. "Take the call here. Suck as much info out of him as you can. Let me know when you're done."

Wendell picked up the phone as Sandford disappeared into his private quarters.

<~<~|~>~>

President Ebu stood on his office's balcony, from which he saw part of the city's collapse. The last time President Sandford spoke to Tawanda's President, the late Adebowale Okoro, the man received a private jet that they found parked on an out-of-the-way landing strip. This time, who knows? He smiled as he said, "Mr. President, how nice to speak with you again."

"President Ebu, this is Wendell Waters. The President's tied up with a terrorist emergency and sends his regrets. I'm acting on his behalf. I hope you will accept his apologies and talk with me."

Ebu's smile faded. No gifts. In fact, this underling substitute downgraded his position. Swallowing his pride to save Damir, and thus Tawanda, he said, "Yes, Mr. Waters. I will speak with you."

"The last reports we had from Peter Powell are four hours old. What is your current status, Sir?"

Ebu said, "I am restoring order and services as quickly as possible. It will take time to get everyone sorted out, establish an inventory of lost lives and property, and find the resources to put Damir on solid footing."

"It sounds like you've got everything well in hand. Very impressive."

Ebu frowned. "Mr. Waters, it is my job. It is what I do."

"Yes, of course. I meant no offense."

Ebu's face relaxed.

Wendell said, "Have the mines been affected?"

"Not to my knowledge. However, they are not operating. I understand the workforce abandoned the site in fear of another sinkhole."

"Thank you for your time, Mr. President. I will relay your words to President Sandford."

The call ended. Ebu seethed with fury. "Mr. Odili." The man flew into the office. Ebu vented as he peered out the window. "The great United States called to interrogate me, not to offer help in Damir's hour of need. I will never forget this affront for as long as I live."

"Yes, Sir."

"You will remind me of this day should I ever forget." Ebu turned away from the chaos. "Bring Peter Powell and his entourage to me."

<~<~|~>~>

Odili found Peter standing on a car parked on the south side of the main highway. Sam positioned himself on a car-hood on the north side. Both directed foot traffic through megaphones. "Safe ground, food, and shelter behind the hotel. Please clear the streets." This announcement alternated with, "Structures five hundred meters or more from the north and south sinkhole edge appear to be on safe ground. Please return home. Looters will be prosecuted."

For some, staying wasn't an option. For others, empty threats fell on deaf ears. They looted abandoned stores and homes.

Taxi worked behind the Damir Hawa. He had organized a growing staff of volunteers. He gridded the area, mapped the sectors. Workers went to each area, recorded the refugee's names, and gave each of them a sector ID card. The hotel allocated computers to the census. They helped make the recordkeeping easier and facilitated reuniting families. As a result, people settled down.

The war refugees had adopted a calm that surprised him until Mayor Yar'Adua explained. "For the first time, we had organized and fought for our freedom. God got angry and swallowed most of us. We forgot to be , and we paid for it."

If Taxi had time, he might have clarified the misconception. Instead, he had to concentrate on the waves of people entering the area. The work felt endless and sapped his strength. Still, he never faltered. The revolution fell on his shoulders, and he had to make it right.

Odili pulled him away from his work.

<~<~|~>~>

Peter, Sam, and Taxi stood in front of the imperial desk while President Ebu remained seated behind it. He said, "As you can see, I have returned to lead my people out of this chaos. Please update me on the situation."

The three men reported in.

Ebu said, "Thank you. I have rounded up police and army personnel. They will take up the task of controlling the crowds and dealing with criminal behavior. You are all free to return to…." He looked at each of the men. "To whatever it is that you do."

Taxi said, "Services have to be solidified. There are civilians and war refugees that need support."

Ebu said, "I will contact the hotel."

Sam said, "The main road is a mess and traffic is using improvised routes to negotiate around the city. Disturbed dry earth particles fill the air causing many to choke and gasp."

Ebu said, "I will take care of it." He looked at Peter, Sam, and Taxi. With no more comments, he stood. "While Damir appreciates your help, I must emphasize that it is I who shall make this city great again."

The three men nodded.

"Good. I am glad we have agreement. Please remain available. Thank you." Ebu sat. With pen in hand, he shuffled papers, signaling the end of the meeting.

The men left. By the time they exited the government building, the police force materialized and took to the streets, establishing as much order as possible.

Peter watched, as did Sam and Taxi. He said, "That was fast. Wonder where they've been hiding for the past twenty-four hours?"

Sam said, "Protecting the savior of Damir, I suspect."

Taxi grunted. "He has no idea what has to be done. Something else is at play."

Peter said, "Pretty cynical."

"I'm a cab driver. Cynical is my middle name."

"Look over there," Sam said, pointing a finger at the eastern exit out of Damir. "The police sent some people to the growing settlement behind the hotel and others to a holding area."

Peter said the obvious. "They're segregating the able-bodied men."

Sam nodded. "Why would they do that?"

Peter said, "You don't think it's to work the mines, do you? I don't want to believe Ebu's financial priorities outweigh his humanist imperative." His mirthless laugh sounded hollow.

Sam said, "Ebu came back to protect Tawanda's only export."

Taxi said, "Do we intervene?"

Peter said, "I don't think we stand a chance of changing anything."

Sam nodded. "We'd only get thrown in jail where we're no use to anyone."

Taxi said, "I'm going back to the refugees. See what I can do. Make sure they are as comfortable as possible and not getting hassled by the police."

Peter said, "Okay. See you later." He watched Taxi leave and turned to Sam. "Interested in taking another look at the sinkholes? If the refugees think there's a connection between their activism and the timing of the catastrophe, maybe there's something to it."

"You think the sinkholes…." Sam couldn't finish his thought. "No. Impossible."

Peter shrugged. "Let's go see what we can see."

<~<~|~>~>

The encampment had been wracked by two sinkholes about the size of six football fields. Peter and Sam walked the rim. The top of the debris rested twenty to thirty meters below.

Sam said, "What are we looking for?"

"I don't know."

Sam sniffed. "Smell that?"

Peter paused. "Not sure. What is it?"

"An explosive propellant of some sort."

"I can't tell. Too faint."

Sam stopped. "Something else. Notice the shape?"

"Of what?"

"The sinkhole. It's almost rectangular."

"Impossible."

"Look."

"Maybe. Could be…or…not."

"Over there," Sam said. "You can see the top of…."

"Of what?"

"Peter, something's wrong here. I've got to do some research. Normal sinkholes are the result of water weakening the underlying structure, consisting of limestone or a limestone-like mineral. Everything is fine until the saturation point is reached. Once that happens, the surface collapses. Sometimes all at once and sometimes gradually. I'm not at all sure that's what's happened here."

"You're telling me you think the sinkholes are man-made?"

"I didn't say that."

Peter said, "If you're right, who?"

"Who indeed," Sam said.

The two men continued their walk around the rim in silence. At their start point, Peter said, "Only the government benefits."

Sam nodded. "Pretty much."

They turned and faced the two other sinkholes that took out Damir's main road and perimeter buildings.

Peter said, "If true, why decimate the city?"

Sam said, "Look at the shapes. Irregular."

Peter took pictures of the sinkholes behind him and those in front of him. "Yes. Different."

Sam started walking around the next rim.

Peter said, "Are you looking for the anomaly? The shadow?"

"Yes. If I'm right, there may be an interconnected cavern system beneath the city. The first intentional collapses triggered the other two."

"This is all just a hypothesis, Sam. We don't know anything of the sort."

"Still, it fits."

"Doesn't make it true. Before we can say anything or accuse anyone, we've got some homework to do."

"You could make it easier, Peter."

"Me? I have no expertise in this field."

"Ah, but you have access to satellite data and technology which might give us a reading as to the subsurface of Damir."

Peter smiled. "I think you may be right. Let's get a beer, and I'll make the call."

Chapter 30 ▶ Observatory Circle, Washington D.C.

Wednesday, 13 May

Dani entered her house. Put her briefcase and bag on the entry table and went into the media room. The boys didn't make eye contact. These were not same kids who visited her at lunch time. She put her hands on her hips and said, "Okay, what's going on?"

Isaac said, "It's bad."

"How bad?"

Ivan said, "Dad's been outed on TV this time and it's not good."

Dani dropped into a chair. "How?"

Ivan picked up the clicker and switched the screen to the local news channel. After a few minutes, it showcased Terence surrounded by reporters and a photograph of Bruce superimposed up in the righthand corner.

Dani's eyes left the screen and went to the boys. "How are you doing?" They shrugged. "Really?"

Isaac said, "We've known since Dad first brought Bruce home for dinner."

Ivan said, "While you straightened up for dessert, we went out with Dad and showed Bruce the farm. We saw them touching hands and standing closer than even we do."

Dani said, "Why didn't you come and tell me?"

Ivan said, "It felt kind of private."

Isaac said, "When we got back to the house, everything went back to normal."

Dani got up. "So, you said nothing."

Isaac said, "Mom, it was years ago. We were kids."

Dani stopped and turned to face them. "You've seen nothing since?"

Ivan said, "We don't hang out with them."

Isaac said, "If we were in the room, they were always doing business."

Ivan said, "We knew for sure the same day you found out."

Isaac said, "Before you were sworn in."

Dani nodded. "I remember." She sat down. "What about tomorrow?" The boys looked puzzled. "At school." They shrugged.

Ivan said, "We'll deal with it. Most of the kids have screwed up families. Teasing will be over by fifth period."

Dani smiled. "You brilliant boys just gave me an idea as to how to handle this. I'm going to say we knew and we're okay with Dad's choices. We're a close family, and we intend to stay that way."

Isaac said, "Really?"

Her phone buzzed. A text from Terence. "Home. Getting ready. Sorry re pix." She read it and put the phone down.

She said, "Does that work for you?"

The boys nodded.

"Good." She picked up the phone and texted her response to the White House Press Secretary. After putting the phone in her pocket, she said, "We'll talk with Dad privately."

Terence joined Dani and the twins before she had time to get up. He stood in front of the dark TV monitor. "I want to apologize to all of you. This is a conversation we've needed to have for longer than I care to admit. I just thought you, Ivan and Isaac, weren't old enough to handle it."

Ivan said, "Dad...."

Terence stopped him. "I'm sorry it blew up today. I thought I'd taken all the precautions to save you any embarrassment. If you need to take time now, or off from school, or want to talk about it, whenever and wherever, I'm here for you, and will do what I can to...."

Ivan said, "Dad, we knew, even before it hit the newspaper a couple days ago."

Terence looked at each boy and then at Dani. She nodded. "It's true. They knew before I did." She pulled out her phone and showed him her text. "That's what the media will say."

His eyes filled with tears as he handed the phone back. "You all agree?"

Dani said, "We're a family and we need each other right now. Do not, any of you, say anything else to anybody."

The twins and Terence nodded.

A special agent came to the door. "Your guests have arrived."

<~<~|~>~>

Rachel and Chris arrived on time. The boys started peppering him with questions before he took his coat off.

Chris laughed. "Hey, guys. Give me a chance to get comfortable. Got a beer in this joint?"

The twins took off, happy to be on a mission for their computer guru. They returned to the sitting room with several selections.

Chris said, "Good choices. Hmm. I'll take this one. Thanks."

The boys double teamed him until Chris threw up his hands. "Okay. Stop." The boys froze. "Good. Now let me reiterate so I can make sure I heard you correctly. Okay?"

Two heads nodded.

"You have found instances of new code, and not necessarily the same code, every time you check your parents' phones."

Nods.

"And on your own phones?"

Shakes.

"To confirm, just your parents'?"

Nods.

"Is it the same code, on the same day, at the same time?"

The boys looked at each other and then at Chris. Shakes.

"Your mother's changes more often than your dad's?"

Nods.

"Do you think it is the same person coding for both phones?"

Dani listened to the exchange. The more she heard, the more she became concerned as to the scope of the problem.

Dani said, "Are you saying you clean our phones in the morning and we both come home with new tags on our phones?"

Nods.

Ivan said, "We've been working on a program to stop any sim card invasion, but we're stuck. That's what we're trying to explain to Chris."

Dani said, "How did I not know you two were so focused on computer code?"

Isaac shrugged his shoulders. "We figured you knew."

"How?"

Ivan said, "When you'd come home and check on us, we were testing our electronics, games, and programs."

"But how...."

Isaac said, "Dad. He financed our hobby."

Dani looked at Terence. He smiled and shrugged. "Bank of Dad."

Dani said, "I can't believe I didn't know any of this until now."

Ivan said, "You were always busy."

"Dani," Chris smiled, "don't feel even a little guilty. I did the same thing as a kid. My parents gave me an allowance which I use for parts. They'd do regular checks of my workshop without a clue. They had no idea what I was up to."

The grandfather clock chimed. Terence said, "Dinner time."

<~<~|~>~>

After the meal, during desert, they started a discussion revolving around the ethics of eavesdropping—a necessary yet invasive form of surveillance.

Rachel said, "It depends what's at stake."

Terence said, "That's why you need a warrant." He paused. "Dani, that's how they found out about me."

"They?"

"The newspapers. Whoever's tapping our phones alerted the photographer and leaked the story to the press."

"You're right," Dani said. "This is all about hurting me politically." She reached for her phone.

Terence said, "What are you doing?"

She said, "If someone is tapping our phones, there'd be a warrant on file."

He said, "Don't. You'll send up a red flag. Let me, the ostensibly aggrieved party, try to find out who's behind this. I'll let you know if I find out anything."

Dani opened the back of her phone and pulled out her sim card. "It may be that it is only for the phones in the White House phone system."

Terence followed suit. "Our private mobile phones are on their own server."

Chris said, "Give me the server info and I'll make sure they're protected from here on out."

Ivan pulled out his phone, sent a message, and Chris's phone buzzed. "It's me. I just sent you the info."

Chris forwarded the message to his team in New York with his comment, "Protect ASAP."

Dani played with the sim card. "What about hacking from within the White House?"

Rachel pulled out her phone. "Chris, do you think our phones have the bug? We've both been at government offices today."

Chris held out his hand and Rachel gave him her phone. He said, "Here boys, go check these. If they have the code, don't take it off, just tell me where. I want to study it firsthand."

The twins took the phones and raced upstairs.

Dani leaned back in her chair and sipped her coffee. "I'm not liking this situation very much. It is out of our control for reasons we do not understand."

Terence's phone rang. He looked at the ID screen and stood. "I'm sorry. Excuse me for a few minutes. I have to take this call." With his phone to his ear, he walked outside.

"Now that we're alone," Rachel said, looking at Chris and Dani, leaning forward, elbows on the table, "would you two please explain the rationale behind microchipping immigrants to the United States."

Dani said, "It's an experimental operation for the DOD and Homeland Security." Chris shot her a look. She said, "Yes, I know."

Rachel said, "Is it satellite controlled?"

Chris said, "No. The chip is dormant until it is energized by a scanner of some sort."

"Like E-Z Pass on our cars or like Vets use on dogs."

He nodded.

Dani said, "With an app on our phones?"

"Possibly."

Rachel said, "So, between the possible medical applications...."

"Which we are not talking about here."

Rachel shot him a look. She absolutely hated to be interrupted or forced down another thought path before she had a chance state her point. "Chris, let me finish." He didn't bother to look apologetic. "Chips will allow the government to put anything they want into the data, and it could be read by anyone with scanner."

Chris said, "Not anyone. The code is encrypted with safeguards in place."

"Anyone can break a code," Rachel said. "Therefore, it is an infringement of our constitutional rights. It feels like Big Brother targeting unsuspecting people. My fear is that as soon as it's instituted, we will all be microchipped. That means our government, any government, has instant access to everything and anything about any one of us at any moment."

Chris said, "You have taken this to a level far beyond the immediate goal. A test. From what you're implying, it will be a worldwide technology before...."

Dani interrupted. "Wait. We're talking possibilities, right?"

Rachel said, "Now you understand why I'm concerned."

Dani looked at Chris. "If taken to a logical conclusion, we'll be walking transmitters."

Terence returned with four glasses and a bottle of brandy. He served and then sat down. "So, what are we talking about? It looks serious."

Chris looked at the women and said, "We're talking about electronic surveillance. Today, it's just your phones. Tomorrow, it could be everybody's phones."

Terence said, "Invasion of privacy and profiling. Not good."

Rachel said, "Exactly. Not good at all. That information becomes gold. People will fight over it, for it, as well as try to circumvent it."

Terence said, "Once it becomes corrupted or co-opted, anything could happen to anyone. Just like it happened to me."

Rachel said, "The ethical question becomes a nightmare."

Chris stood. "Okay. Point made. The good news is that I'm on the project and can take steps to address these issues."

Four feet scrambled down the stairs. Isaac returned Chris and Rachel's phones, "They're clean."

Ivan said, "We think we've got an app that will allow a smart phone to disable an unauthorized eavesdropper."

Chris said, "Let's see it."

Isaac said, "We're close but need your help to figure out the missing branch of the main algorithm."

Chris addressed the adults in the room. "Ladies and gentleman, if you'll please excuse us." Chris snapped a butler's bow. "The twins and I must go now and save the world."

<~<~|~>~>

At the end of the evening, Rachel had to drag Chris away from the twins. Back at the hotel, she said, "How did it go with Ivan and Isaac?"

Chris said, "The boys are smart. They almost solved the problem they were working on. I gave them a couple of possibilities. It'll be interesting to see if they can figure it out."

"Can it be applied to the microchip technology?"

"Not directly, but it gave me an idea."

"You do know that just because we can, doesn't mean we should."

Chris gave her a hug and a kiss. "Don't worry.

She returned his kiss. "Said President Truman to the Atom bomb makers before the he ordered the hit on Japan."

He said, "I'm serious."

"I know."

He gave her another kiss. "Go to sleep. I've got some work to do."

Chapter 31 ▶ Damir, Tawanda, Africa

Thursday, 14 May

At six in the morning, Damir time, Peter called Dani, eleven PM, EST. "I know it's late, but I need a favor."

"I'm still up. What can I do?"

"My friends and I have examined the sinkholes and we think there's an extensive cave system about sixty meters below Damir. If it's true, Damir could literally collapse at any moment."

"Oh, my God. Terrifying."

"The problem is, Dani, we don't know for sure. We need a geological study ASAP. We have to make a decision whether to recommend an evacuation or not."

"I understand."

Peter said, "Can you use U.S. satellites to do a geologic mapping of the area?"

"I'll find out. I'll text you 'yes' or 'no.' Text me your email. If it's yes, I'll get an immediate scan and send you the report."

"Thank you, Dani."

"Be careful, Peter. Your mom expects you home soon."

"No problem. Don't worry."

<~<~|~>~>

Showered and shaved, Peter sat down for breakfast in the hotel dining room. Normally, he found the breakfast staff calm, courteous, and efficient, the food delicious, and the ambience perfect for inner reflection. Today, tension filled the room which put everyone on edge, curt, and apologetic.

Sam and Taxi appeared at the table. "May we join you?"

"Of course."

A waiter appeared, poured coffee, and took the breakfast order. The man made a slight bow and left.

"I have news," Taxi said. "The mine workers, frightened by the collapse, have disappeared."

Peter said, "That can't be good. No production means no money for the government."

Sam said, "Ebu must be sweating the repercussions." He twisted in his chair to beckon a waiter. Seeing none, he stood. "Something's wrong."

Pop! Pop! Rat-a-tat-tat!

The three men hit the floor, crawled to the window closest to the gunfire, and looked for the shooter. What they saw surprised them—eleven policemen. They ran outside. One of the officers addressed a cowering crowd.

"President Kwanh Ebu orders all able males to work in the mines. Everyone who works gets fed. All others must leave the city. Our limited resources must support the police, army, and mines. No exceptions. Those who refuse will be executed on the spot. Foreign visitors and diplomats have twenty-four hours either to leave or work."

After a split second of silence, chaos erupted, the crowd exploding in all directions, gone before the police could react.

Peter, Sam, and Taxi fled to the stairwell and ran up to Peter's room. Behind locked doors, they dropped into chairs and caught their breath.

Peter said, "Taxi, you have to get out of here."

Taxi shook his head, "I cannot. I need to help my people resist."

Sam said, "If you fight, the soldiers will fight back. The people who remain are too old, too young, or too sick to defend themselves."

"Not all who ran have run away."

Peter said, "While I applaud your bravery, I question your goal. What's left here to fight for? The city center is all but destroyed. Anything with value is either residential or mineral."

Sam said, "Peter's right. What's the point?"

"Freedom."

Peter said, "Always. But sometimes, being practical is smarter. At least those who work will have pay and food."

Taxi sighed. "If you believe their words, you would be right. It is more the case that the workers will become slaves. I cannot let that happen."

Sam countered. "Admirable, but I don't think you have a choice."

Taxi said, "Allowing the government to place greed above people is wrong." He turned to Peter. "Can the United States help us evacuate?"

Peter said, "Let me try." He got up and walked into the bedroom, closed the pocket-doors, and called Dani.

She answered, clearing the sleep from her voice and brain. "Peter, what's going on?"

"The government has issued an ultimatum. People must work the mines, leave, or die. Foreigners must evacuate within twenty-four hours. What can we do to help?"

"Can you get to President Ebu to change the deadlines or negotiate for a more moderate emergency plan?"

"Not clear. I'll try."

"Do it, Peter, and then get out of there."

"Dani, the people here have been through enough."

"I'll see what I can do."

Pop! Pop! Rat-a-tat-tat!

The line went dead.

Chapter 32 ▶ Washington D.C.

Thursday, 14 May
Dani watched the monitor as the Senate majority leader addressed the TV cameras.

> "As I have said, the immigration question tops the Senate's priorities. The world is shrinking, the population is growing, the resources are diminishing, and the need for basics is increasing in the global community. Natural disasters and internal politics have strained every nation. Immigrants flood borders. Europe's at the breaking point. There is no end in sight whether we participate as a haven country or not. Therefore, the Senate continues to oppose opening our borders. Our current deficit forbids a financial outlay to transport, accept, and care for immigrants entering without their own financial support."

She didn't hear what the reporter said because she leapt out of her chair and strode to Oval Office, arms by her side, hand balled into fists. The guard opened the door as she approached. He said, "Ma'am, they're expecting you."

The "they" were Wendell Waters, Uriah Henderson, and the President.

Sandford said, "You saw the announcement."

Dani said, "I did. Where did that come from and why now?"

Wendell said, "I'm not sure. The White House had no knowledge."

She said, "I spoke to Peter early this morning. Damir is in chaos. If we don't do something, the refugees who didn't perish in the sinkholes stand a good chance of dying in the mines."

Uriah said, "Was there another sinkhole?"

"I don't know," she said. "It's possible Damir's underlying geological structure has been damaged. No one knows if it will stand up to any further tremors."

Wendell said, "Like blasting at mine sites."

She nodded. "Yes, like that. We must get people out of there. Move them to a safer environment. Offer the help they need."

Uriah said, "We can't. Our hands are tied. It's not our policy to interfere in another country's internal politics."

Dani looked at Sandford. "Mr. President, this is a humanitarian effort. We, the United States, can't let these people die."

Wendell said, "We can't interfere."

Sandford said, "Dani, you know we can't let a wave of immigrants into this country without a comprehensive plan. Based on what we just heard, we have to let President Ebu work this out and hope for the best."

Dani said, "Sir, I accepted the office of the Vice President for two reasons. First, I wanted to help, and, second, I trusted you to always do the right thing. The Senate majority leader is a bully who will do anything to keep you from doing your job and getting re-elected. We can't operate in the people's interests if we're going to let him call the shots."

Wendell shot to his feet.

Sandford said, "Sit, Wendell. She has a point." To Dani, he said, "Let me think about it. We'll talk later."

Dani said, "Thank you, Sir." Talk later, indeed.

On her way back to her office, she pulled out her cell phone. Picked a number and called. "Where are you?" Pause. "Stay there. I'll be right over." No one was going to die on her watch.

Chapter 33 ▶ Harrison, NY

Thursday, 14 May
Lucy watched the tape of the refugee encampment dropping into oblivion over and over again. The decimation exceeded her expectations. Her plan went off without a hitch. Simple. Efficient. The people gone and silenced in a heartbeat. No pain.

However, the marketplace collapse surprised her. She brought up her maps on another monitor. What did I miss? The data did show the initial cavern as an advantageous fluke. It never occurred to her that there might be more.

Lucy turned off the video. Time to move on. She got to work on timelines covering her next several jobs. She put on the news for background noise, until she happened to look up. The evening news showed the footage of Damir's business center collapsing and disappearing in new sinkhole.

Not supposed to happen. Not good.

She had the phone in her hand with Ebu's phone number on the face. I'll call him, explain the chain of sinkholes…hmm. Staring at the phone, she realized she had never apologized to anyone for anything. She set her jaw. I'm not going to start now.

Lucy put the phone face-down on the table and engaged her drone in Damir and flew it around the city. On her monitor, she observed people milling around. Soldiers. Guns. People leaving the back of the hotel in a steady stream, circling the outskirts of the city to the remains of the refugee camp. These people are crazy. The ground is unstable. What the fuck are they doing?

After a while, it became clear. They were scavenging the area for tools, kitchenware, and other things they might need.

Lucy checked her maps. Her last set of explosives were in perfect position to take these people out. Less for Ebu to worry about. Less suffering.

She brought up the activation screen and hovered the cursor over the "go" button. With growing excitement, she waited for the optimum people-per-square-foot moment.

The ground fell away and a cloud of dust rose into the air.

Chapter 34 ▶ Philadelphia, PA

Thursday, 14 May

Vanderhagen watched the Senate majority leader's announcement. He picked up his phone and tapped a contact. At the connection, he said, "Well done. Perfect timing," and ended the conversation. On his laptop, he transferred cash to the agreed Political Action Committee.

A phone in his desk drawer buzzed. He retrieved it and answered.

The caller said, "We're still out of it but not sure for how long."

"Commercial interests must be back in operation without any outside interference."

"That's not what's driving the decision. It's the humanitarian situation."

"Understood. Stand firm."

Vanderhagen finished that call and made another. "President Ebu. Thank you for taking my call."

President Ebu said, "I am, as always, appreciative of the interest you take in our country."

"Are the mines up and running?"

"Our citizens do not wish to work the mines," Ebu said. "Despite harsh penalties, the able-bodied have defied our attempts at conscription, volunteer or otherwise. People fear another cave-in."

"What is needed?"

"Food, medical teams and supplies, clothing, portable...."

Vanderhagen said, "I meant with respect to the mines. We lose, you and your government lose, hundreds of thousands of dollars every day they're closed."

"We may lose more than that."

"Explain."

"The papers are being drawn to end the war with the DRC in twelve days. They agreed to a truce for a percentage of our tariff. If the mines are down and Damir is gone, they will never sign. They will not have to. Tawanda will be theirs for the taking."

Vanderhagen said, "Not an option. The DRC isn't partial to our operations. We must come up with another solution."

"My people will only work if there is an assurance of safety, which we are unable to provide."

"Is my nephew, Peter, still in Damir?"

"Yes, as far as I know," Ebu said. "He was last seen at the hotel."

Vanderhagen said, "I'll make some calls. You make sure he's safe."

Vanderhagen leaned back in his chair, hands clasped over his midriff. He stared at the ceiling. His phone rang. He checked the ID and sat up straight. "Hello, Sir." It was the head of the cartel.

"We have received no payments from Tawanda for the past seventy-two hours."

"Damir suffers from a natural disaster and a pending civil war. The mines are closed."

"Unacceptable."

"Be assured, I'm taking care of it."

The line went dead. Vanderhagen pulled out his handkerchief and dabbed at the beads of perspiration that ringed his hairline. He looked at the presidential portrait of his father above the fireplace. "You made this job look easy. No decision too harsh. Ends always justified the means."

He walked over to the bar and stared at the bottles. He reached for the Scotch and shifted to ginger ale. He needed to be clear-headed when he chose his sacrificial lamb.

Glass-in-hand, he sat at the chessboard table and looked at the unfinished game—his last with his father. He reached for the bishop and stopped mid-air.

Vanderhagen pulled out his phone and called Peter.

"You're call cannot be completed as dialed," the robotic voice said. "Please try again later."

Vanderhagen hit END and texted his nephew. "Mine update."

He sipped his drink expecting a return text within minutes. He got it. "No change. Situation chaotic. Another sinkhole."

Vanderhagen turned on the TV. A reporter interrupted the program. "We have phone video coverage of the aftermath of another sinkhole in Tawanda. It opened at the far end of the refugee camp which was vacated earlier. Victims swallowed and buried were scavenging the area when it happened. Stay tuned."

He turned the TV off and made another call.

<~<~|~>~>

Dani saw the ID and hesitated. Another ring. She answered. "I'm busy."

Vanderhagen said, "We must talk."

"I'm in a meeting."

"This is important."

Dani sighed and signaled Yosef to give her five. She watched him leave and said, "I'm listening."

"Tawanda just suffered another sinkhole. You must get Sandford to commit U.S. forces to stabilize the country."

"We can't. We don't have formal relations with Tawanda."

Vanderhagen said, "A borderless humanitarian effort, then, before Tawanda disappears."

Dani said. "You don't give a damn about the people. What's this really about?"

"The cartel has interests in the region."

"Money," Dani said. "I thought so."

"And Peter. We, you, need to get him out of there."

"I've spoken to Peter, and he's assured me…."

Vanderhagen said, "The situation changes every second. You must move on this. Do something or there will be nothing left."

"Why? What do you know?"

"It is possible that the DRC will seize on Tawanda's weakness and take over."

"We are back to your money, interests, and agenda."

"Dani, it doesn't matter. A sovereign nation is in trouble. The United States must take a stand."

"I've another call."

"Do not dismiss me."

"It's my job."

Chapter 35 ▶ East Side, N.Y.C.

Thursday, 14 May

Sybil lay in her bed, on her side. She watched the traffic on the East River and the Brooklyn Bridge through the floor to ceiling windows. The mesmerizing ebb and flow calmed her, numbing thoughts of Lidia.

Clinking pans, clicking plates, and pinging silverware emanated from the kitchen. Sybil turned over. The smell of chicken soup caused her stomach to growl. She arched and stretched before going vertical. Robed, she barefooted her way toward the living area and the dining table.

"Good afternoon, Mrs. Powell," the nurse said. "I'm glad to see you're up."

Sybil nodded. "Yes."

"Sit, enjoy your lunch." The nurse put the soup bowl on the placemat. "I'll straighten the bedroom while you eat. "When you're done, we'll shower and dress."

"Not necessary," Sybil said. "I'm not going out."

"Of course, you are. It's a beautiful day for our walk."

"Not today."

"Doctor's orders."

"No."

"I'm sure you'll feel better after you've eaten."

"Go away."

The nurse disappeared into the bedroom. Sybil picked up the remote and turned on the TV. She raised a spoon of soup to her lips. The weather report confirmed the nurse's assessment. She sipped the hot liquid, alternating with bites of stone crackers. The next news segment led with Tawanda's last sinkhole tragedy.

Sybil's throat constricted and launched her into a coughing fit. She caught the expelled soup in her napkin and regained control. Her attention returned to the TV. The devastation and armed patrols made her head swim. Where was Peter?

She grabbed her phone and called him. No answer. She tried again. And again. Then she texted. "Are you okay?" She put the phone down, screen side up, and stared at it, willing it to return an answer—the right answer.

She didn't realize she'd been holding her breath until she saw, "Yes," appear and she gasped, "Thank God."

Without thinking of the consequences, Sybil called her brother. "James, you must get Peter home right now."

"Sybil, you know…."

"Don't you dare fuck with me, you bastard. I've lost everyone I've ever loved due to endless Vanderhagen machinations. I can't lose Peter, too."

"You sound over-wrought. Have you taken your meds today?"

"Are you listening to me? Peter's in Tawanda. I want him pulled out and sent home immediately."

"You know I can't do that."

"You can pimp me out at fourteen and ruin my life but you can't save your only nephew?"

"Peter's working. He'll be fine."

"He's not going to be fine. Get him out of there. Now."

"Sybil, I've just told you…."

"Shut-up." Sybil lowered her voice. Through gritted teeth she hissed, "Listen to me, James. If anything happens to Peter, I will personally kill you where you sleep."

Chapter 36 ▶ Damir, Tawanda, Africa

Thursday, 14 May

Peter, with Sam and Taxi, sat in his hotel room looking at the maps imbedded in Dani's email on Peter's laptop. "Look what happens," he said, picking up a stylus, "when I color in, number, and time-date-stamp the cave-ins. The first three look like a collapsing house of cards. The fourth appears out of order."

Sam said, "You're right. The first three move west to east and the last is west of the original. That's surprising. The last one should have been closer to the hotel."

Peter said, "I agree."

The men stared at the evidence in front of them.

Taxi stood. "I can't stay here looking at pictures. My people need a refuge and guns. I have to make that happen."

Sam said, "Why, Taxi? Why is this all on you?"

Taxi said, "I started this whole thing. I listened to an ancient wind-whisperer. I tried to do the right thing. Now thousands are dead, and thousands will be killed."

Sam said, "None of this is your fault."

Taxi grunted and walked over to the window. "The police are back."

Sam and Peter joined Taxi in time to see an officer raise a megaphone to his lips. "People of Tawanda. Your President, Kwanh Ebu, asks only for mine workers. This area might collapse at any moment. The mine camp is much safer. Go there for food, water, and shelter. First shift starts in the morning."

No sound or people responded. Taxi said, "I have to get downstairs. Come see me if you find anything useful." He left without ceremony.

"Drink?" Peter said, holding a bottle of rum. Sam retrieved and held out two glasses. They returned to their seats and the maps.

Sam said, "I can't believe I'm saying this, but it looks like…."

Peter said, "Sabotage."

"Who would do such a thing?"

"What was going on before the first collapse?"

"There had been a massive uprising of the refugees. They spoke of tremors, of the earth moving, and of ancestors urging them to leave."

"You mean leave Damir?"

"Taxi arranged it with the police," Sam said. "He had a permit. No one expected that so many would want to go. I suspect other than the original few, no one knew why they were going."

"Interesting."

"Once they'd collected below the President's office, he came out and spoke to them, avoiding any promises. In response, they sat down. Only after Taxi and a few others negotiated with Ebu, did the crowd disperse."

"What was the deal?"

"Immediate supplies for the encampment, and in two weeks, a plan to move the refugees home."

They sipped their drinks.

Peter said, "I guess that's why Ebu dispatched me to negotiate a peace agreement with the DRC."

"First step in ending the war so the refugees would be able to return home."

Peter didn't disclose the "no return" clause. "Home to what?"

Sam shrugged. "I have no idea."

"So, the plan is that after two weeks, the refugees leave, see the barren wasteland, and do what? Stay and rebuild or migrate. In either case, their survival chances are little to none."

Sam said, "The refugees are strictly baggage, financial and otherwise."

Peter raised his glass and swirled the remaining quarter inch of rum around and around. "If Ebu gets rid of the refugees and makes peace with the DRC, he removes his biggest obstacle to world recognition and United Nations member status."

Sam stood up and went to the window looked out and then back to Peter. "If Ebu's behind this, he'll kill anyone who stands in his way." He turned. "Peter, no one'll get out of here alive."

"Not necessarily," Peter said. "Ebu needs those mines operating. It's his only source of income at the moment." Peter finished his drink, put the glass down, and reached into his messenger bag. He withdrew a map. After unfolding it, he put it down next to the geological map. He began tracing each with an index finger.

Sam watched with interest and sat. "What have you found?"

"A way out of this mess."

Chapter 37 ▶ West Wing, Washington, D.C.

Thursday, 14 May
President Sandford used the interlude between meetings to review his email. His private phone rang. He looked at the ID and answered.

After the brief pleasantries, Vanderhagen said, "How do we stand in Tawanda?"

Sandford said, "We don't. However, we're evaluating the need for aid and exploring African alliances for assistance."

"Tawanda must remain independent."

"That's President Ebu's call."

"The mining must resume."

"James, those issues are out of my control."

"Because you choose to ignore them."

Sandford said, "You must know I have to respect other sovereign nations. I can't commit United States resources to every squabble around the globe."

"Stabilize Tawanda and bring Peter home."

"Orders don't help, James."

Vanderhagen said, "Neither will the release of the pedophile incident, that is, if you're planning a second term."

"We both know it's a lie."

"We both know it doesn't matter."

<~<~|~>~>

For the next few minutes, Sandford stared at his monitor. A knock on the door and Wendell Waters, Uriah Henderson, and Dani Mitchell walked in and sat down. He got up, grabbed a yellow pad and pen from his desk, and joined them. "Tell me where we are in Tawanda."

Dani said, "I've talked to Peter. He said Damir's in an uproar. The President has ordered able bodied men to work the mines, and a fourth sinkhole took the back end of the refugee camp."

Uriah said, "I've had no contact with President Ebu, either directly or indirectly. The silence doesn't bode well."

Wendell said, "I spoke to President Ebu just before this meeting. His focus appears to be the mines. His people's welfare remains secondary, if he considers it at all."

Sandford nodded. "I'm sure you're right." He got up and grabbed a bottle of water from the bar, opened it, and took a long sip. "We can't be officially involved in any way." Returning to the couch, he said, "Send in a team and pull Peter Powell out."

Dani said, "To cover the extraction, let's plan a food and medical supplies air drop under the auspices of the UN's Office for the Coordination of Humanitarian Affairs."

Wendell said, "No interference is better."

Ignoring his negativity, she said, "Or through PRAISE. Rachel Allen arrived in Washington today. I can ask her."

Wendell looked from her to the President. "If we must do something, that would eliminate any political connection."

Sandford regarded Dani. "See if you can work it out with Rachel so there's no hint of U.S. involvement."

"I understand," she said. "One more thing. What are we going to offer the refugees?"

Wendell's face darkened. "No refugees. I believe we've discussed that."

Dani leaned forward. "There are people dying. We can save them. Give them shelter, food, and medical attention."

Uriah said, "There are world relief non-profits headed toward Tawanda right now."

"That won't be enough to get the people to safety."

Wendell said, "Safety is another issue. The Senate's 'no immigration' policy is all over the news. If we bring boatloads of people into our ports, we'll be seen as directly opposing due process."

Dani said, "We're talking about old and young, sick and dying, terrified people."

Sandford put up his hands. "Stop. We can't do everything this minute. Put together the plan to extract Powell and coordinate with PRAISE. See if they'll underwrite a food drop since we have the stores and capability to assemble the operation immediately. Let me know when you're good to go."

Chapter 38 ▶ Observatory Circle, Washington, DC

Thursday, 14 May

On the way home, Dani asked her driver to pick up Rachel at the hotel. The driver parked in front while the other agent went inside to escort Rachel from her room into the car. Dani said, "Just the person I wanted to see."

"Good to see you, too," Rachel said. "What's the big secret?"

With the touch of a button, Dani raised the privacy window between them and the agents in the front seat. She said, "I've the go-ahead to air-drop food and emergency parcels over Damir. There's a small window of opportunity for this humanitarian mission, and we have to use it to our advantage."

"I agree," Rachel said. "This is too important. What can I do to help?"

"Pay for it."

"Just like that?"

"Just like that."

"Do you happen to have any paperwork on this deal?"

Dani smiled. "I do." She opened her briefcase, pulled out a folder, and opened it. "I just finished this." She handed a paper to Rachel. "These are the stats on the estimated numbers of people and the corresponding numbers of drops."

Rachel scanned the document. "How sure are you of the numbers?"

"I've got the stable Damir population numbers and the size of the war refugee population from previous government assertions, minus the current death toll, from the news reports. I realize it isn't one-hundred-percent accurate but it's the best guess I've got."

"Okay. Let's go with it," Rachel said. "What's your target date for the drop?"

"End of May."

"When do you need an answer?"

Dani said, "Yesterday."

"I'm inclined to say 'yes,' of course," Rachel said. "However, I have to make a few calls—make sure our board members are on board."

"I understand."

Rachel said. "I'll give you an answer by noon tomorrow, if not before."

"One more thing," Dani said. "It has to look like your idea, and I'd like it to go out under the auspices of the United Nations. That way, we can help. However, our government can't be connected to this in any way."

"You mean, Sandford."

"Yes. We haven't officially recognized Tawanda, and Sandford wants any support kept under wraps."

"Why the hold up?"

Dani said, "The war refugee encampment was a blight on this earth. The human rights violations doomed Tawanda's application to the United Nations."

Rachel said, "Now it's gone."

Dani caught her breath. "What?"

"Now that the refugee encampment is gone, nothing blocks Tawanda's recognition. That's what you said, right?"

"I didn't hear what I said until you repeated it."

"What did I say?"

"Someone deliberately killed those refugees."

"No way that's true," Rachel said, shaking her head. "I can't believe…." She froze. "Wait a minute. Dani, do you think President Ebu ordered…."

"Yes, to get them off his political and financial back."

"Hold on. This is conjecture," Rachel said. "There's nothing to support your hypothesis."

Dani said, "I'm not so sure. I've got something to show you."

The car pulled up to the Vice President's residence. Dani put her finger over her lips. "Let's not share this theory and see what the others think."

<~<~|~>~>

Inside, they were greeted by the Chris, Terence, and the twins.

The boys ran up and gave Dani a peck on her cheek. Ivan said, "Boy, do we have something to show you." She grinned. This had to be a first since kindergarten. They each took one of her arms to lead her to the sitting room.

Terence blocked their way and said, "Let's let the ladies freshen up and meet us at the table." The boys released her. "Dani, don't spend too much time upstairs. You've quite a presentation waiting for you at dinner."

Everyone was seated except Dani. She came in last carrying a stack of folders which she placed on a side table.

Dinner was congenial. The boys shared their exemplary school interim reports.

Dani said, "I'm so pleased you've turned your lives around."

Terence said, "Great job. I'm proud of you."

The boys grinned.

Rachel said, "Congratulations."

Then, Chris said, "Not too bad." The boys lost their smile. "However, I understand this is a first. You'll have to keep it up or do even better if you want my endorsement on any college, internship, or work applications."

Ivan and Isaac burst into smiles. "Yes, Sir."

"Okay," Dani said. "I've waited long enough. What's the other big surprise?"

The boys stood. Ivan picked up a clicker and pushed a button. "This initiates a white noise to kill any and all listening devices, replacing broadcasts with a local radio signal." He looked at one of the agents who nodded.

"Ma'am," the agent said, "we've tested it and it works."

Isaac said, "We have also written the code, with Chris's help, that allows a phone to scan its own sim card to find and disable a rogue listening device."

Ivan said, "Initial tests were good, and now we want to test it in the field."

Dani and Terence looked at each other and then at the boys. She said, "You want to use our phones?"

Terence said, "Of course. Come on, Dani. It'll be exciting."

Dani laughed and agreed.

Chris said, "Once they came through with that little project, I asked them if they could do a similar app for scanning a Pet ID Microchip." He addressed Terence and Dani. "If it's okay with you, I'd like to set Ivan and

Isaac up in their own business under the ICU's new consumer applications division. Umm, that is, if they keep their grades and behavior up to your standards."

<~<~|~>~>

When the boys left the table after dinner, Dani said, "Chris, you've done wonders with Ivan and Isaac. I've never seen them so happy and engaged."

"They're good boys, Dani. They just needed a direction." Chris looked at his watch. "I guess it's time...."

"No," Rachel said. "Dani has something to show us."

Dani got out of her seat, collected her folders from the side table and placed them on the large dining table so they could stand on one side and see the whole image.

Terence said, "This looks like a geological survey. We had one done for the farm."

Dani said, "It is. I'm interested in what you see."

Rachel looked at the maps and then stepped back, giving the men time to analyze the image.

Terence said, "It looks like a land mass resting on a string of hollow structures deep beneath the surface."

Chris nodded. "I agree."

Dani said, "What if I told you that this," she pointed to the encampment area, "structure collapsed."

Chris said, "What was on top of it?"

"No buildings. Just tents and people."

"Hmm."

Terence said, "It collapsed on its own?"

Dani nodded.

Chris said, "No way it happened by accident. The pattern doesn't hold true for the domino effect. Besides, people reported tremors between the first and second. I do think the third and fourth resulted from the first two. However, the fifth one was man-made."

Dani said, "What do you think happened?"

Terence said, "I've worked with explosives. So, I can say with some authority that for that sequence to implode, there would have to be several well-timed explosions to weaken the walls to the point of collapse."

Dani said, "To be clear, we're talking about human intervention, right?"

Terence looked at Chris. They both looked at Dani.

"Okay," Dani said as she collected the papers. "For now, this stays between us. I don't want to start a world war over supposition."

Terence walked over to his wife. "Dani, be careful. Whoever orchestrated this has powerful connections."

"I know." She smiled. "But so do I."

Chapter 39 ▶ Philadelphia, PA

Friday, 15 May
Vanderhagen walked into his study. A phone's muffled sound came from his desk drawer. He retrieved the phone and sat. Another ring. He answered without saying a word.

"This is the chef. You have a party for me?"

"Elite and immediate."

"Good. I'm available. Text coordinates."

"Fees per usual?"

"Agreed. Bon appetite."

The conversation ended. Vanderhagen texted info to the calling number and tossed the phone back into the drawer. He pulled out another and made a call.

President Ebu said, "Mr. Vanderhagen."

"Mr. President," Vanderhagen said. "What progress have you made regarding the mines and my nephew?"

"Peter is fine. He's staying at the Hotel Hawa. As for the mines, I can assure you we are bringing order back to Damir. You will know as soon as they are operational."

"Must I remind you that every down hour costs your country thousands of dollars?"

"The cave-ins have impeded process. Am I assured that this catastrophe has run its course?"

Vanderhagen said, "I'm not the person to ask."

"Your recommendation as I recall."

"An optional referral."

"You are cutting hairs," Ebu said, his voice without warmth.

"Careful, Mr. President. You tread on quicksand." Vanderhagen ended the call. He slapped his phone down on the desk. "Splitting hairs, you moron. Splitting hairs."

He went to the bar, threw ice in a glass, and grabbed the bottle closest to him. He poured a couple of fingers and gulped half down. Ledgers lay on his desk. Letters waited for his response. The chessboard beckoned.

Walking to the table, his eyes flicked to the empty chair—his father's—and back to the chess board. Vanderhagen sat down to play a game, imagining his father as his opponent. He set his drink to the side and moved a piece. "Ah, Father, that's your favorite opening. I'm not surprised."

He moved another. "Now, don't assume this is a replay of our last game. That would be a mistake. I've learned a lot since then."

He moved a knight. "Daring, Father. Not like you. You let people get into their own trouble. This move is more like me. Aggressive. Forcing weakness."

He countered with a pawn. "This ought to stop you. I can see where this attack is going. You taught me well. I will use your defense against you."

He leaned back in his chair, waiting for inspiration, sipping his drink. "This is a tough one, Father— juggling the cartel's interests with the life of my nephew. If Peter were home, I'd let Ebu's damn country implode. We were doing just fine with the DRC. The extra points are not worth the aggravation."

Vanderhagen swirled the ice around the glass. "I know, I know, Father. Emotions should never get in the way of business. I understand that, believe me. Except I'm not you." He drank the last of the liquor as he observed the chess board. His phone rang. Dani. He answered.

"This is a nice surprise."

Dani said, "Business. I want to know what you're doing in Tawanda."

"I'm in Philadelphia."

"Specifically, what's your involvement with Damir?"

"Your intel must be flawed."

"Don't play games with me," Dani said. "I know Peter's representing your interests. I want to know what's going on. Thousands of people have died, and the country's on the verge of civil war. The only outcome is chaos—your middle name."

"I'm offended at your insinuation."

"Clean-up your mess."

"Your rampant paranoia colors your judgment."

Dani said, "Play your games if you must. If I find your name attached to anything other than the cartel's mines, I'm coming after you."

Vanderhagen said, "Careful. You may find your interests and mine are one and the same."

Chapter 40 ▶ Gramercy Avenue, N.Y.C.

Friday, 15 May

Rachel sat on the couch, her computer on her lap, and Zeus resting at her feet. Her attention centered on food-drop packages—size, variations, weights, and cost. However, a part of her brain kept track of Chris through the various sounds that accompanied his morning routine.

The running water stopped. He'd finished his shower. Short metallic pings relayed clothes hangers being moved about. A click meant he shut the closet door. The release of mattress air said he sat down to put on his shoes. A slap of leather against leather and she looked up, returning his smile.

"What's up for today?" Chris said, adjusting his belt. "Are you planning to stay in?"

Rachel shook her head. "I've got to go see Sybil and let her know what Dani's up to. Even though I'm the acting executive director, Sybil is ultimately responsible."

"How's she doing? I hope she's back on her feet."

"I'll find out today. Still, don't be too harsh. Everybody has to mourn in their own way."

Chris said, "Sybil needs something to do besides vegetate in that apartment."

"Maybe she'll want to come back to work. I'd love that."

"Tired of being the 'working girl' already?"

"I've got to say that I much prefer the job of writer."

Chris leaned over and gave Rachel a kiss. "I'm on my way."

"Anything exciting?"

"Not out of the ordinary. Code to write, people to see, places to go."

"I see," Rachel said. "Sounds busier since Washington."

"I have to make up for lost time." Chris put on his jacket and opened the door. "Call me if you need anything."

"Okay. See you later."

The door shut and Rachel frowned. Zeus looked up at her and whined. "You caught that too, didn't you?" She put the computer aside and leaned down to scratch behind his ears. "Wonder what people he's seeing and where he's going." The dog sat up and put his chin on her knee. "He hardly ever leaves the building." Zeus licked her. "Guess we'll have to wait. Find out tonight." He cocked his head, put his paws on her knee, and thrust his head onto her lap.

Rachel laughed. They snuggled for a bit before she got up. "We have to get ready to go see Sybil." She walked into the bedroom with Zeus at her heels.

<~<~|~>~>

Ninety minutes later, Rachel and Zeus entered the lobby of the penthouse apartment. She knocked on the door. No answer. She rang the bell. That did it. She heard movement behind the door. "Hi, Sybil, it's Rachel. Open up."

Rachel entered the foyer, Zeus's leash pulled tight. He leaned against her. "Sybil? Are you all right?"

"Come in. Have a drink," Sybil said, as she reclined on the couch.

Rachel sighed in relief and released the taut leash. Zeus relaxed.

"Pull up a chair." Sybil waved toward the side chair.

Rachel sat, with the dog on the floor beside her. "Have you had breakfast?"

Sybil held out her glass. "Having it now."

Rachel took the glass out of the woman's hand and walked to the kitchen. "As good as this must taste, I'm going to prepare some real food—coffee, eggs, and toast."

"Don't bother. I'm not hungry."

"Tell me why?"

"Peter's not home. He hasn't called. Nobody tells me anything. Even Lidia's been silent."

"She's gone, Sybil."

"Her spirit used to come every day. No more. I'm alone, deserted, and without purpose. I used to think the world needed me. I thought if I didn't look out for the marginalized peoples on this earth, no one would. I mattered…and…then…I didn't. I know that because here I sit, the world's savior, ignored, unnecessary, dismissed, abandoned, and alone."

"Sybil, that sounds like a speech from an old Bette Davis movie."

"Rachel, not you, too."

Rachel returned with a tray and placed it on the coffee table. "Here. Eat."

"I can't."

"Do it. You'll need your strength."

"For what?"

"I have a job for you."

"I'm not ready. I can't."

"What you can't do is sit here any longer. The isolation and self-pity is going to kill you if the liquor and pills don't do it first."

Sybil rolled her lower lip out. Rachel braced for the pouting tirade. Instead Sybil started to laugh. "Good one, Rachel." She pointed a finger at her friend. "This is a tough-love intervention, right?"

"It's time. You are needed."

"I'll listen," Sybil said, picking up a piece of toast. While she ate, Rachel related the disasters in Tawanda, what she knew of Peter's situation, Dani's request, and PRAISE's role in the operation. "Well?"

Sybil wiped her mouth and said, "I think we can do the food drop. Any figures?"

Rachel reached into her handbag and withdrew three folded sheets of paper and a thumb drive. "Here are the estimates I did this morning on hard copy as well as on this drive."

Sybil took the information and studied the papers. "Not too bad."

"No."

"If I coordinate this with Dani, there's a good chance Peter will get out of that wretched place unscathed?"

"That's what the plan is for."

"I've not had much contact with Dani. Can you trust her? Is she James's puppet or on her own?"

"I think she is estranged from James, but that's up to you to find out." Rachel handed Sybil a business card. "This is her contact information. Her private line is on the reverse side. I have given her your number so she will take your call."

Sybil looked down at the information. "You've certainly done your homework." Without raising her head, she lifted her eyes to Rachel. "Why me? Why don't you do this on your own? You have no need to include me."

Rachel leaned forward, hands clasped, elbows on her knees. "I hate being Executive Director of PRAISE. I don't like the responsibility. I don't like going to the office. I don't like all the administrative crap that has to get done on an operation this extensive and important."

"Why don't you say what you really think?"

"Sybil this is your baby and you're very good at what you do. The organization needs you back at its helm. I'm a terrible substitute."

Sybil regarded her friend for a moment. "You need to get back to your writing, right?"

Rachel sighed and leaned back. "Yes. I have to do what I do best ,and you have to do the same."

Sybil stood. "Can you wait?"

"What for?"

"I'll get dressed and you can drop me off at the office. Apparently. I am needed."

Chapter 41 ▶ Damir, Tawanda, Africa

Friday, 15 May

In his hotel room with Sam, Peter closed the laptop and stuck it in his messenger bag. "Let's go."

Sam nodded. "Think he'll buy it?"

"Not sure he has a choice if we're going to stop the impending carnage."

They took the stairs to the lobby and found Taxi by the reception desk. He said, "You'd better get out of here. No one's volunteered for the mines. It's going to get ugly."

Peter said, "I have an idea that may solve the problem."

Taxi said, "I'm listening."

Sam said, "Not here." He pointed at the table in the far corner of the bar. "There."

When they were seated, Peter opened his computer and brought up the satellite geological maps. In a hushed tone, he explained his proposal. "See, the caves extend under this whole area. I think we can be fairly certain that if we gain access here," he pointed to the map, "we can exit there." He shifted his finger and looked at Taxi. "The access point is in the mine workers' village, and the exit point is on the far side and outside the mine's gates."

Taxi said, "How does that help us?"

Sam said, "Convince the men to work and bring as many refugees as they can claim as family to live in the village. While they work the mines, the families will be our workforce to dig into the cavern."

Peter said, "I'll negotiate a common tented area. The women will dig and remove the soil in bags hidden under their clothes."

Sam said, "Peter and I will organize another group of diggers, beyond the hills. We will also dig. As soon as we have access, we'll explore the caves and make sure the passage is clear."

Taxi smiled. "Now, I see. An underground escape route which allows everyone to leave. We can be across the border before anyone realizes."

Peter said, "Yes."

Sam said, "If you agree, we need to negotiate with President Ebu—men for village amenities." He looked at Taxi and Peter. "One of you needs to make the call."

Taxi put up his hand. "One moment, please. I must talk with the other leaders."

Peter said, "You must be sure of their loyalty. If anyone leaks the plan, it'll mean permanent enslavement or worse, death."

Taxi said, "What do I do after the deal? Walk away?"

Peter said, "Are you kidding? You're the key to the whole thing. You must make yourself the intermediary, with unlimited daily access to the village, speak for the people, and guard their rights as promised by the government and the mine owners."

Sam said, "That way you'd be able to monitor the work on the hole."

Taxi nodded. "Yes, that could work. Me and two associates." He stood. "Give me five minutes. I'll be back."

After he left, Peter said, "What do you think?"

Sam stroked his chin. "I don't think there's any other choice. We both know it's risky."

Taxi returned with two other men and said, "We have discussed your proposal. While we have serious concerns, we think it is a better idea than being murdered." The two men nodded imperceptibly. "I will talk with President Ebu." He pulled out his phone and walked away, followed by his two associates.

He returned. "Ebu has agreed. He will have the mine owners prepare the village for the workers. After I inspect the facilities and they meet with our agreement, the workers will return with their extended families."

Peter said, "You're not smiling."

"There aren't enough provisions to care for the remaining refugees."

Peter held up his phone. "My mother's organization agreed to a food and supplies air drop. We can expect it within forty-eight hours."

Taxi's shoulders dropped and a smile cracked his tired face. "Thank God. I had no idea how I was going to tell half the people they would live and the other half that they would die."

<~<~|~>~>

President Ebu called Vanderhagen. "We have an agreement with the mine workers."

"Excellent. I will open the mines."

"This is not without conditions."

"I'm listening."

"The worker village must be expanded to include their extended families. They will not work if they cannot be sure their people are cared for."

"How does this affect the owners?"

"Increased supplies at the village store and daily rations—including water, health care, and sanitation as well as community tents."

"You agreed to this?"

"It seemed little enough to insure production."

"I will commit to half the cost."

"Mr. Vanderhagen, I insist you shoulder the entire cost as Tawanda must devote the rest of its treasury to rebuilding Damir and caring for the other refugees. I can see no other way of meeting your needs and ours."

"Be careful, Mr. President."

"I am not prepared to order the public execution of my own people. If that happens, we will both lose much, in addition to time, labor, and money."

"I will guarantee three months."

Ebu said, "One year to insure the city's revitalization."

"Agreed if, and only if, the exports meet or exceed previous numbers."

"I will make sure the workers understand."

Vanderhagen said, "In that case, we have a deal."

<~<~|~>~>

Peter finished his calls to his mother, Dani, and the State Department. He looked at Sam and said, "Mom's on board. The government's happy there'll be no civil war. It's one less insurgency to deal with."

Sam smiled. "It's hard being the gatekeeper of the world."

Peter shook his head. "At least this situation got resolved without war or voiding the peace treaty with the DRC."

"What'll you do?"

"Depends if they call me back or not."

Peter's phone rang. He looked at the ID and answered. "Uncle James."

"Peter, glad to hear your voice."

"What's going on?"

"I'd like you to monitor our interests at the mines on the owners' behalf. We're opening and expanding our worker village to help relocate families. I need you to make sure our operations manager, Musimbwa Bakama, carries out the necessary adjustments."

"Umm. I'm not sure I'm the man for this job. Bakama tried to kill me last time we met."

"A misunderstanding. I will take care of it. Keep me informed of your progress."

"Certainly." Peter hung up and grinned. "Sam, I'm to oversee the creation of the expanded village. Care to assist?"

Chapter 42 ▶ West Wing, Washington, D.C.

Monday, 18 May

Dani sat at her desk in the West Wing. She reviewed the day's calendar and created her "to do" list. A knock on her door. She looked up. Yosef poked his head in and said, "Your presence is required in the Oval Office."

"Do you know why?"

"Didn't say."

Dani rose, put on her jacket, and paused, wondering if she needed to bring anything other than her phone. She decided no information meant no folders. As she approached the Oval Office, a guard opened the door for her.

Upon entering, Dani felt she had interrupted a meeting in progress, President Sandford, Wendell, Uriah, and the Head of the Joint Chiefs of Staff, General Jefferson Clemmons, sat on the facing couches.

Sandford stood and said, "Come on in, Dani. I believe you know everyone." Dani nodded and sat down, as did the President, who said, "Uriah, bring us up to date."

Uriah said, "Tawanda has sidestepped civil war. An agreement has been reached with the new mine workers. It will offer relief to many refugee families affected by the encampment collapse."

Dani reacted as if she hadn't talked with Peter earlier. She said, "That's good news. What about the remaining refugees?"

Wendell said, "We're here to discuss that very issue with General Clemmons."

The general said, "Call me Jefferson, please."

Sandford said, "As you know, Congress wants to end undocumented immigration, regardless of cause—political or humanitarian—to our shores." He paused. Heads nodded in response. "Jefferson, please present your thoughts on this."

"Thank you, Sir." Jefferson cleared his throat. "My people at the DOD have been working on a microchip ID project. We are ready to test its effectiveness."

Dani fought to keep her face passive and not reveal her knowledge of the project.

Jefferson continued. "We feel the Tawandian people would be an excellent target group for several reasons. First, their government can't support them. Second, their very presence impedes Tawanda's acceptance into the United Nations."

Wendell said, "Why do we care? Tawanda started the war, created the refugee problem, and has spent little to nothing on rehoming."

Jefferson said, "We care because we can use it to our advantage. We believe President Ebu will allow us to evacuate them to ease his fiscal burden. Our people would go to Damir, create papers, record information on the microchips, and inject the data along with the standard travel immunizations."

Dani said, "With or without the subject's knowledge?"

"Wait a minute," Wendell said. "Why go through the bother?"

Jefferson said, "We need to test the microchip and delivery process, Wendell." He turned to Dani. "They will know. Each will receive an ID card with their picture and a unique twenty-digit code that matches the code on the chip and their documentation."

Dani said, "Does the Senate majority leader know?"

Uriah shook his head and said, "No. We want this action to be seen as an essential humanitarian action, not an immigration issue."

Dani turned to Sandford, "Except that it's not either. It's a Department of Defense testing ground for human tracking."

Sandford said, "This is not up for debate. It's an essential component to our national security initiatives. However, it does fall under your scope of work. I'd like you to make the announcement when it's time."

Dani said, "Me? I'm surprised. I thought surely, Sir, this would fit in perfectly with your human rights initiative."

Sandford smiled. "It does. With your participation, it will show that you and I are in complete agreement that human rights trumps any and all other considerations."

Dani said, "What about a person's right to privacy?"

Wendell said, "Our collective thinking is that it's a small price to pay to guard our borders."

She eyed each person in the room. "I see," she said. "You've already strategized this endeavor without including me."

Sandford said, "Not at all. We wanted to present you with a clear, well thought out plan."

"In that case," Dani said, "I'd be happy to make the announcement…after I've been briefed on the details."

"Of course," Sandford said. "You have twenty-four hours until the press conference. My press secretary will do the write up."

Dani stood. "Jefferson, my office please, with a detail summary, in ten minutes."

She left the room, entered her office, and escaped into her private restroom. She turned the tap on, pulled out her phone, and called Rachel. Before the first ring, Dani ended the call. Her downfall had come sooner than she expected and would leave her exposed to unfathomable anger and verbal abuse. This one speech would end her political career by putting her in the spotlight as an advocate for targeted mass immigration. The liberals would be aghast at the targeting, and the conservatives would be furious at any immigration at all.

Dani was doomed to failure, and she knew it.

<~<~|~>~>

Peter got the message from Uriah Henderson at bedtime. First thing in the morning, he met with President Ebu. "Mr. President, I bring you good news from my country."

"Sit down, Mr. Powell, and tell me."

Peter sat. "My country has offered to take the displaced refugees."

"Take them where?"

"To our country. We will fly them out and see to their resettlement."

"On whose authority?"

"Sir? I'm afraid I don't understand. Haven't the refugees always been a problem?"

"Does your President think he will be doing me a favor by taking over my problem?"

Peter said, "I can't answer that. I'm only the messenger."

Ebu said, "His offer makes me look weak. It says I cannot take care of my people."

"I'm sure that wasn't his intention."

"It does not matter. It is how it will be perceived," Ebu said. "My people have suffered enough. Now, they will be the labor force that rebuilds Tawanda."

"Sir…."

Ebu put up his hand. "They will be nominally paid, and I will see to it that they have housing, food, water, and sanitation. No one is too old or young to help. Please relay my appreciation for the offer and my formal refusal."

Peter stood. "I understand." He walked to the door, stopped, and turned. "Will you also refuse the food and supply drop?"

"Please explain."

"Non-profits are working to assemble pallets of canned goods, wound dressings, and health care items to be air-dropped."

"I see."

Peter waited.

Ebu said, "I will accept the supplies on behalf of my people. Thank you." With a wave of his hand, he ended the conversation, and Peter left.

<~<~|~>~>

As soon as Dani arrived at her West Wing office, Yosef told her the President wanted to see her.

"Good morning," Sandford said, handing her a sheet of paper. "This is the text we received from Peter."

She read the message out loud. "Ebu refuses refugee evac. Needs work force to rebuild. Air drops OK."

She put the paper on the desk. "I guess that's it then. Our hands are tied."

"Dani, I'm confused. I thought you were passionate about getting those refugees out."

"Get them out, yes. Use them as a security experiment, not so much."

"Still, everyone would be safe—a win-win situation."

"You're right, Sir," Dani said. "Shall I make the air-drop announcement?"

"Not necessary. PRAISE and the UN will handle it." Sandford looked down at his desk and picked up a sheet of paper and handed it to her. "I'd like you to work with Jefferson and find another population to target for our prototype."

"Sir, are you sure the United States needs to go down this path? The imbedded microchip may violate some constitutional privacy issues."

"I've put a team on this to make sure that we observe all the laws and ethics related to this technology."

"Is there any chance it could be misused?"

"Not under my watch."

Dani nodded. "I'll be happy to work with Jefferson."

"Good. I think you two will make an effective team."

Dani walked slowly back to her office thinking about the President's take on the tracking microchip. He'd never be able to control it.

Back at her desk, Dani decided to concentrate on the task at hand, for her own piece of mind.

Her phone buzzed. She saw the ID and answered. "Peter, where are you?"

"In Tawanda."

"You need to get out. We're sending...."

"I can't leave, Dani."

"Why?"

"The city is quiet, for now, but I don't know for how long. I've got a plan to evacuate as many refugees as we can. I'll know more once it gets underway."

"Peter, you should tell President Sandford."

"Not yet. I need about week to set it up and a week to execute. During that time, I'll oversee opening of the mines for Uncle James. I'm hoping you can create a fourteen-day diversion to take everyone's attention away from Tawanda. It has to seem like the country is doing business as usual."

"You don't ask for much, do you?"

"Trust me," Peter said. "Will you do it?"

She said, "I have something in the works that could do the trick."

"Thanks, Dani. We'll have a long talk when I get back."

"You just make sure you get back."

"No problem."

Chapter 43 ▶ Gramercy Avenue, N.Y.C.

Monday, 18 May

Zeus jumped off the couch, and Rachel woke with a start. "What's..." She didn't finish her sentence. The answer walked in the door.

Chris said, "Sorry, I'm late. I forgot the time."

"Why? What time is it?"

"Almost eight. Hope you didn't eat." He held up a big paper bag. "I brought dinner."

Rachel sat up and stretched. "I must have fallen asleep."

Chris, without giving her a kiss hello, took the packages into the kitchen and unpacked the bags. "How'd your day go?"

Rachel got off the couch and sat on one of the counter stools. Still no kiss plus very little eye contact. "Not too shabby. I encouraged Sybil to get back to work."

"I bet that took all day." He took down a couple of plates and pulled out silverware.

"No, not really. I made her breakfast and told her PRAISE needed her skills more than mine."

"She believed you?" Chris opened the containers and plated the food.

"Maybe, maybe not. Either way, she believed that I really hated running the office and wanted to get back to my writing," Rachel said. "This smells delicious." She reached over for a taste.

Chris tapped her hand. "Bad habit. Wait. It has to be heated." He put the dishes in the microwave for three minutes.

"You must have gotten Sybil on her best day yet." He cleared the debris from the countertop.

"I guess. She didn't call, and I got to write without worrying about anything else."

The microwave dinged and Chris pulled the plates out. "Here at the counter or the couch and TV?"

"Couch."

"Grab a couple of beers and we're all set."

Rachel got the drinks from the fridge and joined him. He handed her a plate and said, "Enjoy."

She took a bite. "This is good. Where's it from?"

"A new Hungarian restaurant on the lower West Side." He picked up the clicker and nodded toward the screen, "Ready for the next episode or...."

"Down by my warehouse?"

"Yes. I hope you don't mind. We had talked about renting that space out, remember? I wanted to take another look." He clicked through several screens picking options for viewing.

"Without me?" Rachel put down her fork.

"You were out." He found two more movies. "Is that a problem? Keys were on the wall."

"You didn't ask."

"Whoa," Chris said, turning to look at her. "Did I do something wrong?"

"I don't know, did you?"

"Rachel, I just wanted to scope out the space. No big deal."

"Why didn't you ask me first?"

Chris turned to stare at her. She watched his face soften. He said, "You're right. I should have asked. I guess my mind was preoccupied on a possible new venture."

Rachel picked up her fork and said, "What venture?"

Chris picked a show and clicked the remote. The screen filled with opening scenes. "It's nothing, just an idea right now."

Rachel took a few more bites of her meal, put her plate on the coffee table, and picked up her beer. After a few sips, she put the bottle down next to her plate. She wriggled into the corner of the couch, tucking her legs under her. She now had a full view of Chris.

He ate his meal and finished his beer as he watched the story play out, glancing at her every now and then, without saying much. The show ended. He stood up and collected the plates. "Rachel, you didn't eat."

"I wasn't very hungry."

"Give it to Zeus or save it?" The dog jumped to his feet at the mention of his name. Tail wagging, he stared at Chris.

"Save it."

"Sorry, boy. No scraps tonight. Have a treat instead."

Zeus plopped his butt on the floor and waited. Treat in mouth, he lay down by Rachel to enjoy it.

Chris did the dishes and put them in the drainer. He picked up the dish towel and dried his hands, leaving it folded on the counter, and returned to the living room. Pulling out his phone, he said, "It's getting late, and

I've got some work to finish before my morning meetings."

Rachel didn't move.

He said, "Oh, I forgot. C'mon Zeus, last walk before bedtime."

<~<~|~>~>

Thirty minutes later, Chris and Zeus walked into Rachel's apartment. The dog ran to Rachel. and she gave him pats on his side and scratches behind his ear.

He said, "I looked for you in my place. What are you doing here?"

She said, "I needed my own space. I felt like I was intruding on yours."

"You've got to be kidding." Chris held out his hand to her. "C'mon. Let's go."

Rachel didn't accept. "Do you realize you've dismissed me all evening...again?"

Chris dropped his hand. "Dinner and TV? It's our thing. We've been doing that since we met."

"You don't talk to me anymore."

"I'm confused. What's this about?"

"It's about the warehouse and your secret venture."

"It's just business. I'm a little wrapped up...." Chris phone buzzed. His eyebrows raised and his shoulders shrugged. He pulled out the phone and looked at the ID. "Sorry, I have to take this."

Rachel got up and went into the bathroom. In the middle of brushing her teeth, Chris appeared at the doorway, smiled, and held up his phone. "Important." She kept on brushing. He put the phone in his pocket and leaned on the door jamb, arms crossed over his chest. She spat into the sink and rinsed with mouthwash. "Honey, I can't stand here all night."

Rachel wiped her face and said, "I know. You're busy."

Chris stood up straight and dropped his arms. "This is about my work?"

She looked at him and tried to walk past him.

Chris blocked her. "We don't talk about work. Yours or mine."

"So," she said, brushing him aside, "this warehouse and venture is like the microchip development."

"What do you mean?"

"You don't want to tell me because it'll make me upset."

Chris said, "It's business, Rachel. Since when do you care about electronic security?"

"I don't."

"Why are you asking?"

"Because you're shutting me out. Before, you left business at the office. Now, you're hiding it—closing computers, taking private phone calls, and sneaking into my warehouse…even resorting to vagueness about this new venture."

Chris laughed. "That's nothing new. You're seeing all this because you're living with me. You're making way too much of the whole situation." Again, he offered his hand to her. "Let's go."

She held up her hands. "I can't. I know it's irrational, but I feel pushed away."

"Rachel, you know that's not true."

"I need some time."

"You want me to go?"

"Up to you," Rachel said. "I'm going to bed."

Chapter 44 ▶ Damir, Africa, Tawanda

Monday, 18 May
Peter called Sybil. "Hi, Mom, how's it going?"

"Much better. I'm back at PRAISE."

"Good for you. It's about time."

Sybil agreed and said, "How are you? Where are you?"

"I'm fine and still in Damir. I need a favor."

"Name it. I'll do anything I can."

"I'm going to need transport for one thousand people over the course of three to four days."

"Ground or air?"

"Ground would cause less attention. Air would depend on where the plane lands. Many can't walk far."

"Peter, what are you up to?"

"Helping refugees escape a dangerous situation."

"I'll make some calls."

"Not to Uncle James or the government. I don't want to jeopardize his position or U.S.-Tawanda relations."

"Don't worry. I'll text you when I've got something lined up."

"Good. I'll keep you up to date with our time frame."

Peter hung up and brought up his maps on the computer. A knock on the door. Peter identified his visitor through the eye hole and let Taxi in. "Take a look at this." Peter turned the computer screen toward his friend.

Taxi said, "Do we have time?" Peter checked his watch. "Sam will be downstairs in ten minutes."

Taxi nodded and looked.

Peter said, "See this?" He pointed to squiggles. "It says the cave is closest to the surface at this point. Looks to me like ten meters. An easier dig than I expected."

Taxi said, "Our diggers can do it in less than a day. Where is it?"

"At the far end of the workers' village. A perfect place to erect the community tent. It'll hide the activity."

Taxi nodded. "What about the other end?"

Peter moved his finger over the cave system and stopped. "We will dig here. Again, the map shows the cavern's ceiling near the surface. We'll have to dig sooner or be faster than the others. Our job is to make sure the caves can be inter-connected and easy to navigate."

"If not?"

"We're no worse off than we are now."

"Not necessarily good," Taxi said. "I will think about another option."

Peter nodded and looked at his watch. "Sam's downstairs."

<~<~|~>~>

The three men arrived at the gated entrance to the mines. The guards checked their papers, made a call, and let them enter. They walked to the administration building. Peter stepped up to the secretary's desk and addressed her, "I don't know if you remember me. I'm Peter Powell, representing the mine owners. Please let Operations Manager Musimbwa Bakama know we are here for our appointment."

She said, "I do remember, Mr. Powell. Please take a seat. I will let him know."

Bakama made them wait fifteen minutes. It gave Peter time to remember the airport incident several weeks ago. Bakama had tried to kill him. Now they had to figure out a way to work together.

The secretary said, "He will see you, Mr. Powell. The others can wait."

Peter entered the office. Bakama remained seated and didn't speak. Peter took the initiative. "Mr. Bakama, I'm here with two others to walk the worker village site."

Bakama gestured for Peter to sit. He leaned forward, elbows on the desk, and said, "You did not report me to the police?"

"No."

"I have also heard nothing regarding possible irregularities in the rough diamond count."

Peter said, "I made a choice."

Bakama nodded. "I will have one of my men drive you to the site."

Chapter 45 ▶ Gramercy Avenue, N.Y.C.

Tuesday, 19 May

Rachel opened her eyes and saw Zeus's happy face. He licked her jaw and nose. His tail wagged and his body wiggled. "Bet you're ready for breakfast." He barked. "Okay, I'm up. Let's go." He jumped off the bed and waited.

She slipped into a jogging suit and walked to the dining table and paused. On its surface, she saw Zeus's bowls, filled with food and water, a wildflower bouquet, breakfast from Alfie's, the diner across the street, and a note. "I'm sorry for my insensitivity. I hated sleeping without you. Please forgive me. Will be gone most of the morning. Let's plan to have lunch. Love, Chris."

Rachel put on Zeus's leash. "Let's walk first—eat later."

They rode the elevator down to the lobby. Nikolai greeted them. "Good morning."

"Hi, Nikolai. We're going for our morning walk."

"I see."

"Need anything?"

He shook his head. "You?"

Rachel stopped, her hand on the door handle. "Me? No, I'm good." She pushed the door open, and Zeus led the way out.

They walked to a nearby park. After Zeus did his business, she sat on one of the benches. Zeus jumped up next to her and laid his head and upper body across her lap. She stroked his back. "What am I going to do?" The dog grunted. She smiled. "You're such a good listener." She gave him a hug. He snorted. "If we have lunch in either apartment, make-up sex is likely to obliterate any actual resolution. Right?" A low, short whine. "Okay, we agree. Plan B. I'd better pick a restaurant and let him know." Zeus's tail beat a rhythm on the bench.

She pulled out her phone and texted Chris. "Meet at Luigi's at noon."

<~<~|~>~>

When she arrived with Zeus, Chris welcomed her with a kiss and a hug. "I like your choice. We haven't been here in a while."

The maître de seated them. Zeus relaxed under the table. The busboy filled their water glasses, and the waiter took their order.

Rachel said, "Thank you for breakfast."

Chris reached for her across the table. "I love you, Rachel."

She put her hand in his. "I love you, too."

He said, "I want you to know I've never felt more connected to anyone. I've always kept business out of our relationship. Not because of you, but because it distracts me from you. Since you've moved in with me, it's hard to separate the two."

"Your time and our time?"

"Yes. Exactly. Isn't it the same with you?"

"I haven't entered my critical writing stage yet, but I know it'll be hard to shut it down once I'm there."

"What do we do? Not work at home. We could lose a lot of together time."

Rachel wrinkled her nose. "I wouldn't like that, but I hate feeling intrusive."

Chris said, "What do you mean? I haven't changed since the day you arrived to rent one of my apartments."

"That's not true," she said. "You've stopped working on projects around the building."

"Tarek's helping Nikolai." He squeezed her hand. "That gives us more time together."

"It doesn't feel that way."

The waiter brought drinks and garlic bread. Rachel took a piece. "You used to be a techie who loved coding. You worked in the open around me because you knew I had no idea what you were doing. You never wore a suit unless we went out."

"I'm still that guy."

"Look at you, you're wearing a suit."

"Like it?"

"Very funny," Rachel said. "That's not the point."

Chris smiled. "So it's not a bad thing."

"It's not about how you dress. It's about your business becoming more important than us, eating up your time, and...." Rachel stopped in mid-sentence.

"What?"

"I just realized it's making me jealous."

Chris laughed. "You have nothing to worry about. I'm just a little preoccupied right now." He moved closer to Rachel and lowered his voice. "I'm considering an expansion and taking on partners for a new venture. It's in the early conceptual stage, and I'm working out the kinks—hence the warehouse. Going there without you or your permission was wrong. I apologize."

The waiter appeared. "May I take your plates?"

Rachel looked down. She hadn't remembered being served or eating.

"Would you like dessert? Here's the menu."

Chris scanned it and said, "Two ice cream sundaes."

Rachel smiled. "Very endearing."

"I'm trying. Is it working?"

"This new venture, is it an outgrowth of your DOD project?"

Chris stopped smiling. "I'll tell you all about it, privately, at home."

The waiter brought the hot fudge sundaes. Rachel tasted hers and put her spoon down. "You know I have ethical issues concerning that project, right?"

He nodded, "I do, and I think they are offset by the larger picture of life-saving possibilities."

She picked up her spoon. "The venture. You're going to commercialize it, aren't you?"

"Rachel, you have to trust me on this."

She looked up. "Chris, I do trust you. I don't trust what people will do with the technological possibilities."

He said, "I'll think about that," as he motioned to the waiter for the bill. He paid and stood. "Let's go."

They walked back, hand in hand, Zeus by her side.

In the lobby, Chris said, "I've got to talk to Nikolai, so go on up. I'll see you later for dinner. Tonight, I'll surprise you."

<~<~|~>~>

Chris's Fortune 500 internet security company made it possible for him to purchase three contiguous buildings on Gramercy Avenue, 213, 215, and 217. He had hired Nikolai right away. They rehabbed his acquisitions. First, they did Chris's duplex office and his triplex apartment in 215. Next, they fixed the apartments in 213 and 217.

Rachel lived on the fourth floor in 213. She moved in almost two years ago, after Chris agreed to change the original floor plan into a loft-like space as part of the rental agreement. After that, he and Nikolai expanded the lobby to cover for all three buildings and added an office on the first floor for J&J car service.

Chris, in the middle of his conversation with Nikolai about the next planned renovation, said, "Hold on, my phone." He pulled it out and read Rachel's text. His jaw clenched.

Nikolai said, "Something is not going your way?"

Chris said, "I wanted to buy Rachel's warehouse on the lower Westside. She just texted me. She refuses to sell."

"Hmm."

"What's that mean?"

"I didn't say anything."

"You 'hmm-ed' me."

"It is odd to me that Rachel would refuse you anything."

"She's changed."

"I see."

"What do you see?"

"Growing together pains."

"Good," Chris said. "Go explain that to her."

"I am happy to do this for you because you are my friend. I do, however, need one more piece of information."

"What's that?"

Nikolai said, "How have you changed?"

"I haven't."

"Hmm."

"What?"

"How has she changed?"

"She feels, as she explained to me today at lunch, left out," Chris said. "In fact, she's so unhappy that she left my apartment and slept at hers last night."

"Do you have any idea why she would choose to make such a decision?"

"She admits to being jealous of my work and disagrees with my plans for a new venture."

Nikolai said, "I understand. You have always made your own decisions and been very successful on your own."

Chris nodded. "Exactly."

Nikolai continued. "It is not important if Rachel is proud of what you do or not. Therefore, it should not be important to you that she likes to kill rats in the basement with her bare hands."

Chris did a double take. "Wait. What?"

Nikolai ignored him. "It is good to get these issues resolved. In a relationship, compromise is important."

"Nikolai," Chris said. "Are you being sarcastic?"

"People from my country do not know what that means."

Chris raised an eyebrow. "Okay. Point made. What should I do?"

"I have no idea," Nikolai said, shrugging his shoulders. "She is not mad at me."

Chris ran his fingers through his hair. "Spit it out. You know I don't do self-analysis."

Nikolai pursed his lips and, after a few seconds, said, "I will ask if you are treating her like the models you used to bring home for extended stays or are you treating her like the wife she will be in six months?"

Chris's mouth dropped open. "Are you kidding me?"

"Never. I am horrified you would even suggest such a thing. Although, I will admit I am a little bit in love with Rachel myself. So, if you do not figure out a way to make her happy, you will have to deal with me and my extensive arsenal of repercussions."

"Oh my God, you're right."

"If you say so."

"I can't believe I've been so stupid."

Nikolai didn't answer.

Chris said, "How did you know?"

"I didn't. You figured it out."

Chris stood. "Give yourself another raise."

Nikolai returned a broad smile. "It is good for me you suck at relationships. Soon I will be part owner of these buildings."

"You're a good friend and a smart man, Nikolai. Thank you."

"You are wasting valuable time."

Chris started for the elevators. Stopped. Turned and strode to the front doors. "I've got an errand to run. Be right back." He flew through the doors and turned right.

Rachel appeared in the lobby with Zeus by her side as Chris disappeared around the corner. With no enthusiasm, she said, "Afternoon walk. Be back soon."

Nikolai said, "Could you stop at the hardware store for me?"

"Sure. What do you need?"

Nikolai scribbled several items on a yellow sticky-pad, tore off the top sheet of paper, and handed it to her. "This will help me. I must stay here until Tareek returns."

"No problem."

"Go to the one near the shoe place. He knows me. He will call if there is a problem."

"I can call, too."

"I will not argue. Go. I am busy."

Rachel and Zeus went through the doors and turned left.

Chapter 46 ▶ Washington D.C.

Tuesday, 19 May

Dani thought about Peter's phone call. He needed time and she needed increased face time with the President to establish her political standing and power. She looked over her notes from the past week. The immigration issue had been put on hold. Not good. She'd work out an approach and present it. She stared ahead, while wiggling her pen between her forefinger and thumb. She caught the pen and focused on her phone.

Who was listening and why? As much as she wanted to know, Dani wasn't sure who she could trust to find out. She let that problem drop and took on a new one—immigration policy.

Her plan centered on the Senate majority leader— turn his outrageous policy into a negation of his leadership abilities and shine a positive light on Sandford. Pulling out a yellow pad, she did a rough campaign analysis, mapping out key actions, expected outcomes, and supportive research.

Dani identified at risk populations throughout the world and made the case for the United States to offer refuge. If Sandford accepted her premise, the public would see the President as the leading human rights advocate in the free world, the Senate majority leader as an ancient isolationist, and the ultra-conservative Congress as obstructionists.

She filled the yellow pages with words, lines, and circles. The jumble made perfect sense. The clock in her office chimed. Startled, she looked up, grabbed her pad, and flew out the door. Dani rounded a corner and almost collided with the President.

He said, "What's the rush, Dani?"

She said, "Sir, may I join you in your walk around the grounds?"

Sandford's eyebrows shot up. "I…of course."

Outside, they walked in silence for thirty seconds. "Sir," she said, "I know this is a bit irregular, and I thank you for trusting me."

Without turning his head, he said, "Go on."

"Sir, I've come up with a plan to establish you as the global leader in human rights. It would entail a declaration of sanctuary for refugees escaping from countries that are politically oppressed, war-torn, or suffering from natural disasters."

Without missing a stride, he said, "The Senate will not authorize such an announcement."

"How far are you personally prepared to go?"

"I can't promise what I can't deliver. You know that."

"What if you could?"

Sandford glanced down at the yellow pad in her hand, "Is that what you've got there?"

"Yes," Dani said. "I have outlined the economic recovery of our poorest states through a government sponsored clean energy, clean air, and fresh food initiative fueled by an immigrant homestead act."

"A program that's been rejected in those states more than once?"

"Because it hasn't been coupled with a work program. The economic benefits would increase the dollar circulation within the towns, the federal aid based on population, and free community energy resources, not to mention the safety of thousands."

"Does this have anything to do with Tawanda?"

"I don't know at this point."

The President stopped and turned to Dani. "Let me read your notes. If I think it'll work, I'll address it at today's afternoon meeting." He reached for the pad.

"Not these." She held it back. "I'll copy them in a more presentable form and have them on your desk by the time you return."

<~<~|~>~>

Sandford kept his word. At the end of the meeting with Wendell, Uriah, and Dani, he brought up the immigration initiative.

"Dani, I want you to formalize an economic plan based on rehoming refugees seeking asylum, current and estimated future counts. We simply can't close our borders. It would be inhumane. However, with a workable plan for distribution, I think there are parts of America that could reverse their poverty-stricken communities into a positively thriving, robust economy."

Wendell said, "The Senate majority leader is opposed to any such suggestions."

"Do you have a reason not to at least consider a methodology that could benefit thousands of Americans?"

Wendell shook his head. "No."

"Good. Dani, please keep us updated as to your progress."

Chapter 47 ▶ Gramercy Avenue, N.Y.C.

Tuesday, 19 May
Chris paced his living room, waiting for Rachel to return for her laptop. He held the small jewelry box containing a peace offering in one hand, turning it over and over with his fingers. He put it down, opened his laptop.

His lawyer emailed, "New company papers ready for signing."

His real estate guy emailed, "Several spaces to show. Name a time."

His manufacturer emailed, "Prototypes available for testing. We're ready to go when you are."

His new head of marketing emailed, "Interest growing in new technology. Waiting for release date. Have several contracts waiting."

His headhunter emailed, "Have found three suitable candidates that fit your specs ready to interview. Say the word. Will send resumes and set up meetings."

General Clemmons emailed, "Looks like immigration revamp a reality. Move release date up."

The doorknob turned. The latch clicked. Before he could turn around, Zeus thrust his head into Chris's lap.

Chris killed the screen and spun around to face Rachel as her smile disappeared.

"There, you've done it again."

"What?"

"Turned your screen off as soon as I entered."

"Honey, you know I'm involved…."

She raised her hand to stop position. "New venture. Don't worry. I'm not prying. Just here to grab my computer." She walked over to the desk and reached to pick it up.

Chris covered her hand with his. "Wait."

"For what?"

Chris said. "I want to apologize."

"You don't have to. I was out of line."

"What?"

Rachel said, "We're adults and can agree to disagree. I'm a human rights advocate and you're a businessman. I get it."

Chris removed his hand and leaned back in his chair. "Reeeally? I see you've given this a lot of thought since lunch."

Rachel's eyes widened. "What do you mean?"

"Don't play games with me. You'd never give in this easily. There's got to be something else."

She picked up her laptop. "I don't want to argue."

Chris jumped to his feet. "Tell me, Rachel. This is not going keep us apart for another night."

Rachel shook her head. "I don't have the right or knowledge to tell you what to do."

"But…," Chris said.

"No buts."

"There is definitely a 'but.' Tell me."

"Okay. Fine," Rachel said. "You're rich enough. You don't need to make more money by using people's pain, or intruding on their privacy, or helping to target at-risk or minority populations."

"Is that what you think I'm doing?"

"I believe it's where the technology will go, how it will be used. The world is data hungry. Computers gladly gobble up 'in case' information because some day someone might need to know my shoe size. With your venture, the government could decide to target, investigate, interrogate, or deport everyone with a microchip ending in '123.' It'll be downhill from there. Personal freedom, as we know it, will disappear."

"Hmm." Chris walked over to the windows and back. "What if I could stop that from happening?"

Rachel said, "I don't think you can. If it's not you, it'll be someone else."

She picked up Zeus's leash and started for the door. "Rachel."

She did a quarter turn. "I'm not mad. I've got writing to do and you've got work. We'll see you later."

He watched her go. He'd won. She wasn't mad. She didn't want to interfere. She understood. Business is business. She'd be back later. He ran his hands through his hair. No kiss. No hug. Not good.

<~<~|~>~>

Rachel entered her apartment and put the laptop down on the table. She pulled out her phone and considered calling her mother. Maybe time away from here would cut through her mood. Maybe a shower.

The shower felt good, but she still felt hollow. Dressed in sweats, she walked over to the kitchen and opened the freezer. She saw a half-gallon of ice cream encrusted in frost crystals. She didn't care and pulled it out. Two maybe three scoops left. Enough.

She thought about eating it right out of the carton. Zeus whined at her feet. She answered him. "I'll give you some, just wait a minute." Zeus's tail thumped on the floor. "I need hot fudge. Let me see if I can find any." Zeus snorted.

Rachel checked. None. Cursing that she hadn't left the place stocked for such an emergency, she tore through her cabinets. She found jam, peanut butter, and Jells. In another cabinet, she had corn flakes, oatmeal, and cocoa. "Hey Zeus, I could use cocoa. It's not the same, but in a pinch?"

She waited for his response. Hearing nothing, she looked down. Zeus was gone. Rachel turned to look for him and gasped. Chris stood in front of her, hands behind his back. "What are you doing here?"

He said, "I'm having a hot fudge sundae moment. Nuts and whipped cream. Extra hot fudge. With a dab of caramel." He showed her one hand holding the confection container. "However, I didn't want to eat it alone. So, I bought two more." He held out the other hand. "One for you and a vanilla cup for Zeus."

In two steps, she was in his arms.

He whispered, "We're going to figure this out."

She took a step back and said, "Ice cream first."

Chapter 48 ▶ Damir, Tawanda, Africa

Friday, 22 May

Bakama's crew took two days to prepare the village for the workers and their extended families. On day three, people arrived. Work began at the mines, in the community tent, and behind the rocky formation beyond the mine fence.

Inside the tent, the work was slow and steady. The art of terracing seemed part of the people's DNA. It made digging the staircase into the cavern easy. All diggers wore a rope—one end tied around their waists, the other attached to an elevated crank and axle, like that of an old wishing well.

Excavated soil went into small containers, hidden under clothes, and carried out. The workers dumped their loads at the newly instituted village run brick-making operation. Due to the varying agility of the elders, the constant flow of people in and out of the tent didn't cause any undue concern.

The exit dig outside the fence behind the rocky outcrop went faster. With Peter's guidance and Sam's help, the diggers opened an entrance to the cave by midday.

<~<~|~>~>

After lunch, Peter, using a rope, dropped into the cavern, followed by Sam. They switched on their head lamps and pulled out telescoping probing sticks.

Peter retrieved the map and said, "We're here. The next cavern is here. We need to find the weakest point in the common wall."

Sam looked and nodded. "The floor is smoother than I expected."

"Probably worn down by prehistoric streams."

"Still, use your probe stick. We have no assurance this place is safe."

The men made their way across the floor to the far wall. Peter used a whistle to signal for help.

A worker, equipped with a headlight and three pickaxes, dropped to the cave floor. He joined Peter and Sam at the wall. He gave them each an axe.

Peter and Sam explored the wall with their gloved hands, chucking loose rocks into a pile. Peter said, "I don't see any natural opening."

Sam tapped the wall with his pickaxe. All three listened for a difference in resonance—the higher pitch indicated a thinner divide. He found it. "Let's dig here."

Forty-seven minutes later, they'd opened a small hole.

Peter blew the whistle.

Another worker came to help them widen the passage. It took three hours to open a doorway into the next cavern.

Peter looked at his watch. "I suggest we go back to the surface and explore number two in the morning. The air is stale. We need fresh air and this place needs time to breathe.

Sam said, "Agreed. Still, it wouldn't hurt to take a look."

They went through the opening and stood in the second cavern. It was larger than the first. Sam took a few steps. "Are you sure you want to stop?"

Peter said, "Yes. If I'm right, this cavern connects with the one under the worker village. We'll be there by this time tomorrow. We don't need to push ourselves and risk our lives to find out."

<~<~|~>~>

Back at the hotel, Peter entered his room and did his routine room-scan for listening devices. He found three which he flushed down the toilet. "It's okay. Come in."

Sam and Taxi walked over and sat down at the table. Peter handed them a menu. "We'll order in. This is the quietest and safest place in the hotel."

Taxi put the menu down. "Don't bother. Food stores are low. They have only one meal."

Peter called the concierge. He ordered three meals and three beers. He ended the call and said, "Be here in half-an-hour."

Peter sat down. "Boy, I didn't realize how tired I was."

Taxi said, "How's the dig site at your end?"

Peter said, "We're making good progress. We're in the second cavern and I expect we'll get through to the third by tomorrow."

Sam said, "The floor isn't too bad. Our guess is that it was a riverbed because it sure isn't road smooth."

Peter said, "The ceiling is high enough so that people don't have to stoop or crawl. My concern is the air quality."

Sam said, "I think it'll be okay. Once the village entrance is complete, the fresh air should blow through."

Taxi rubbed his chin. "Bad air. No light. Over a mile underground. Do you think the refugees can make it?"

Peter nodded. "We'll know more tomorrow. I'll bring several candles with me and see if they'll light and stay lit. That'll give us a better reading on conditions."

Sam said, "Taxi, if you had to estimate, how soon will the village diggers break into the cavern?"

Taxi said, "Days. Maybe a week. They are old and not very fast."

"Hmm," Sam said. "How often do supply trucks enter the village?"

"Maybe three a day."

"Are they checked going in and out?"

"Only the trucks going in."

Peter sat up. "Are you thinking of taking people out by truck?"

Taxi said, "There are almost two hundred workers and eight hundred family members."

Sam said, "If we can get the families out by truck, the workers can escape through the caverns in under an hour."

Peter said, "It could take up to four days, figuring sixty people per truck load, and that's if the trucks have high sides and a tarp cover."

Taxi added, "If the guards don't check. Once they do, the whole operation is blown."

Sam said, "Taxi, what's the security in the village? Armed guards? Cameras? What?"

"I have not seen armed guards," Taxi said. "It's not a prison. The mine people just want the workers to show up every day. To that end, there is one rotating camera mounted in the center of the village. The fence is electrified, and perimeter lights are on motion sensors. People are not going anywhere."

Sam said, "If we want to cut through the fence, we can install an electrical bypass on it to maintain current and not alert security."

Peter said, "We can create a loop for the camera."

Taxi said, "It will be easier if we make it look like the camera is malfunctioning. After a while, whoever is monitoring it will figure it is just being temperamental. No one will come out at night to fix it."

Sam said, "I guess the big question is can we move a thousand people on the ground in one night without anyone noticing?" He looked at Peter and Taxi. They shook their heads. "I guess we're back to a steady stream underground."

Peter stood, stretched, and walked over to the window. As he watched the city, he said, "Taxi, the sinkholes are disappearing."

"Yes. The rebuilding is going surprisingly well. Our refugee bucket brigade is constant if not fast."

"How are they holding up?"

"They are supplied with water and meals. For most, it is more than they have had in many years."

"What happens after the sinkholes are filled?"

Taxi said, "That, my friend, is the big question. I wish we could take them all."

Peter shook his head, "Me, too," and returned to the table. "How long to bus refugees to the Arua Airport?"

Taxi said, "An hour on the Adumi Road, assuming Uganda border guards will let us pass."

Peter said, "What do we need to make that happen?"

Sam pulled out his phone and started tapping. "I have an idea. Yes. If we can get an Emergency Relief pass for the bus from the Unite Nations Refugee Agency, the border guards won't stop us."

"How likely is that considering we don't want to alert President Ebu or the mining company about the evacuation?"

Sam smiled. "I know a guy who knows a guy. How many do we need?"

Chapter 49 ▶ New York City, NY

Saturday, 23 May
At PRAISE, Sybil leaned back in her chair, after several days of hard work. She'd forgotten how good it felt to be engaged. Her phone rang. The ID made her smile. "Hello, Peter."

"Hi, Mom. You sound great."

"I am. How are things with you?"

"We're making progress on all fronts, including an evacuation plan. I'd like to run it by you to see if we can make it work. If not, it's back to the drawing boards."

Sybil said, "I'm listening."

"I've got approximately a thousand refugees. We figure we can move one-third to the Arua Airport in Uganda in three nights. If you can get me two Boeing 737's, we'll be golden."

"Why that specific plane?"

"It's standard at the Arua Airport. Anything larger may arouse questions. We want to keep this low key until everyone is out of Tawanda."

"Including you?"

"Yes, Mom. I will be on the last flight."

"What about the rest of the refugees?"

Peter said, "They've volunteered to help fill the sink holes."

"By volunteered," Sybil said, "I assume you mean forced into slavery."

"I do. However, they are getting food, water, and shelter. In some ways, it's better than what they had."

"Can we get them out?"

Peter said, "Not this time. They're under constant supervision by the police and soldiers."

"Do you have the buses?"

"I do."

Sybil said, "Excellent. I will make sure the two planes are available for as long as you need them. What's the start date?"

"I figure we'll be ready in two days."

"I suggest a test run into Arua."

"Why?"

"You might want to connect with the Ugandan police. You don't want to run into any border issues."

Peter said, "Good idea. I even know the chief of police."

"Remember, we're seven hours behind. Give me a ten-hour window to get the planes to Uganda."

"I will. Thanks, Mom."

"For you, Peter, anything."

<~<~|~>~>

The next morning, Sam drove Peter to the exit cavern's entrance. Taxi greeted them, pointing at two extension ladders by his side. "I thought these might be better than trying to raise and lower each person in and out of the caverns."

"Easier and faster," Peter said. "Are you coming down with us today?"

Taxi shook his head. "I am checking out the worker village to see how close they are to breaking through. Afterwards I need to speak with the sinkhole workers. I don't trust the mines or the government to keep their promises to the refugees."

Peter said, "Good luck. We'll talk later." He watched Taxi drive away, got into his gear, and followed the others down the ladder into the darkness.

One man stayed by the ladder. Halfway to the pass-through in the far wall, Peter lit a candle and set it on the floor. It flickered and stabilized—its flame strong. At the pass-through, another man. Peter lit a candle and placed it on the floor to the left of the opening. "I'll give a shout if we need another man." The man nodded.

The second cavern felt wider and shorter than the first. Peter lit a candle halfway and joined Sam and a digger at the far wall. They pulled loose rocks away, listening for any telltale sound of collapse. Sam tested for thickness. The wall did not give up any answers.

Peter said, "Since we have no idea where to break through, let's dig the opening in line with the other breakthrough."

They tunneled four meters in before they broke through. It took them two hours to create an opening large enough for an upright person to walk through.

Peter asked their digger to remain at this doorway and lit candle. Halfway, another candle. Peter and Sam walked, lighting their path with a flashlight. They knew they were under the workers' encampment and had to locate the entrance. Every few steps, they'd stop and listen. About fifteen meters from the wall, a steady thump-thump echoed above them.

"Hear that?" Peter said. "It's the diggers above."

Sam nodded. "This might work after all. Come on. We have to clear any obstructions, figure out how to light this path for up to six hours, and bring the second ladder to this entrance."

For the rest of the day, they prepared the underground passage.

Peter went to bed exhausted. His muscles ached from wielding the pickaxe. His hands hurt from blisters across the palm and in the crook between his thumb and forefinger—all in spite of wearing work gloves.

With eyes at half-mast, he reached for his phone and texted. He was asleep as soon as he pressed "SEND."

<~<~|~>~>

Dani's phone vibrated. She picked it up and viewed her text message. 3planes@320ppl-ea,ETD2days.

Chapter 50 ▶ Damir, Tawanda Africa

Saturday, 23 May
This morning's walkthrough went well," Peter said. He stood next to Sam's car, Sam in the driver's seat. "From the time the first person descends the ladder into the cavern, walks the underground path, ascends the ladder, and exits here, I estimate two hours at most."

Sam said, "That's about right."

"The buses will fill and take off."

Sam said, "That's my cue." He turned on the engine. "Let's go and time this route."

Peter walked around the car and got in. "Do you have the documents for the bus drivers and the planes?"

"In the glove compartment. We need to register everyone on each bus and again on each plane."

Sam drove around the backside of the rocky outcrop and on a back-road heading east. "This route is out of the way. Chances are good we'll avoid any surveillance radar." At the next intersection, he turned onto the Adumi Road. Forty-five minutes later they were at the border. Tawandian guards on one side and Ugandan guards on the other.

Peter said, "I somehow forgot about this side."

Sam said, "What do you think? Bribes?"

"No. Too much exposure for one crossing much less three. Let's back-up and think about an off-road crossing."

"Not going to be easy at night."

"Damn. Okay. Let's finish the drive to the airport and talk to Taxi when we get back."

Ten minutes after the border check, they parked at the airport.

Peter said, "How are we going to get busloads of people through the airport check in? It's going to be a mad house."

"Maybe we can highjack the gate and take them right up to the plane."

Peter smiled. "Sure. I'm sure nobody, especially those heavily armed guards over there, will try to stop us."

"I see your point."

"Come on. Let's go over to the police station."

Sam shook his head. "Not a good idea."

"We need police cooperation," Peter said. "How else are we going to get six buses onto the tarmac three nights in a row?"

"The more people we involve on the ground, the less likely it's going to work."

"Then, my friend, we've got a lot of unsolved problems."

Sam said, "We could do a different border crossing every night. That might eliminate one problem."

"Doesn't matter what we do. Once we break through the airport's gate, the police will know and Ebu will know. He needs the refugee labor in the mines and in the city. He isn't going to let anyone out of his country if he can help it—at least right now."

Sam said, "You want to call it off?"

"No," Peter said. "We need a different solution."

Sam started the engine, put the car in gear, and headed back to Damir. A phone buzzed.

"It's mine," Peter said. He read the text aloud. "Taxi says the village diggers have gotten through."

Sam said, "Are you going to tell him?"

"Not yet," Peter said. "There's got to be another way."

<~<~|~>~>

That night, after dinner with Sam and Taxi in Peter's room, the men talked.

Taxi said, "I have no idea what I'm going to tell the people."

"Nothing yet," Peter said. "We're not defeated, just waylaid."

Sam said, "Crossing the border is out of the question."

Taxi said, "Busing a thousand people out at one time is impossible. We don't have enough vehicles."

"That leaves us with walking or flying," Peter said. "Walking is out of the question, so we're back to flying. That means we have to use the Tawanda Airport."

Sam laughed, short and quick. "There's no way Ebu won't see the refugees. Every uniform in the place reports to his commanders who report to him."

Peter said, "If David Copperfield can make the Statue of Liberty disappear, we can make the refugees disappear."

Taxi said, "Who is this David Copperfield?"

"A magician who makes his audience believe the logical impossible is true."

"You can do this kind of magic too?"

"Yes, I think I can if my cousin will help me secure the props."

Sam said, "In what time frame?"

"I won't know until I talk to her," Peter said. "Let me make some calls. I'm sure you two have things to do."

Sam and Taxi protested being evicted before finishing their beer.

"Take the beer," Peter said. "Breakfast, here, at seven sharp."

Peter closed the door after the men left and texted his mother. "Hold food and supply deployment. Checking possible ground distribution. Will call within hr."

He punched in another number.

Dani answered. "Hi, Peter. Are we all set?"

"We have a situation. After a trial run, we're certain there'll be complications if we cross borders. So, I came up with another plan." He told her.

Dani listened. "I think that could work. I'll have to talk to a few people."

Peter said, "If it's a go, Mom could contact President Ebu to get his permission for the planes to land to distribute the PRAISE packages under the UN program, for assistance."

"I'll get back to you."

<~<~|~>~>

Dani, phone in hand, walked toward the Oval Office. She encountered Jefferson and Chris in the hallway. She looked at her watch. "What are you two still doing here?"

Jefferson said, "We figured while we were here, we'd work out a strategy for the refugee intake process."

Chris said, "The process is taking longer than we thought."

"But well worth it," Jefferson said. He turned to Chris. "Thank you for coming down on such short notice. My presentation and your input helped the President see our strategy and security."

"You're welcome, Sir. I will keep you updated on progress and delivery." He turned toward Dani. "A pleasure."

She smiled and nodded. Chris left.

Jefferson said, "It went well. The President is pleased. Your support made a big difference."

"As we discussed, it's a two-way street," Dani said. "Do you have a little time for a walk and talk?"

Jefferson checked his watch. "Yes."

They left the White House and walked toward the Potomac River, tailed by the Secret Service.

Dani said, "The refugee evacuation plan has to be modified to maintain its low profile. We must use Tawanda's Okoro Airport, which is, as you know, directly under the President's control. Do you have planes available to bring in supplies and move approximately one-thousand people out?"

Jefferson said, "Now?"

"Next day or so. I've got the supplies. In two days, they'll be housed on pallets fitted inside large wooden crates. All I need is transport information."

"I believe we have two aircraft that can fly round-trip between Tawanda and our base in Qatar all day, retrieving and depositing goods. We could finish the job in less than twenty-four hours."

Dani said, "We have to limit ourselves to night flights, so it may take two nights."

Jefferson pulled out a card and a pen from his pocket. He wrote on the back. "Give this number to…."

Dani said, "Sybil Powell, executive director of PRAISE."

"Have her text me and we'll coordinate. Also, share this number with your ground organizer."

"My cousin, Peter Powell."

Jefferson said, "Have him text me to coordinate the exchange. I'll forward it to the base commander who will handle it from Qatar."

They stopped outside the side entrance to the West Wing.

Dani said, "Thank you, Jefferson."

"No need. This operation serves both our needs."

The general got in the rear seat of his chauffeured car, closed the door, and rolled down the window. "A pleasure working with you, Dani."

Before she could answer, his car pulled out and sped down the road.

<~<~|~>~>

Peter got a text from Dani just before his ten o'clock bedtime. "Have air support. Coordinate text 555-328-4691. Call Sybil in fifteen." His raised his arms in celebration.

Fifteen minutes later, he called his mother. "Did you speak to Dani?"

"I did. I think the two of you were born under a lucky star."

"We couldn't do this without you."

"We're a good team, what can I say?"

"Is the cargo ready to go?"

"Yes. I'm calling President Ebu first thing in the morning to get landing clearance. If all goes well, I expect the first delivery to be in two days. Text the number Dani gave you and you'll have more current information."

"I will."

"You owe me a dinner."

"It's a deal."

Chapter 51 ▶ Gramercy Avenue, N.Y.C.

Sunday, 24 May

Zeus greeted Rachel and Chris at the door. She gave him "hello" pats while Chris walked right past.

He said, "That little gathering certainly didn't go well." He took his jacket off and threw it on the chair. "Drink?"

She said, "Sure." She hung up her coat. "I thought our parents got along, for the most part."

Chris raised his eyebrow. "Which part? They agreed on nothing."

"That's an exaggeration. The problem was more a matter of tone and intensity."

"We're going to have to plan two weddings—one for each set of parents."

"No, we're not. It's going to work out. My mother had to get the feel of the opposition. She's worked with reluctant clients before."

"My parents were in shock."

"I'd say, Midwest meets Westchester."

"Hrumpf." Chris handed her a glass of creamed sherry. He poured himself a shot of vodka neat and took it down in one gulp. He poured another.

Rachel said, "It's all about red, gold, and orange versus pink, yellow, and peach."

"You mean, understated versus over-the-top." He sat on the couch.

"Mother will make it work and your parents will be happy, I promise."

"She'd better do it soon. My parents are texting me every five minutes."

Rachel smiled. "They'll stop. Just say, 'It's out of your hands.'"

"That's no lie."

Rachel sat next to him. "If we stay neutral and supportive, our parents will be fine."

He put his arm around her and gave her a kiss. "I'll go with that."

Chris squeezed her. "I've got a present for you."

She closed her eyes and held out her hand. He put his phone in it.

She opened her eyes. "Your phone?"

"Read the text."

She did, out loud. "A chip reader application for mobile phones."

"It'll read microchips and be able to interfere with a scanner. It'll give anyone with the app control over who gets to read what."

"Does this mean a person can control their privacy?"

"That's exactly what it means."

Rachel said, "You did this?"

"My new start-up company did," he said. "You see, I've invested in the twins."

"Ivan and Isaac?"

"The very same."

"You did this for me?"

"I wanted you to know that individuals will be able to be in charge of their own information and control what others may see or know about them."

Rachel smiled. "You're very sweet."

"I try," Chris said. He pulled out small velvet box.

"For me?"

"I'm always thinking of you."

Rachel took the box, opened it, and gasped. She stared at a two-carat diamond pendant set in platinum. She held it up. Pave diamonds studded the chain. "Chris, this is breathtaking."

"Here," he said, holding out his hand. "Let me put it on."

Rachel brushed her hair off her neck and leaned toward him. She felt his breath on her neck, the cool chain on her skin.

He kissed the nape of her neck and her lips as he sat back. "Perfect."

Rachel dropped her chin and gazed up at him, her lips parted as her tongue moistened them. She said, "I'm not sure this outfit does justice to this necklace."

"Really? I think it looks great on you."

She reached out and put her index finger over his lips. "I think I can do better."

He embraced her and said, "I love you just the way you are."

"Shall I show you here or in the bedroom?"

He kissed her. "I hate tough choices."

She wriggled free and stood facing him. "I'm good either way." She unbuttoned her blouse.

He stroked his chin. "Interesting."

She turned away from him and let it fall to the floor. Looking over her shoulder, she slowly rotated her body toward him as she slipped her bra straps off her shoulders. "And now?"

"More light. More sparkle."

With hips swaying, she unzipped her skirt with deliberate slowness.

He contained his smile with a crooked grin. "I like the shimmer."

Rachel peeled it off her hips and leaned over to push it off her knees, giving him an up-close and personal view of her cleavage set off by the diamond pendant.

Chris jumped to his feet, scooped her into his arms, and said, "Enough. Bedroom it is."

Chapter 52 ▶ Washington, D.C.

Monday, 25 May
Dani arrived early and sat on the couch with President Sandford. Wendell, Uriah, and Jefferson arrived a minute later and sat across from them. The staff brought in coffee and Danish. The President thanked them and began the meeting.

Sandford said, "As I mentioned in the memo, Dani has developed a plan for incoming refugees that I'd like you to hear. I'm very interested in your comments."

Dani handed a flowchart to each person. "I've constructed a very doable process for integrating small to large influxes of immigrants into our society." She went on to describe her plan, emphasizing the economic advantages and benefits for the town, the people, and the new settlers. "By working together, there will be an increase in jobs, production, the area tax base, and commerce via circulating money and the growth of support businesses."

Wendell put the paper down and said, "Nothing changes the fact that you're defying the Senate majority and violating the substance of the new policy. The result will be an internal political war, from which our party may never recover."

Dani said, "Native Americans and immigrants form the foundation upon which our country is built. Their determination, handed down through generations, brings an ability, sensibility, and work ethic that supports us today. We can't let fifty-four senators jeopardize this country's growth."

Uriah said, "The refugee problem plagues Africa and the Mideast. Huge encampments drain their governments' resources. They can't stay and they can't go home when their war-torn country of origin is still in a state of war. Are these the populations that could benefit from your refugee plan?"

Dani nodded. "Yes, among others."

Wendell said, "This whole discussion is pointless. There is no money to support our current indigent population much less thousands more. With our proposed federal tax reduction, which we expect to go through, we'll have even less. That means the states targeted by Dani's proposal, the poorest in the country, will have to carry the burden."

Jefferson said, "From a military and national security perspective, I see a huge problem vetting an influx of people with no papers and no history, with no way to check. In other words, your plan may unleash a crime wave of proportions we've never seen."

Dani said, "These people are starving, sick, and abused, not counter-terrorists."

"To your knowledge," Waters said. "Who knows?"

"I know," Dani said. "Most terrorist crimes in this country are committed by white males. I can have supporting data on your desk by the end of business."

Jefferson said, "I see you're looking to re-open military bases for intake and initial housing."

Dani said, "Yes, those in southern coastal cities. They would be the perfect environment for societal indoctrination."

Jefferson said, "Not a small investment."

Dani countered. "It's a small investment when you consider we are invigorating parts of this country that have already died. The people who live there just don't know it."

Uriah said, "Do we have diplomatic relations with the African countries we are assisting in this manner?"

Dani said, "Some."

Wendell said, "You're saying we may be assisting people who are, for all intents and purposes, enemies of their state. In essence, we'd be granting them political asylum."

Dani said, "In some cases."

Wendell said, "Mr. President, this whole concept puts us in an untenable position. We could be risking World War III."

"I disagree, Sir," Dani said. "These countries are in turmoil and lash out at the neediest within their boundaries. There's not enough money in their faltering economies to take care of their own population, much less fund a world war."

Jefferson tapped his phone over and over again. He looked up and said, "Mr. President, I've just estimated what it would take to open a closed facility." He leaned forward to hand Sandford his phone. "Do you honestly think it is worth it?"

Sandford said, "Yes."

Wendell said, "It doesn't matter what the number is, we don't have the budget. I think this whole thing is wishful thinking. My vote is to honor the immigration ban."

Uriah said, "I agree with Wendell. I see no advantage to accepting untold numbers of refugees."

Jefferson said, "The plan is weak. Implementation uncertain."

Dani sighed. "I see. Everything is too hard, too expensive, or too difficult. It is not our job to offer aid and comfort to people in need. Sad, really."

Sandford put up his hand. "Dani, I'm going to stop you there." He looked at the other men in turn. "I have reviewed this idea since Dani brought it to me several days ago. I think it bears further thought and discussion. Each of you needs some time to make your "upside-downside" lists. Let's meet again this afternoon." He stood. Everyone else did too. "General, will you please stay for a few moments?"

Once they were alone, Sandford said, "Jefferson, how is the DOD's microchip project going? Is it ready for testing?"

Jefferson said, "I believe it is."

"Could we use it on the first wave of refugees to arrive under Dani's initiative?"

"I can find out."

"Please do. Let me know ASAP. That means before our afternoon meeting."

"Of course. I understand." Jefferson saluted and left.

Sandford walked over to the windows, then to the door. He opened it and stepped outside. He gripped the balcony railing as he whispered the words of the 23rd Psalm.

Chapter 53 ▶ West Wing, Washington, D.C.

Monday, 25 May

Dani's lunch sat on her desk. Her nerves killed her appetite. She believed in her program of societal integration and hoped the others would see its huge benefits. Radical or not, it bucked the over-riding philosophy, "Don't make waves." Taking on the Senate majority leader, after his public announcement, would cause problems. She'd have to smooth it over in a painful quid pro quo.

If the group decided against the plan, and Sandford liked it, he'd tell her to make the decision. It would be a brilliant beginning or ignominious end to her career. Although she had never smoked, she wanted a cigarette. Instead, as she paced the room, she took in deep breaths and released the air to a count of six. Her anxiety dropped after five repetitions. She did three more for good measure.

The phone's intercom emitted a sigh. Dani stopped. "Vice President, Ma'am, the President would like to see you in his office."

<~<~|~>~>

Dani entered the Oval Office. Sandford said, "You know Jefferson." She nodded. He continued. "This is Christopher Gregory, of International Computer Utilities and Security."

She said to Chris, "Nice to formally meet you."

He said, "Likewise, Madam Vice President."

Sandford said, "Dani, sit down with us. I think they have a critical component to your proposed immigration initiative."

Dani said, "I've renamed it the Societal Integration Initiative, SII. This way it won't look like a direct assault on the Senate majority leader."

Sandford smiled. "Brilliant." He turned his attention to Chris. "Please explain your concept."

Chris used the next five minutes outlining the reasoning behind and process for microchipping incoming refugees and others migrating to the U.S. "In the end, it will create a tracking database that can be used for all kinds of statistical data to improve services."

Dani said, "Very impressive."

Chris said, "If the first few tests prove as successful as we anticipate, the government can decide if this technology should be made available for other purposes."

Dani looked at Sandford. "If you would like to test this on the first wave of refugees, I have no problem with it."

Sandford closed his eyes for five seconds and then looked at Dani, then Jefferson, and then Chris. "Let's see if we get a consensus at our meeting at two."

The President extended a hand to Chris. "Thank you for your service to our country."

Chris blushed. "Thank you, Sir."

<~<~|~>~>

At two, Dani, Jefferson, Wendell and Uriah returned to the Oval Office.

"So," Sandford said, "have you re-examined our options?"

Uriah said, "I think it could work. It's certainly better than throwing people into a city with a few thousand dollars and a handshake."

Wendell turned to look at him. "What?"

Jefferson said, "Given the difficulty of normal vetting issues and the time constraints, this plan gives us an opportunity to work with the refugees, give them a health care work-up, do a complete indoctrination, and ease their way into society. It is a good use for our closed bases, and it will serve to reinvigorate the surrounding communities."

Wendell said, "I don't know what changed Uriah's and Jefferson's minds, but I'm resolute and vehemently opposed to any program of this nature. I believe we have taken in enough refugees and allowed unprecedented immigration that must be stopped. Opening our country to more foreigners is neither productive nor intuitive. Our research shows that not only do communities resent foreign invasion, but crime rises where competition for jobs increases. I beg you, Mr. President, not to go forward with this, or any other plan, which will wreck our society."

Sandford said, "Wendell. Please...."

"No, Sir. I've tried to envision Vice President Mitchell's proposed utopian plan and come up blank. Refugee settlements injected into America's heartland will disrupt life as our people know it. There isn't enough money to buy their pride. The stress alone will cause tempers to flare and perpetuate actions, until now, unheard of in those parts." Wendell cleared his throat. "I say let this proposal die here and now."

Sandford said, "Anyone else?" No one said a word. "Yea or nay?" He looked at each person present as they responded in turn. "Dani, I believe you have your answer."

<~<~|~>~>

Dani left the Oval Office, elated by her plan's approval. Her phone buzzed. She looked at the text from Peter. "Tomorrow: 1st plane ETD 3:30 PM EST. 2nd plane ETD 5:30 PM EST. 14 hr flight. Destination?"

She turned and saw Jefferson walking with Chris. "Jefferson, may I speak to you for a minute?"

Jefferson excused himself and met Dani in the hall. "What's up?"

She said, "I've got two plane loads of refugees coming in the early morning in two days. At which base can they land?"

Jefferson pulled out his phone and tapped some keys. "Your phone number?" She gave it to him. He said, "I texted you the info. Keep me apprised of your timeline as you know it."

"Thank you, General. I will."

Dani texted the information to Peter as she walked back to her office.

She had no idea if Jefferson would relay their conversation to the President or not. Either way, Sandford could claim deniability if the whole thing blew-up. It didn't matter. She knew she would be able to live with the outcome.

She texted Peter again. "Total rescue?"

He answered. "Approx. 1000"

She texted Jefferson. "Plan for 1000 over three days." At her desk, she put her phone down and got to work.

Chapter 54 ▶ Philadelphia, PA

Monday, 25 May
James Vanderhagen paced back and forth in front of the empty fireplace. Juggling the economic forces around the world seemed like child's play when his father did it. Now one crisis after another plagued his every moment.

A phone buzzed. Vanderhagen recognized the number and answered. "Good news, I hope."

"Sorry. The immigration policy is at risk. Sandford is considering letting the Vice President handle it. Keep his hands clean and still be credited with the humanitarian effort."

"Unacceptable."

"I understand."

"Talk to our man in the Senate. He should be able to convince the White House to drop this project."

"Sandford?"

"No, I'll take care of that."

"Mitchell."

"Yes."

The conversation ended.

Vanderhagen picked up his own phone and made a call.

"Father, I can't talk."

"Then, perhaps you'll listen."

Dani said, "I don't have time for this."

"Stay out of Tawanda."

"I don't know what you're talking about."

"People may get hurt."

"Are you threatening me?"

"No," Vanderhagen said. "Reporting the situation."

"Why me? Why now?"

"Do not interfere in Tawanda's domestic issues."

"I have to go."

The connection dropped.

Vanderhagen had done his job. He'd warned his daughter of the rocky road ahead. The senator would have to deliver the death blow. He pulled out a throwaway phone and made another call. "Mr. Bakama, what's the status?"

"Sir, all is good. The workers have returned to the mines. Production is back on track."

"Call if anything changes."

Another sip and another phone call.

"Congratulations, President Ebu. The mines are up and running."

Ebu said. "Yes. I made it my priority."

"Excellent. We will commence payments and tariffs as per our agreement."

"With our economy at a standstill, our mineral output is all that sustains us."

Vanderhagen said, "Keep the mines open. It's the only way your country will survive."

Two sips and his last call.

"Everything under control."

“Good.”
“My position?”
“The cartel will vote next week.”
“Need I worry?”
“No.”

Chapter 55 ▶ West Wing, Washington, D.C.

Tuesday, 26 May

While being driven to work, Dani reviewed her plan for the refugee immigrants. It had to be as seamless as possible. She pulled out her outline and identified which agencies handled what areas and who she had to call.

She opened her laptop and started her project management software and added the beginning and end dates for each phase, realizing that there were enough unknowns to make the whole exercise meaningless. Still, she had to start somewhere.

Her driver said, "Three minutes."

Dani made her morning's "to do" list, finishing as the car pulled up to the West Wing. She got out, went to her office, and put her pocketbook and briefcase on her desk.

"Madam Vice President."

She spun toward the deep impatient voice of the Senate majority leader. He had a scowl on his face, tension in his body—hands fisted, jaw set. Dani knew the only way to survive his onslaught was to remain in control, maintain her physical space, and defuse all intimidation tactics with calm assertiveness. Her position as Vice President and the fact he chose a face-off in her office, gave her leverage. She intended to use it.

He said, "Madam Vice President, I understand you plan to countermand my cease-and-desist immigration order, in place until the Senate finishes the particulars on the new policy."

Dani removed her coat and walked over to the closet. She hung it up with prolonged deliberation, aware he watched her every move. His agitation increased with each second delay.

He said, "Are you going to answer me?"

Dani looked at the man. Determined not to mirror his anger, she spoke with a neutral tone colored by courtesy. "First, I don't believe you asked me a question, and second, do you prefer coffee or tea?"

"I'm not here for breakfast."

Dani smiled. "If you'd made an appointment, my aide would have explained that I don't discuss business until I've had my second cup of coffee." She sat down at her desk, pressed the intercom button, and said, "One coffee, please, and a fresh corn muffin." She released the button. Looking up at the senator, she said, "This won't take long. Would you like to have a seat?"

She retrieved her cell, tapped record, and placed it on her desk.

The man walked up to the visitor's chair as if to sit. Instead, he put his hands on her desk and leaned his bulldog face toward her. "Have you defied my announcement and made plans for the U.S. to receive immigrants?"

"No."

"Have you authorized the opening of a closed army base?"

"No."

"I don't believe you."

"And why is that?"

A knock on the door. The senator straightened and walked away. Yosef brought in coffee and a muffin. He eyed the visitor and said to Dani, "Do you want me to stay?"

"That won't be necessary, Yosef. Thank you." The aide left.

The senator turned to her and said, "I happen to know that an order went out late last night to open our coastal Virginia base."

Dani sipped her coffee, took a bite of muffin, and another sip. She said, "If true, how and why do you know that?"

He returned to intimidate. He put his hands back on her desk. "It only matters that I know. I've spent years in this town developing my power base. You can bet that I'm not going to let you, a political neophyte, undermine my authority."

"Did you say 'let'? I don't need your permission to do anything."

The senator stood and crossed his arms over his chest—a father lecturing a child. "You have not been forthcoming. I can't let that go unchallenged. Therefore, I'm going to censure your actions on the Senate floor in today's session."

Dani took another bite, followed by a sip. "Are you choosing to release classified information to the general public?"

The senator leaned on her desk, putting his face as close to hers as he could. "Don't you dare try to turn this on me. You are defying me, and I'm not going to stand for it." He stepped back, pivoted, and marched toward the door.

"Senator," Dani said. The man stopped without turning. "Leaking classified information is treason. If you utter one word, I will haul your ass in front of a federal judge faster than you can spell your name."

He spun in place, raised his hand, and shook his finger at her. "You have no idea whom you're threatening. It is you, not I, who is in the wrong. It is my job to stop this violation in its tracks."

She picked up the intercom. "Two agents ASAP."

"No need. I know my way out."

Dani stood. In a voice hard and even, she said, "You will wait."

"I have no intention...."

The agents arrived. "Ma'am, you called."

"I did. Please take and hold this man in detention. He has admitted to treason." The agents restrained him.

The senator said, "You...you...you can't do this to me. I've got to be in chambers in an hour."

Dani said, "I will extend your apologies."

The senator tried to break free. "Your accusation is preposterous. I will sue you for false imprisonment."

She said, "Please allow the agents to escort you. I will speak to our legal advisors as to how to best proceed. Until then, agents, no communication."

The senator's red face, narrowed eyes, and hyperventilation limited his ability to respond. All he could say was, "Bitch."

Dani stood tall and raised her chin. She wanted him to know that she now had the upper hand and had no intention of letting him off the hook. "I'm terribly disappointed that you chose to put your own agenda ahead of the President's and this country."

The senator's mouth dropped, and he stopped struggling.

Dani said, "Thank you," sat down, and began reading the folders on her desk. Once the room cleared, she put her finger over the "Stop Record" icon. Wendell ran in, and she changed her mind.

"What's going on? The senator's screaming for a lawyer."

Dani said, "I'm sure he is."

"He's a United States Senator, for God's sake. You can't just throw him in jail."

"At the moment, I've just detained him."

Wendell plopped down in a chair. "Okay, tell me."

"He said he'd expose classified information on the Senate floor."

"About?"

"That's classified."

"By who's order?"

"The President's."

"We'll see about this." Wendell stood up. "Come with me."

Dani remained seated. "I beg your pardon?"

"Madam Vice President, please come with me to see the President."

<~<~|~>~>

At the door to the Oval Office, Wendell knocked and opened the door. He said, "I'm sorry to interrupt, Mr. President, but this can't wait."

Sandford looked up. "This is not…."

Dani entered first, while Wendell had his hand on the doorknob. Wendell caught up and said, "Sir, this woman," he pointed to Dani without looking at her, "ordered the Senate majority leader put into solitary confinement."

Sandford leaned back in his chair. "I'm sure there's a reason."

Wendell looked at Dani. "Tell him."

She moved forward and said, "The senator blind-sided me this morning. He was in my office before I arrived." Dani put her phone on the President's desk. "This is the conversation." She hit "Play."

"Ridiculous," Wendell said at the end of the recording. "The man was just doing his job. Mr. President, she can't do this."

Sandford said, "In this case, I think she can. Perhaps, Wendell, you should go down and let him know that his status is being reviewed. Assure him the information he holds is indeed classified, and we have made his case our top priority."

"Sir, as Chief of Staff, I would like to be informed as to the nature of this classified project."

Sandford said, "I understand. We will talk. For now, please ease the senator's apprehension, and let him know his stay with us will be as brief as possible."

Wendell did not take the President's rebuff well. His body stiffened and his jaw set before he bolted from the room.

Dani recovered her phone. "Sir." She turned to leave.

Sandford called her back and said, "You actually accused him of trying to undermine my administration."

"He's a bully. I didn't want him to think it was a secret."

"What do you want to do with him?"

"I don't know how much information he has. For now, he needs to be isolated because any leak could jeopardize the operation. That means we need to have two to three days of his silence."

"Not going to be easy, Dani."

"Mr. President, he has voiced his intent to commit treason, which means federal prison. I'd say that gives you some leverage to negotiate a few troubling issues in our favor, along with his memory loss."

Sandford smiled. "Send me the recording."

Dani did as he asked. "Done."

Sandford looked at his computer screen. "Yes. Have it." Then, he looked at Dani. "You handled yourself well. I'm glad you're on our team."

"Yes, Sir. So am I, Sir."

Chapter 56 ▶ Damir, Tawanda, Africa

Wednesday, 27 May

After the evening meal, the slowest, the old ones, went down the ladder first. The community revered and honored them for their wisdom, ancient secrets, and knowledge of culture, healing, and history. They descended from twilight sky into cavern darkness, eyes taking time to adjust to the underground torch lights.

A guide carrying a lantern led the way, cautioning and encouraging. The cool temperature calmed their anxiety regarding this strange journey. The dry, stale air intermingled with fresh air vented through the open shafts. Hair wisps danced in the fragile breeze.

At the bottom of the exit ladder, Peter and Sam waited for sign of the refugees—the guide's glowing lantern. Out of the darkness, it appeared. Sam checked his watch. "This is going faster than I expected."

Peter said, "They must be in better shape because they've been eating better."

"We figured two hours to walk the mile," Sam said. "It's more like ninety minutes." He looked at Peter. "When's the plane arriving?"

"I have to go up top to get a signal. I'll let you know."

<~<~|~>~>

President Ebu stared out the window at the arc of illumination above the Okoro Airport. Every so often, he spotted plane lights as they climbed into and out of the sky. "Mr. Odili, do we have the landing schedule for the UN relief shipments?"

"It is on your phone, Sir."

Ebu unlocked his phone and handed it to Odili. "Bring it up for me."

Odili found the information and returned it to Ebu. "These are the times."

"Do we have an import office at the hangar?"

"Yes, Sir. We are handling all the deliveries as you ordered."

Ebu said, "Is there someone there to receive payment?"

"Sir?"

"Taxes. Tariffs. Gratuities."

"I know of no such invoice, Sir," Odili said. "This is rescue effort."

"Create such an invoice and bill the donors. The resources will not be distributed until the money is paid."

"Sir, you will be seen as putting your people at risk."

Ebu said, "This government has rules and regulations. I would be seen as weak if I did not uphold my own laws."

"Perhaps, in this case…."

Ebu held up his hand. "My decision is made. Do it."

Odili said, "As you wish."

<~<~|~>~>

Peter's phone buzzed. "ETA 10:30pm 1/hr x5," as the first person emerged from the cavern. It was eight forty-five. It would take time to load the buses. Sam followed and walked over. "How're we doing on time?"

Peter said, "If we can leave here by ten, we'll have plenty of time." He crossed his fingers. Tonight's plan was the boldest one yet. He had no idea if they could pull it off, but he knew they had to try.

One by one, the old ones emerged. They moved from the exit to the buses, where helpers took names and gave out ID numbers. As each the bus filled, the engine sputtered into a hum. Armed volunteers sat on top, lying between the baggage railings. No one expected trouble, still....

Peter, armed, rode inside the first of six buses which would run relays all night. He wanted to make sure the transfer from bus to plane went according to plan.

The buses took the western approach to the airport. It went away from the city and around the sparse outlier population, circling to the back of the airport to reach the far hangar. The Boeing C-17 Globemaster III sat near the building.

Peter got out of the bus and tried the gate. It was open. He breathed a sigh of relief and motioned for the passengers to leave the bus and enter the hangar. Once emptied, Peter watched the bus leave to pick up the next group of refugees.

"Mr. Powell?"

Peter turned to an American soldier with a clip board who said, "Here's how we plan to make the exchange."

Peter knit his eyebrows. "Exchange?"

"Yes. We've placed our supplies in large wooden crates, which we'll remove from the plane and bring into the hangar. We have equipment to remove the contents and replace them with people. We will then bring the crate back to the plane and the people will exit the box for seating. All that will be visible are boxes going in and out of the transport."

Peter smiled. "Good plan."

"After this plane is full, it will go back to the states, and another will land. The government has loaned this mission five C-17s for twenty-four hours."

"That's a big change."

"Less chance of a screw-up."

"I'll make sure this happens." Peter walked away and pulled out his phone and texted Sam and Taxi. "Everyone's going tonight!"

Peter and Sam worked to make sure buses ran unimpeded roundtrips all night. Taxi remained in the worker village to make sure everyone got out. He'd leave with the last of the workers. By sunrise, the worker village would be empty.

<~<~|~>~>

In the administration building, inside the locked gates of the mines, the seated security guard monitoring the worker village camera woke with a start just before sunrise. The village was quiet. He closed his eyes and stretched his arms, legs, and back. He glanced at the screen one more time, got up, and went to the bathroom. He emptied his bladder, washed his hands and face, and brushed his teeth.

Awake and back in his seat, he waited for the signs of morning activity. The routine never varied. Every day at first light, breakfast fires sent up ribbons of smoke, people lined up for the toileting area, and returned, in no formal pattern, to their quarters to eat.

The guard's job included watching the time. At precisely one hour after sunrise, he'd blow the shift horn. The workers would stream into the village center, hop on the transport trucks, and head out to the mines. His job finished, he'd clock out, and go home.

Today, expecting the usual routine, he sat back in his chair, watching the screen, aware of the lightening sky. The sun's first rays pierced the windows. He adjusted the blinds and checked the screen. There was no activity. No morning toileting, washing, breakfast preparation, or scampering children.

The guard sat up straight and used the joystick to rotate the camera. The village appeared empty. He scratched his head. He scanned the area again. His stomach tightened. This was not good. He swallowed the bit of bile that made it to his throat and made the call.

<~<~|~>~>

Musimbwa Bakama, still in bed, rolled over to answer his phone.

"Who is calling me at this ungodly hour?"

"Mr. Bakama, it is the night guard at the mines."

"Why do you call?"

"I do not see any activity in the village. I think everyone is dead."

Bakama sat up and swiveled on his butt. His legs hung over the side of the bed and his feet touched the floor. "Do you see bodies?"

"No, Sir. I see nothing."

Bakama stood. "Send security in with gas masks. Be sure to record. I will be there in twenty-three minutes."

He arrived at the administration building in seventeen. He said to the guard, "What has happened?"

The guard said, "Nothing."

"Where is security?"

The guard pointed to the monitor. "There. See. At the edge of the screen."

"What are they waiting for?"

"I think they are just being cautious."

Bakama said, "Give me the microphone." Over the loudspeaker he announced, "This is Operations Manager Bakama. Get in there and tell me where the workers are."

He watched the men on the screen move faster. They poked heads inside tents and looked at the camera shaking their heads. They checked the buildings and the community tent. Bakama's phone rang. "Mr. Bakama, sir, there is no one here."

"Check the fencing."

The security guards spread out along the fence line, checked for breaks, and reported back. "Mr. Bakama, Sir, there are no breaks. The people have simply disappeared."

"Impossible. I am coming out there." Bakama put the phone in his pocket and ran out the door. He got in his car and took off, leaving waves of dust in his wake. He tore down the road in a fury, skidding to a stop below the camera post. He jumped out and marched to the guards. "Show me."

The head guard walked him around. "See. No one in the tents. No one in the store. No fencing broken or damaged. No footprints outside the fencing—anywhere. They have vanished."

They wound up in the community tent. Although there were chairs around the perimeter, Bakama chose to sit on the edge of the table in the middle of the room. The table sat on a rug. His weight didn't shift the piece. In an off-handed manner, he said, "This table is heavier that it looks."

"Sir?"

In that instant, Bakama realized the import of what he said. He got off the table and leaned against it. It remained in place. He looked at the guard. "Move it."

The guard put his hands on either side of the table and tried to lift it. It didn't budge. He tried to move it with his hip. Nothing. He looked at Bakama's darkening face. He dropped to his knees to examine the legs. "Sir, Mr. Bakama, the table legs are nailed to the rug."

"Pick up the rug."

The guard lifted a corner. "Sir, Mr. Bakama, the rug is nailed to a piece of wood."

Bakama stamped his foot in frustration and said, "Idiot, pick up the wood."

Further attempts revealed the wood was hinged. The guard flipped it open and uncovered the escape shaft. Bakama said, "What's that doing in here?"

The guards' silence and shrugs said it all. "You mean nobody knows about this?"

Heads shook.

"Do you know where it goes?"

More head shaking.

"Shine a light down there."

A guard ran to his jeep to retrieve a flashlight and handed it to Bakama, who directed the beam into the hole. He looked at the guards, "How could a thousand people disappear down that hole overnight?"

Shoulders shrugged, faces blank.

Bakama hit the head guard in his midriff with the flashlight. "Take this. Get a ladder and get down there." He stepped away and pulled out his phone. Tapped the screen and said, "Mr. Odili, I need to speak with President Ebu."

"I am not in the office. What time is it?"

"Get to the office. All the mine workers and their families have disappeared."

"Did you say….?"

"Do not repeat my every word. We are in crisis. I must speak to President Ebu."

Odili said, "Right away. He'll call you."

Bakama's phone rang. He said, "Ah, Mr. President. The workers have disappeared underground."

"Mr. Bakama, it is early. I have returned your call as a courtesy. I assure you I have no idea what you are talking about."

"I am telling you there are no men to work the mine."

"They are gone?"

"Everyone is gone. The village is empty."

"Where are they?"

"I have no idea."

"Find them. The mines cannot shut down again." The phone went dead.

<~<~|~>~>

Ebu, now wide awake, raced to his office. Odili was waiting for him. Ebu said, "The mining workers are gone. In fact, the whole camp is gone. Disappeared down a hole."

Odili said, "Where are they?"

"Good question. A thousand people can't just disappear."

"More than a thousand disappeared into the sinkholes."

Ebu's energy soared. He clapped his hands together. "Mr. Odili, you are a genius. They must have found another underground space."

"A sinkhole?"

"No, a cavern."

"Is that where they are?"

"No, but that's a good point." Ebu walked over to the window. "I see nothing unusual going on in the city. If they're not here, where?"

"They wouldn't get very far on foot."

"Hmm. You're right."

Ebu's phone rang. "Sir, it is Bakama. We now know they escaped underground and exited outside the fence, in the Northwest corner of the mining property."

"Anything else?"

"Tire marks. Trucks or buses."

"Going west?"

"Yes."

"Chase them down, Mr. Bakama. They are going to the airport, and you haven't much time."

Ebu hung up and made a call. "General. We have mine workers escaping the country. I believe they are headed toward the airport. I want them stopped and returned to the mines. Use our soldiers working on the sinkholes and police, if you need to. Just don't let them leave the country."

<~<~|~>~>

The last bus, commandeered by Taxi, crossed the main road and headed toward the airport. That's when he saw dust clouds on the horizon behind them. He slung his rifle over his head and shoulder, climbed out a window, and hoisted himself onto the rooftop luggage rack. He dropped to his belly, beside three other men. "Think they're coming for us?"

The men grunted.

Taxi said, "Me, too."

Taxi freed his weapon and pulled out his phone. He called the bus driver below and said, "Floor it." He called Sam, who rode in the bus ahead. "They're coming after us. Airport fast. All rifles out and ready."

Sam said, "Got it. Wait. Someone's coming at us from the south."

Taxi said, "Not good."

Sam said, "We can make the gate. I'll get the buses moving faster."

Taxi said, "The plane has to be ready to go. Tell Peter."

<~<~|~>~>

Peter answered his phone and ran to the aircraft as soon as he heard the situation. He motioned to the pilot to get ready by waving his hand in a circle above his head. The pilot started the engines. The crew prepared to assist.

Bolt cutters hung on the side of the hangar. Peter grabbed them and took off for the cargo gate. Smaller than the other gate, it'd shave critical seconds off the bus route. He made it as the buses came into sight.

He did an awkward version of "jumping jacks" to get the drivers' attention. The buses turned. He cut the lock, swung the gate open, and jumped aboard the first bus. The gate slammed against the fence and rebounded. The bus crashed into it and ripped it off its hinges.

An airman directed the vehicles around to the back of the plane. Another soldier took over and sent them up the tail ramp, into the cargo hold. As soon as the last one cleared the ramp, the plane started rolling. More airmen appeared and locked the vehicles in place while the tail ramp closed, and the plane taxied down the runway.

Tawandian army and security guard vehicles slid, skidded, and bumped as they converged and swerved to make the gate. Once on the runway, the pursuers fired warning shots to stop the plane.

The plane's speed increased. The ground vehicles outran the C-17, surpassed it, and formed a barrier. The plane reached airspeed. Soldiers leapt from their jeeps as the C-17's wheels grazed their windshields. Frustrated ground troops fired at the belly of the C-17.

The U.S. transport never wavered, soaring into the waking sky like an eagle—bold, powerful, and strong.

Chapter 57 ▶ Damir, Tawanda, Africa

Thursday, 28 May
President Ebu paced around his office, his hands behind his back, the right hand holding the fisted left. He stopped and went to the window upon hearing the first shots.

Gunfire. Silence. Gunfire. The silver Boeing C-17 rose above the horizon, sunlight bouncing off its polished surface.

Odili rushed into the presidential office. "Sir, I have the general on the office phone."

Ebu released his right hand and picked up the receiver. "Tell me."

The general said, "They got away. We thought we had…."

Ebu ended the call, stone-faced.

Odili said, "Sir?"

"They got away. The mines are down."

"We can get diggers from Uganda, Sudan, or The Central African Republic."

"Outsiders."

"A problem?"

"They may not understand or accept our ways."

"Once you sign the peace agreement with the DRC, we can divert our soldiers."

Ebu turned, his face animated. "You may have solved the problem. Although reassigning soldiers is not an optimum choice, it may be the only one if Tawanda is to avoid bankruptcy. This course of action will weaken our defenses. Furthermore, if the DRC finds out, we may lose the war."

"Then, Sir," Odili said. "We will not tell them."

"Leave me. Let me think." He watched Odili leave and pulled out his cell phone. His heartbeat against his chest. He had to make the call. Before he could, the office phone rang.

Odili's voice came through the intercom. "Operations Manager Bakama, Sir." Ebu took the call.

Bakama said, "It was a covert operation, Mr. President. We had no idea. What can I do?"

"Nothing. The people are gone. Have you reported the situation to Mr. Vanderhagen?"

"No, Sir. I've just returned from the airport with our security guards."

"Excellent. I have decided to order some of my soldiers to work the mines until you can amass another permanent crew."

"Thank you, Sir. I understand. There is no reason to call."

"I will not forget this, Mr. Bakama."

Ebu hung up and pushed the intercom button. "Mr. Odili, get me the status on our soldiers. I want to know how many are where and doing what."

"Right away, Sir."

Twenty minutes later, Odili walked in with the report. He said, "We have two-hundred-fifty troops in Damir assigned to sinkhole reconstruction and refugee management. Two thousand troops patrol our DRC border. And nine hundred troops defend the Valley of the Old Ones."

"A collection of rocks, tossed by mourners to honor a relative's life."

"Sacred, Sir. It is a tribal monument."

"Worth over twenty years of fighting?"

"A question of honor and commitment."

Ebu said, "I will call the general and move two hundred men from the Valley to the mines. We will do it in stages. No one will know."

<~<~|~>~>

At nine AM in Philadelphia, Vanderhagen sat at the chess table, and stared at the board. It calmed him. Today, his invisible opponent had him in CHECK. A phone rang—its muffled sound came from within his desk drawer. With a sigh, he left the table and lowered himself into his desk chair. He extracted the phone, saw the ID, and answered.

"President Ebu, how nice to hear from you."

"I am calling to give you an update on the mining situation."

"No problems, I trust."

"A small but corrected problem."

"I see," Vanderhagen said. "Tell me."

Ebu cleared his throat and said, "The workers who agreed to return to the mines are gone. I am…."

"What does that mean?"

"They have abandoned the mines."

"All of them?"

"Yes."

"Their families remain, right?"

"No. Their families are gone, also. I plan…."

"Impossible. I would have heard."

"You will, soon. I am sure Mr. Bakama will fill you in."

"Where are they?"

"My people tell me they left onboard the UN mission planes."

"The UN doesn't have an air force."

"They use United States Air Force transport."

"And you don't know to where?"

"No. However, I will supply diggers in the interim. They will report for work tomorrow."

"Everyday costs us money, President Ebu."

"I am aware."

"This happens as you say, or I cut your percentage in half." Vanderhagen ended the call. Before he could put his phone down, it rang in his hand. He looked at the ID and answered. "Bakama, explain."

"Sir, you know?"

"I just spoke to President Ebu. Now, you tell me."

Bakama gave him the details and said, "Mr. Vanderhagen, I assure you, we had no idea. One day the workers are here, the next day they are gone."

"I find that very hard to believe. Send me the security footage. I will decide for myself."

"Sir, I will, immediately after our call."

"I also want more security so this can't happen again."

"I begin today. The village will be secured."

"It better be. Next time, if there is a next time, you will be gone, too."

<~<~|~>~>

Vanderhagen made a call to Washington D.C. "I thought we had an understanding."

The voice said, "We did. I announced the 'No Immigrants' edict and tried to enforce it. For my efforts, the Vice President ordered me detained without contact."

"And now?"

"I've been silenced."

"By whom?"
"The President."

<~<~|~>~>

Vanderhagen made another call, this time to the White House. "Want to tell me what's going on?"

The voice said, "About what?"

"Tawanda."

"Nothing has changed."

"I hear differently," Vanderhagen said. "My digger workforce has left aboard a U.S. transport."

"I had no...."

"I pay you handsomely to stay top of situations like this."

"I have. I've been in meetings with Mitchell and Sandford. There's no...."

"Tawanda must remain independent or there will be immediate repercussions."

"Not in my...."

"Fix it, or else."

Chapter 58 ▶ Military Base, VA

Thursday, 28 May

The first plane landed on American soil at nine AM. The Tawandian refugees disembarked, exhausted from their trip, yet animated by their new surroundings.

Soldiers escorted the group to the barracks quad. The reception team assigned each refugee to a building where they found sandwiches, milk and water, showers, toilets, loose-fitting clothing, and beds.

Interpreters explained. "You are invited to relax after your difficult journey. Official entry processing will start tomorrow morning. For now, medical personnel will be here to help you if you have any questions, needs, or concerns."

Every hour, another transport arrived. By one in the afternoon, the last one touched down. Peter, Sam, and Taxi disembarked last.

Stepping on the tarmac, Peter said, "It feels good to be home."

Right behind him, Sam said, "Not sure. It's been a long time."

Taxi looked around. "I need to get on the next plane back."

Sam shook his head. "You may want to reconsider. After what we just did, we're not going to be welcomed for a long, long time, if ever."

"Don't worry," Peter said. "We'll find a way to help the refugees left behind."

They walked to the rear of the plane where the soldiers unloaded the buses.

Taxi smiled. "Chariots of freedom."

A soldier said, "That may be, but you're damned lucky. These wrecks ran on hope and a prayer. I'm not sure they'll even start."

Taxi said, "I'll be back to take a good look at them. If at all possible, they need to go back."

"Sirs," another soldier approached them. "Please come with me." He did an about face without waiting for an answer and marched toward the hangar. Peter, Sam, and Taxi followed. He led them through a door, down a hall, and into an office suite—a main reception area with three closed doors and a hallway around its perimeter. He spoke with the information officer, who got up, knocked on the middle door, and opened it.

"The men are here, Sir," he said and returned to his desk.

An imposing figure appeared in the doorway and indicated they should enter. "Gentlemen, I'm General Jefferson Clemmons. Please take a seat."

"Welcome home." A disembodied voice said.

The general said, "One minute, Madam Vice President. I'm going to put you on the big screen."

<~<~|~>~>

Dani smiled. "Again, welcome. I'm glad to see you made it."

Peter spoke for the group. "Thank you, Dani. We couldn't have pulled this off without your help."

"General Clemmons is the one you need to thank. He took personal responsibility for this rescue operation, supplied the planes, and opened the base."

The general said, "Thank you, Madam Vice President."

Dani said, "I plan to visit the base tomorrow. We can talk then." She paused. "Oh, I almost forgot. Peter, don't forget to call your mom."

She ended the connection and called her aunt. "Hi, Sybil. Peter's safe and in the U.S. He'll call you as soon as he can."

"Thank God," Sybil said. "When can I see him?"

"After his debriefing. It shouldn't be long."

Dani ended the call. She heard a knock on the door and looked up.

Yosef walked in and said, "Yes, Madam Vice President."

Dani said, "I didn't call."

"Sorry," Yosef said. "Is there anything I can do?"

"No. I'm good for now."

<~<~|~>~>

Rachel and her mother sat at the dining room table, looking at the laptop and paging though wedding dresses. Her phone rang.

"Hi, Sybil. You okay?"

"Of course. Just wanted you to know Peter called and he's okay."

"Good news. Let's plan a celebration when he gets back."

Sybil said, "Great. I could use more fun in my life."

Rachel ended the call and turned to her mother. "So, what do you think?"

Helene pursed her lips and said, "Your selections are all over the place."

Rachel said, "You hate them."

"It's not that. The styles are all different."

"Well, there's a part of each dress that I love," Rachel said. "I thought we could start there."

Helene said, "Let's do this. It could take up to six months to get the dress you want."

A knock on the door and Chris walked in, dragging an overnight case. Rachel said, "Where are you going?"

He said, "Virginia for the DOD trial. I plan to return this time tomorrow. If it's going to take longer, I'll call."

Rachel stood and walked over to him. They embraced and kissed. She said, "I'll miss you."

He said, "Me, too," and kissed her again. They separated and Chris put his hand on his luggage handle. "You two have fun. The dads and I will pick out our tuxes next week."

Helene said, "Not alone, you won't."

He said, "I don't...."

Rachel jumped in. "We'll make an afternoon of it. It'll be a bonding thing."

Chris raised his eyebrow at her. "Really?"

"Yes, absolutely. Mom's got the vision, and she's in charge of the details."

Helene, eyes on the computer screen, "Rachel's right. I wouldn't be able to live with myself if anyone in the wedding party looked out of place."

Rachel planted a kiss on Chris's lips before he could answer. He gave in, kissed her back and pulled away. "I'm going. See you ladies very soon."

Zeus looked around the corner of the couch and barked.

Chris laughed. "You too, buddy. Take care of Rachel."

Zeus barked.

Helene said, "I swear that dog understands everything we say."

Rachel sat next to her mother and patted the dog. "He does."

"I guess," Helene said, "we'll have to get him a tux too."

Zeus plopped his head on his paws and whined.

Rachel laughed, "Maybe not."

Chapter 59 ▶ Tawanda, Africa - Phila-delphia, PA

Thursday, 28 May

On the battlefront between the Tawandian and DRC troops, the guns were silent. Peace treaty rumors calmed both sides. The colonel relaxed in his tent, playing solitaire on his phone. An aide rushed in, slid to a stop, and stiffened at attention. "Orders from President Ebu, via the general, Sir."

The colonel read the instructions. His eyes brightened, and his body came to life with each word. "Lieutenant. Get in here. We have an immediate, promotion-worthy, tactical maneuver to pull off."

Under the colonel's leadership, they planned an evacuation that added a truck full of soldiers to each supply convoy leaving the front lines and sent another at random times in between. On the ground, it looked like normal activity. From the air, not so much.

Experienced DRC helicopter pilots spotted the difference. They knew the enemy's routine better than the enemy. They reported their observations to their Commander-In-Chief who deployed scouts to monitor the transports. Their reports to headquarters confirmed Tawandian soldiers were leaving and not returning.

Darkness provided cover for DRC reinforcements. Early the next morning, the Tawandian forces awoke to an overwhelming attack. Before lunch, the DRC took the stronghold and marched into Damir. By late afternoon, on Friday, May 29th, Tawanda ceased to exist.

The announcement reverberated around the world, with little, if any, pushback—except in a few private and powerful circles.

<~<~|~>~>

Vanderhagen found out Tawanda had fallen from a BBC news broadcast on his ePad while eating breakfast on his home's veranda, surrounded by gardens.

> "This reporter is standing in front
> of a partially filled sinkhole, watching
> what appears to be a bloodless takeo-
> ver by the DRC. Ex-President Kwanh
> Ebu's inexplicable withdrawal of
> troops remains a mystery. This is a
> breaking, and we will keep you ap-
> prised of any new developments."

He turned the live-stream off and made a call. "Tawanda has fallen."

"I've explained…."

"Explanations do not change facts. Financial sabotage is unacceptable."

"I can fix this. We have diplomatic relations with the DRC. We can help renegotiate terms…."

"The President's dalliance with a pre-teen goes viral at midnight unless you spare him this embarrassment."

"Spare him…." Vanderhagen heard a sudden intake of breath. "You can't ask me to do that."

Vanderhagen said, "I'm not asking." He hung up and prepared Sandford's exposé for immediate media release. Satisfied, he stood, stretched, and walked into the study's private bathroom, closing the door behind him.

<~<~|~>~>

The study door opened as the bathroom door's latch clicked. The visitor, wearing a wig and sunglasses to avoid CCTV coverage, and thus, outage, slipped in and shut the study door while holding the knob to insure silence. Once closed, she released the latch without a sound. She walked over to the desk--footsteps absorbed by carpet. With lab-grade gloves covering her hands, she extracted a vial from her pocket. The label said, "VX-Toxic," with graphic skull and crossbones underneath the words.

She opened the eyedropper top, filled one third of the glass tube with VX, and picked up Vanderhagen's phone. She squeezed out a drop on the face and back of the device, spreading it around with the dropper tip. Done, she put the phone back, face down, as Vanderhagen had left it. She closed and tightened the bottle top.

While holding the bottle in her left hand, she slipped the glove off and over the VX. She knotted the top of the glove and dropped the package into her pocket.

At the sound of the toilet's flush, she sat down in the visitor's chair with one arm across her lap and the other by her side, gloved hand in her pocket, fingers around the butt end of a gun. If she lost sight of his hands, he'd be dead in a second.

<~<~|~>~>

Vanderhagen emerged, deep in thought, headed for his desk. He jerked to a stop at the sound of a female voice.

"James Vanderhagen. How nice to meet you at last."

He didn't recognize the woman. "Who are you? How did you get in here?"

Vanderhagen sat down and stared at her across the desk.

The woman pulled off her disguise. "I'm Lucy Kilmer."

"Not possible," Vanderhagen said.

"Ah," she said. "You must be thinking about the unfortunate hitman who tampered with my water system and garage."

Vanderhagen fought his anger by tensing and relaxing every muscle in his body to maintain a physical presence of calm and control.

Lucy said, "It's clear, that between the acid shower and the garage implosion, my presence is indeed a miracle. To him and to you."

Vanderhagen leaned forward, elbows on the desk, arms crossed. With the top of his hands visible, his thumbs curled around the edge, one resting on an ivory-headed button. "I had no idea. I thought you were under house arrest."

She offered a faint smile. "I'm not accusing you. Hundreds of miles separated us."

"Exactly. Besides, why would I wish you harm? You're too valuable an asset."

Lucy uncrossed her ankles and crossed her legs at her knees for a clearer shot. "Yes, I know. I've enjoyed working for Ted Donovan, Kwanh Ebu, and you."

"Me?"

"Your projects. Your referrals. Your direct orders. I did my research."

Vanderhagen said, "Not thorough enough. Your misunderstanding of Damir's underlying geophysics created chaos, which lead to Tawanda's downfall. Not the outcome the cartel expected or wanted."

She leaned forward, her left elbow resting on her knee. "Are you're saying it's my fault."

Vanderhagen said, "There's no other conclusion."

"I beg to differ." Lucy inspected her exposed fingernails. "The cartel attributes Tawanda's loss to a major error in judgment for which they hold you entirely responsible."

"How…." Vanderhagen felt his heartbeat quicken.

Lucy said, "I've been in touch with them ever since the attempts on my life. I now work directly for the board."

"I doubt that. They'd never hire a woman."

Lucy raised her chin in defiance. "I'm here to step into your position while you are, as they say, re-evaluated. As of this moment, you do not speak for the cartel—I do."

Vanderhagen tightened his thumb and pressed the button. He leaned back as the trigger launched a hollow point bullet down the gun barrel hidden under the desktop. It passed through the silencer and into Lucy's chest. The impact sent the chair backwards two feet into the back of the couch. The jolt caused Lucy's body to lurch forward.

Vanderhagen relaxed in his chair. "Bitch. You could never do what I do."

He picked up his phone and punched in the cartel's contact number. Before he heard the first ring, he felt a twinge at the small of his back. By the second, his muscles froze.

The phone dropped to the desktop. He lost his ability to breath. Helpless, he vaguely sensed his body spasm—with such force that it broke his back as it launched him out of his chair and onto the desk. His skull cracked as it slammed into the wood. Another spasm sent his body into a fetal position, causing it to roll off the desk, toward the fireplace.

Vanderhagen was dead before he hit the floor.

Chapter 60 ▶ West Wing, Washington, D.C.

Friday, 29 May

Wendell rapped on the Oval Office door, opened it, and stuck his head in.

Sandford looked up and said, "Come in." He pushed the intercom. "Nancy, mid-morning snacks, please."

Wendell said, "Tawanda has fallen to the DRC."

Sandford picked up the phone. "Get Uriah Henderson in here ASAP." He hung up the phone and found a live news feed on his laptop.

"What can Uriah do?"

Sandford said, "He can advise us as to our response."

"Will you please tell me why we had to deal with the refugee issue and why you didn't include me in the process?"

Sandford made a call. "My office ASAP." He ended the one-sided conversation and said, "Dani will be here, too."

Wendell leaned on the President's desk. "Can't you just say? I mean, we've been friends for years. Gone through some tough elections and made, I thought, a pretty good team."

"We are a great team, Wendell. However, this wasn't my operation. It's not for me to explain."

"You knew all about it. You could have given me the heads-up. Even let me help."

"It had to be on a need-to-know basis for it to work without endangering the lives of the refugees or the United Nations mission."

"Did Uriah know?"

"No."

"But Dani did. Right?"

"It was her operation. Your idea, remember, to put her in charge of a no-win effort to keep her from gaining any points that could propel her into the presidency."

A knock on the side door. It opened and a person from the housekeeping staff rolled a cart into the room and placed it between the end of the couches and the President's desk. "Thank you," the President said. "Wendell, coffee? Bagel? Danish?"

Wendell glanced at the spread, shook his head, and continued. "Dani's scope was immigration, which at the time was being completely controlled by the Senate majority leader."

Sandford said, "Refugees are part of the immigration picture. She did not step outside her boundaries on this."

"Dani should never have gotten her hands on such a sensitive situation."

Sandford said, "I approved, and she did a great job."

"Sir, we need to address the fallout before...."

"Before what, Wendell?"

"Before we lose the next election."

The President stood and turned to look out the window. He waited several heartbeats before pivoting to address Wendell. "How did you know?"

"Know what?"

"About the refugees?"

"From the Senate majority leader."

"How did he know?"

"I have no idea."

Sandford said, "I think you do. You have always counseled against human rights issues. I want to know why."

"You know why, Sir," Wendell said. "Multinational corporations have always relied on an oppressed workforce to ensure cost-effective products to sell at competitive prices. The lower the bottom line, the higher profits, market-share, dividends. Hungry people will do pretty much anything to feed their families. The world economy depends on it."

Before Sandford could respond, Dani arrived. Yosef followed her in, carrying her laptop and several folders.

She said, "Yosef, please put everything on the coffee table."

Sandford said, "As long as you're here, Yosef. Tell me about your assignment to Vice President Mitchell's staff."

Yosef's eyes darted to Dani, Wendell, and settled on the President. "Sir, Mr. Waters assigned me."

"You were on his staff?"

"Yes, Sir."

"Do you still report to him?"

"I'm not sure...."

"Yosef, are you spying on the Vice President and giving the information to Mr. Waters."

Yosef didn't flinch. "Yes, Sir. At first." He glanced at Dani. "However, when I observed her agenda focused on saving lives and insuring rights, I stopped."

Wendell, flushed with anger, got in Yosef's face. "It wasn't up to you to filter the information."

Dani took two steps toward the two men and said to Wendell, "You've been spying on me? For my father? You're working for him?"

Wendell said, "I do not work for anybody except the President."

Sandford addressed his Chief of Staff. "Why did you feel the need to monitor Dani?"

Wendell turned to face the President and walked up to the desk. "I've already explained. My concern was for the United States to maintain its support for global economies which, in turn, support your election coffers. I am fighting for your second term so you can complete your plans for the health of our country."

"Wendell, we've never formally discussed the U.S. position on economies outside our own. In fact, I don't ever remember making a statement to that end."

"Mr. President, are you making an accusation?"

The President moved around the desk until he positioned himself two feet in front of Wendell. Sandford said, "I know you're the mole."

Wendell's faced exploded with sweat. "Not true." He pulled out a handkerchief and wiped his brow. It didn't help.

Sandford said, "You not only stopped me from taking the lead in the human rights campaign, but you also hid the information that Dani," he nodded toward her, "was James Vanderhagen's daughter. Now you're advocating against helping refugees in favor of a possible new world economic order and campaign financing."

"In your best interest, Sir, at all times."

Sandford said, "I beg to differ." He reached for a folder. "I have here…."

<~<~|~>~>

Dani stood trying to process the revelation that Wendell worked for the Vanderhagens—first her grandfather and now her father. She took a step toward the two men. She wanted to see the proof Sandford had in his hand.

Out of the corner of her eye, she sensed danger. She turned to see Wendell grab a knife from the cart. He slapped the paper away from Sandford with his left hand and with the other, using his weight and shoulder strength, shoved the knife in, under, and up into Sandford's ribcage.

Dani yelled, "Wendell, stop!" She ran toward the President, "Help! Someone get help!"

Wendell withdrew the knife and stabbed Sandford again. Yosef flew at Wendell and knocked him to the floor.

Agents burst through the door.

Sandford held on to the desk for a second or two before collapsing. Dani ran to his side and cushioned his head, dropping to the floor with him.

Wendell went down fighting as Yosef wrestled the man to dislodge the knife.

Nancy opened her access door, saw the commotion, and screamed.

Dani turned to her. "Go get help." Nancy stared at her. Dani said, "Now!" and removed her jacket. She pressed it down on Sandford's wounds, trying to stem the blood flow.

Agents surrounded Dani. She said, "He's hurt. It's bad." One agent pulled her away and another continued to put pressure on the wound. Still another barked orders.

Free from attending to the President, she saw Yosef, kneeling over Wendell. Her aide looked at her and shook his head and stood. Dani saw the knife sticking out of the dead man's chest.

A split second later, the medical team rushed in. Two agents approached her. "Ma'am, we have to go."

"No. I want to…." Dani twisted her body so she could see the medics. "Is Sandford dead?"

"Ma'am…."

Yosef approached her. "Let them do their job. We'll know soon enough."

She looked at him and nodded. The four of them, Dani, Yosef, and two agents walked to her office.

The whole wing was shut down. She heard bits of conversation.

"No phones."

"Is everyone okay?"

"Back away from your desks."

"What's happened?"

"Were those shots?"

"No questions."

"I have to call my daughter."

"We will interview everyone."

<~<~|~>~>

The Special Agent in Charge of the Presidential Protective Division stood in her office, waiting for her. He assigned an agent to take down Yosef's version of the events in the outer office and spoke to Dani. "Please sit down, Madam Vice President. Tell me what happened."

Dani looked at one of the other agents. "Water please."

He brought her a glass. As she raised it to her lips, her hand shook. She had to use two hands. After taking a drink, as she lowered the glass, water sloshed all over her pants. She looked down and saw Sandford's blood.

Covering her mouth, she ran to the bathroom. Leaning over the toilet, she wretched until it felt her insides were rubbed raw. That's when she saw her bloody hands for the first time.

The special agent stood by the door. "Are you okay?"

She nodded. "I'd like to shower and get cleaned up. I have another set of clothes in the closet."

"First, the interview. Then you may change. A federal judge is already on the way."

Dani said, "Does that means the President's dead?"

"Yes, Ma'am."

Chapter 61 ▶ Gramercy Avenue, N.Y.C.

Friday, 29 May

Rachel and Zeus entered her fourth-floor apartment. Helene called out, "Coffee is hot."

Harry sat at the dining table, in the seat that allowed him to both read the paper and watch the news on television. "Sit. Your mother has the rest of the day planned. Enjoy the peace and quiet while you can."

Helene laughed. "It's not that bad. It'll be fun." She brought the carafe of coffee to the table and sat between Harry and Rachel.

"Mom, you remembered."

"Of course. All your favorites." She pointed at each as she recited the fare. "Bagels, a little whitefish salad, egg salad, nova, onion, tomato, and lettuce. Look. I didn't forget the cream cheese and Jarlsberg."

"This is too much, Mom."

"Don't be silly. Eat what you want. I promise it won't go to waste."

Rachel reached for a bagel.

Harry said, "Wait. Something just happened." He made the sound louder. "Look. I think the reporter just said President Sandford is dead."

Rachel twisted in her seat to see the screen. "Louder, Dad."

"President Sandford is dead. I repeat. The President is dead. His Chief of Staff, Wendell Waters, assassinated Franklin Tyler Sandford this morning. Waters died at the scene. Not much more is known as to why or how. We hope more information will be forth coming.

"As of thirty-five minutes ago, Vice President Dani Mitchell succeeded to the Presidency. She was sworn in by a federal judge in the Vice President's office with her family present.

"President Sandford's body will lie in state for twenty-four hours in the Capitol Rotunda, starting tomorrow morning. His funeral service and burial will follow."

Rachel pulled out her phone and called Chris. "Did you hear?"

"Yes," he said. "Peter, General Clemmons, and I are heading to the White House. Wait. Peter is shaking his head. Oh, okay. The General is going to the White House. He and I are going to Dani's house. Can you get a hold of Sybil and bring her down?"

"Yes. Tell Peter not to worry."

"Good. Take the copter. Let me know your ETA and I'll send a car to meet you."

As soon as the call ended, Rachel called Sybil. "Where are you?"

Sybil said, "I'm home. I just got terrible news."

"I know. I can't believe Sandford's dead."

"President Sandford?"

"Yes. You said you knew?"

Sybil said, "All I know is James is dead. His house-keeper called. The police were all over the study and his body's now at the coroner's office. There has to be an autopsy because they're not sure what killed him."

"I'm so sorry."

"Don't be. I'm glad he's gone."

"You can't mean that."

"I do. Now, he can't hurt Peter."

"What about the funeral?"

Sybil said, "Peter will handle it."

"How are you doing?"

"I'm fine."

Rachel said, "Feel like taking a trip to Washington with me?"

"To wish Dani well? You bet."

"Get ready. I'll pick you up in an hour. Peter and Chris will meet us at Dani's."

<~<~|~>~>

Showered and changed, Peter relaxed in the general's conference room waiting for Chris. An officer came in and delivered an envelope. "For you, Sir. Special delivery," and left.

The envelope had no markings other than his name. He opened it and pulled out a letter from the international law firm representing the Vanderhagen family, dated today, and addressed to him.

> In the case of James Vanderhagen's
> death, effective immediately, you are
> his named successor and CEO of
> Vanderhagen Holdings and Invest-

ments. As such, you immediately assume VHI positions on boards and
global projects.

You will be contacted with further
instructions. Any immediate questions
may be directed to the undersigned.

Peter gasped. He read the letter again, then called the Philadelphia house.

The housekeeper said, "Vanderhagen household."

"This is Peter Powell."

"I'm sorry for your loss."

"What happened to my uncle? Was it a heart attack?"

"I don't think so," the housekeeper said. "The police have taken his body to the coroner for an autopsy."

"I guess we'll have to wait for them to come up with the cause of death."

"Yes."

"Was anyone with him?"

"I discovered him alone, on the fireplace hearth. I called 911 right away."

"Thank you for that," Peter said.

The housekeeper said, "When will you arrive?"

Peter swallowed. "I'm not, I mean, I haven't made any plans. I'm going up to Washington, D.C. in a few minutes. After, I'll return to New York to spend time with my mother."

"Do you have any instructions?"

"Me? No. Why? Is there urgent business?"

"Not that I'm aware of," the housekeeper said. "Take your time. I'll be here."

<~<~|~>~>

The housekeeper ended the call and made another. "He got the letter and called immediately."

The voice on the other end of the conversation said, "Good."

"I gave him no more information than will be on the police report."

"He'll be updated as needed."

"I've had the house thoroughly cleaned and the trash picked up."

"Out with the old, in with the new."

The housekeeper said, "I estimate his return to the family home in ten days to two weeks."

The voice said, "Noted."

Chapter 62 ▶ Observation Circle, Washington, D.C.

Friday, 29 May

Dani, Terence, and the twins left the swearing in ceremony and returned to One Observatory Drive. She said to the boys, "Go ahead. You can change. We're expecting Aunt Sybil, Peter, Rachel, and Chris for dinner."

They took off for the stairs. On the first riser, Isaac turned to look at her. "Mom, are you okay?"

Dani forced a smile. "I'm...."

Terence put his hand on her arm and took over the answer. "Mom's doing the best she can under the circumstances."

The twins smiled and fled upstairs. Dani looked at Terence's hand. He dropped it. "Sorry."

She said, "I'm going upstairs to change. Please let the kitchen know the number of dinner guests."

Terrance opened his mouth to say something. He hesitated. Before he said anything, Dani spoke. "I'll see you at five in the sitting room, no, the garden room. I'm in the mood for light and airy."

<~<~|~>~>

The clock chimed five times. Dani waited until it ended and entered the room. Everyone stood and raised a glass in her direction.

Terence said, "To the new President of the United States, Dani Mitchell."

Dani smiled. "Thank you for coming and for your support." She and held out her hand. Terence filled it with a glass of her favorite drink. She nodded to him and said, "This one is for our late President Sandford--a good man and a good President. May he rest in peace."

All present agreed and sipped their drink. Dani walked over to Sybil. "You okay?"

Sybil said, "Yes. You?"

Dani said, "Shaken, for sure. Sandford's murder...I'm not going to forget that. James is another thing entirely."

Sybil said, "I'm glad he's gone. Sorry, Dani, I know he was your father, but that's the truth."

Dani said, "I haven't said more than two sentences to him in years. He tried to ruin my life, order me around, and force me to prostitute myself for his own ends."

"So, no tears?"

"No. Not one." They clinked glasses in agreement. Dani sipped her drink. "How's Peter taking it? He and James were close."

"He seems okay."

"I'll talk with him. He's had a very busy day."

Sybil said, "Thank you for getting him home unharmed."

"That's all on him," Dani said. "He did a great job getting the refugees out of Tawanda."

Sybil smiled. "He's the best thing I've ever done."

"Yes. He's very special." Dani looked around the room and caught Rachel's eye. They met in the middle of the room. "Rachel, thank you for taking care of Sybil. I know she's still affected by Lidia's death."

Rachel said, "I think she's doing much better now that she's back at PRAISE."

"I agree," Dani said. "What about you?"

"I'm back to writing and getting ready for the wedding."

"After the wedding, would you be interested in a new challenge?"

"I don't understand."

Dani said, "I'll be modifying cabinet posts and advisors over the next month. I'd like you to consider working with me."

"Dani, I'm honored."

"Good. We'll talk."

The women clinked glasses and sipped their drinks.

Chris walked over and put his arm around Rachel's shoulder. "Ladies. Dani, I can't imagine how you're feeling after a day like today."

"Shaken. I'm still processing. My plan is to take the weekend off and schedule some professional counseling."

"Good idea. I know you'll work through this and be a great President."

Rachel said, "Chris, Dani's asked me to work with her administration."

Chris smiled and said to Dani, "As long as she's around for our wedding."

"Absolutely," Dani said. "We wouldn't miss that for anything."

Rachel said, "Does that mean you're coming?"

"I think Ivan and Isaac are already packed and waiting for the date."

Rachel said, "Second Saturday in October."

Dani pulled out her phone and saved the date and put it away. "There. Done."

Sybil walked over to them and said, "Rachel, may I talk to you?"

Rachel excused herself. Dani said to Chris, "How's the project you're running for General Clemmons?"

He said, "We'd only processed one barracks before I had to leave. Injections and scans caused no problems."

"A good outcome."

Chris nodded. "Thank you for backing the project."

The twins ran up. Ivan said, "Mom, can we show Chris something? It won't take more than five minutes."

Dani smiled. "Of course. Don't keep him long and don't be late for dinner."

Terence approached her, with Rachel on one arm and Sybil on the other. "I'm going to show the ladies the garden. Would you like to join us?"

"You go ahead. I'll find Peter and join you."

She watched them walk out of the room, across the veranda, down the steps, and onto the lawn. Next time, the Rose Garden.

She looked around the room. Peter had vanished. Dani walked outside to check the deck. Peter stood twenty feet to her left. She joined him. "Enjoying the quiet?"

"I am," he said. "It's been a brutal week."

"A bit terrifying, I hear."

"Dani, when those army trucks came out of nowhere and the guards started shooting, I didn't know if we were going to get that last bus onto the transport or die."

"I heard that was your idea."

"You mean the buses on the transport?"

She nodded.

Peter said, "The Air Force guys encouraged me. Their quick thinking made me look good."

"What's important is that everyone's safe."

"Not everyone. Have you heard anything about Kwanh Ebu and Oliver Odili?"

Dani shook her head. "I've gotten updates, but none mentioned their whereabouts."

Peter said, "I think Ebu ordered the refugee encampment's destruction. I know for certain they were triggered by expertly placed explosions."

"Can you prove it?"

"Sadly, no. Still, someone's responsible for the loss."

"We may never know who," Dani said. She paused several heartbeats. "Peter, I'm sorry about James. I know you two were close."

"I feel badly. I know I disappointed him," Peter said, dropping his eyes to the railing that ran around the veranda. "I tried to do the right thing."

Dani said, "You chose humanity over money."

"Still people died."

"Yes."

Peter pulled the letter from his pocket. "Dani. You're James's daughter. I don't want to keep anything from you. I got this just before I left the base. It came in an unmarked envelope." He handed her the folded letter.

Dani opened it and read the message. She handed the paper back to him. "I'm happy for you, Peter. You earned it."

"By rights, the position is yours. I'm not sure I want the responsibility. I planned to come home and work with Mom. There are a lot of people out there that need the safety net PRAISE provides. I want to make sure they get it."

"Peter, with the Vanderhagen money and prestige, you may be able to do even more. Just because your grandfather and uncle chose to sit in their office and manipulate other people's lives, doesn't mean you have to. It's in your power to make the world a better place."

Peter looked at her. "Yes, that's what they always said."

"Peter, you're in the prime of your life with enough energy to do PRAISE and manage the Vanderhagen interests."

"Let's hope so," Peter said, "What about you?"

Dani smiled. "Don't worry about me. I'll be fine."

Peter nodded.

Dani hooked her arm in his and said, "Let me show you the gardens."

Peter's phone buzzed. He pulled it out. "I need a minute. It's General Clemmons."

"Sure." She disengaged. "Go ahead. I'll wait here."

She watched Peter go inside and retrieved her phone. She went to an encrypted site, entered a phone number, and texted. "Accepted. Confirmed. Collateral damage?"

The answer text said, "Cold storage. Hardware updated."

Dani put her phone away and placed both hands on the railing. The FBI would find Lucy Kilmer in her Harrison swimming pool. As a final precaution, the housekeeper replaced the weapon under the desk to insure no rifling matches. No ties. Fresh start.

She saw Terence with the women, chatting and laughing. She smelled the lilac scented air and took a deep breath. She wanted to remember this moment—the apex of her life—so far. Another deep breath.

I made it. A Vanderhagen in the White House. The first woman President of the United States. I'm glad, Philip and James, you're not here to see it. I won't have to deal with your smirks, snide remarks, and pathetic attempts to manipulate me. Peter will be a great CEO. The Vanderhagen empire will continue to grow at an unprecedented rate. Want to know why, you stupid, misogynistic, whore-mongering, dead old men? It's because I didn't become a lawyer for nothing. I own it, all of it.

Peter returned, offered his arm. "Ready to show me the garden, Madam President?"

Dani gave him a big smile, looped her arm in his, and said, "Let's go."

The End

A Note from the Author

I hope you enjoyed reading ISOLATION as much as I enjoyed writing it.

If you did, please consider leaving an unbiased review on Amazon or the site where you are a verified purchaser.

Love, Loss, Leverage, Murder

A Novel by C.L. BLUESTEIN
Seduction series-Book #4

Chapter 01 ▶ Harrison, New York

Friday, 25 May, 9 a.m.
Special Agent Eric Jerrod answered his phone as he walked to his car. "What's up?"
"My partner and I just arrived at Kilmer's Harrison house. We can find no evidence subject is on premises. She didn't answer the door and offer us coffee like she usually does."

Eric slid into the driver's seat, strapped in, and engaged the motor. He hooked up the flashing red light and attached it to the roof of his car.

"No ankle-monitor pinging."

"Right. No monitor heartbeat either."

Eric said, "I'm on my way. Wait for me. Stay in touch by phone."

"Will do. Line is open."

Eric pulled into traffic, exited to the highway, and sped northward to Westchester, leaving New York City behind. He heard the agent's monitor crackle.

"We got something. She's alive. Going in."

Eric heard car doors open and shut, and footsteps pounding on concrete. Three thuds and a crash. The front door gave in. He said into his phone, "Your shoulder okay?"

The agent said, "It will be."

Eric smiled. He'd busted more than a few doors in his time. It hurt like a son-of-a-bitch.

"Not in the house. Around back. We're going down the side path. Through the back gate. I see her. She's in the pool."

Eric said, "Get her out. Call the EMTs. Be there in ten."

He wove in and out of light traffic, making good time. He and Lucy Kilmer were not strangers. He had tried, in vain, to muster enough evidence to convict her for the Meyerson family California murder. Five missing people. All he had was circumstantial evidence and a photo from a dead man's phone. All she got was a year of FBI-monitored probation. Under his breath, he said, "I've finally got her. Breaking probation isn't a lot but it's something."

<~<~|~>~>

By the time Eric arrived, the EMTs were working on Lucy. Her fully clothed body lay on the ground, face up, as one EMT pumped fluids into her body and the other cut away her wet clothes, replacing them with blankets. An agent held a plastic evidence bag containing a bullet-proof vest with a massive dent in the chest area.

Eric approached the medics. "Is she bleeding anywhere?"

One EMT looked up. "No. She took a serious blow to her rib cage, which appears to have impacted her heart."

The other said, "I'll call Base." He looked at Eric. "We're taking her to White Plains Hospital."

Lucy's eyelids fluttered.

"She's gaining consciousness."

She moaned, shivered, coughed, and opened her eyes as the EMTs transferred her to a stretcher.

Eric said to Lucy, "I'm going with you." To the EMTs, he said, "She does not leave my sight."

<~<~|~>~>

When she opened her eyes, she had to squint. The golden light streamed through the window on her right. IV infusion bags hung on a stand, wires hooked into a machine and tubes sending life-saving fluids through the needle taped to the back of her hand. A male voice said, "Miss Kilmer, you want to tell me what happened?"

She turned her head toward her visitor and smiled. "Special Agent Eric Jerrod."

Eric said, "I'm not here on a social call. You violated your parole and I want you to tell me what happened."

"I have no idea." She licked her lips. "Water."

Eric handed her a paper cup with a bent straw. "Here you go."

Lucy filled her mouth with water before swallowing. Handing the cup back to Eric, she said, "You tell me."

"Miss Kilmer, we've been monitoring your every move. Last night, you went to bed early. This morning we lost your infrared image and turned on our sound. We found you in the pool, in shock, wearing a damaged bullet-proof vest."

"I don't, can't, remember." She shivered, pulled up the blanket, and tucked in her chin. "I'm cold and my chest hurts."

Eric said, "You get a pass for now. There'll be men stationed outside your door. I'll be back later to hear the whole story."

He left and a nurse appeared. She fussed with the blankets, offered water, and fiddled with the infusion. "A little something to help you sleep." She lowered the window shade and turned off the lights as she left the room.

Lucy drifted into a dream state. Her phone buzzing. Not her phone. Still, buzzing until it stopped. She was moving. Fast. Silence interrupted by more buzzing. Nausea from unfocused undulating landscapes. Swaying and weaving. Pain. Something, someone poking her. She pushed it away, again and again. Annoyed, she grabbed it.

"That's my finger. May I have it back?"

Her eyes popped open. A doctor stood by her side.

"You've suffered quite a chest bruise. The good news is, no bones are broken. The bad news is it will hurt every time you move for two to three weeks. Questions?"

Lucy shook her head.

"Good. I'll check on you tomorrow and see when we can send you home."

After he left, the nurse came in. "Are you alright?"

Lucy said, "I'm fine," closed her eyes, dozed off, and entered a dream state.

It was twilight. After dinner.
One of her unregistered phones
buzzed. She answered. A voice
she didn't recognize outlined her
next contract. It told her who,
where, when, and how much had
been wired to her account. She
slipped into a thermal suit to hide
from the infrared scanner outside

and clicked on the heating pad arrangement under her covers to mimic her body temp. She overrode the door sensors, slipped out of her suburban house into her SUV, and sped down the highway. Every second counted because she had to be back by morning.

Within hours, she sat facing her next victim. When he left the room, she got up, prepared his phone with a lethal contact poison, and returned to her seat by the time he returned. Without looking at him, she knew something had changed. His breathing came faster. His step more confident. His stride more commanding. He even smelled excited. He passed her and sat in his executive chair behind his desk and across from her. He leaned forward, placed his left elbow on the desk, paused, and gave her a "fuck you" smile. Blackness.

The nurse said, "Wake up. We have to take vitals, blood, and your lunch is here."

She administered the tests, left, and returned with a tray. "How's your chest feeling? Are you having any pain when you breathe?"

Lucy put her hand to her chest. "Not too much. I guess I'm feeling okay."

"It's the medication. It also makes you unsteady. Miss Kilmer, don't get out of bed without help. Use the call button. Although you should be all set since your catheter will expel liquids while you hydrate. The doctor will remove it tomorrow."

"My phone?"

"Tomorrow. Today you rest."

Lucy nodded. "Okay, you're the boss."

The nurse smiled. "You have a visitor."

Eric walked in. "It's been several hours. I thought you might like to tell me where the ice crystals in your blood came from."

Her eyes widened. "Ice crystals?"

"Our pathologists seem to think you might have been frozen."

"Frozen?"

"Like you fell through the ice."

"Flash frozen?"

"From what I understand. Anything you want to tell me?"

"No. I'm as confused as you are."

Eric gave her a wry smile. "I doubt that." He walked to the doorway, paused, and turned to look over his shoulder. "However, I will find out. With or without your help."

<~<~|~>~>

Two days later, Lucy Kilmer sat in her living room, listened to soft rock, and sipped her tea. Better and quieter to be home than in the hospital. She held the hot mug chest high and stared out the windows. Her memory had returned.

James Vanderhagen, spokesman for a global cartel, commissioned her to plan, organize, and carry out the mass genocide of thousands of African war refugees living outside Damir, Tawanda's capital city.

Despite her success, the Tawandian government's insatiable greed undermined their momentary advantage and caused its collapse. Their error had cost the cartel billions of dollars. In retaliation, the cartel hired her to execute James Vanderhagen, which she did with a fast-acting army grade contact poison.

She shook her head. Dwelling on the past would only hamper her intention to go forward. Clients, including Tavius Global, waited for her unique set of skills and trained teams to deal with their high-status targets. Lucy loved the work she excelled in. Her fees were high. Her work impeccable. She lived as others could only dream of.

Lucy looked down at her new ankle-bracelet, courtesy of the FBI. It hindered but did not stop her. Her professional life lay in technology hidden beyond the back wall of her clothes closet and in the hollowed-out attic beams. She had threaded her internet connections through a web of servers located all over the world.

Still, there were ice crystals. Only the ninja housekeeper could shed light on this anomaly. Lucy made the call. "You froze me?"

In even tones, the housekeeper said, "Cartel orders. Remove you and trace evidence before police arrived."

"So, you froze me."

"No, 'chilled.' Used a meat freezer."

A knock on the door forced Lucy to end the call.

A muscled young man in gym clothes entered. "Are you ready?"

She shook her head. "Ultan, I can't do a massage today. I've been in the hospital. Bruised ribs."

"Hospital. I thought you were on a job. What happened?"

Lucy explained, ending with, "So, you see, I need a few days."

Ultan said, "I understand. Perhaps Thursday."

"By the way, did we have any contracts this weekend?"

"One. In Phoenix. The team eliminated the target three hours after the alert. We used the Emergency Meeting Protocol with no outside contact. He packed his bags for a two week stay and said good-bye to his family. In the SUV, the team applied standard practice—anesthetic, gas, and woodchipper. As of today, he is lizard food. As far we know, no inquiries have been made as to his whereabouts, but it's only been a week."

Lucy smiled. "Did you monitor the operation from here?"

"Of course. You taught me well."

End of Chapter 1

To Continue reading Book #4 of the Seduction Series, click the link below:

DECEPTION Love. Loss. Leverage. Murder

Or search: C.L. Bluestein Deception

ABOUT THE AUTHOR

C.L. Bluestein lives in Slingerlands, New York. Her ideas for projects are fueled by absurdity and puzzles—i.e. how, why, and how come things work—whether it is functional or mental, psychological or physical, political, or just plain interesting. She is a member of the International Women's Writing Guild (IWWG)(2008-), https://iwwg.com/ and a writer for The Good Men Project 2016-), https://goodmenproject.com/ Other writings available at http://carolbluestein.com/

Check out the rest of the political thriller Seduction Series featuring Rachel, Chris, Beth, & Eric.

#1 SEDUCTION – Love, Loss, Leverage, Murder

#2 PERCEPTION – Love, Loss, Leverage, Murder

#4 DECEPTION – Love, Loss, Leverage, Murder

You Want Me To Do What? Walk in the sandals of our ancestors through this engaging interactive contemporary scripted Story of the Exodus/Passover for Jewish and Interfaith Families. Targeted but not limited to tweens.

REVIEW: "You Want Me To Do What" is the most innovative addition to the Passover literature I've seen. This is not just another pretty Haggadah....these interactive mini-dramas will make ANY Seder using any Haggadah come alive for all ages." Cantor Charles Bergman, Los Angeles, CA **Free download** at http://carolbluestein.com/

Twitter: @clbauthor
FB: Carol Bluestein
Web: http://carolbluestein.com/